CORINA'S WAY

CORINA'S WAY

a novel

ROD DAVIS

NewSouth Books

Montgomery

NewSouth Books
P.O. Box 1588
Montgomery, AL 36102

Library of Congress Cataloging-in-Publication Data

Davis, Rod, 1946–
Corina's way : a novel / Rod Davis.
p. cm.
ISBN 1-58838-129-3 (hardcover)
1. Women clergy—Fiction. 2. School chaplaints—Fiction.
3. Mambos (Voodooism)—Fiction. 4. New Orleans (La.)—Fiction.
5. Voodooism—Fiction. I. Title.
PS3604.A98C67 2003
813'.6—dc21
2003003685

Design by Randall Williams
Printed in the United States of America

Some fragments of song lyrics in this book are excerpted from
"Oh Happy Day!," Hawkins. *Oh Happy Day!,* Pair records, 1969; and
from "Love and Happiness," Green/Hodges. *I'm Still in Love With You.*
Hi records. 1972.

TO

JENNIFER, MORIAH,

AND PEACE

1

I T WAS THOSE Cubans again. Twice this morning and two more times this afternoon. If they drove past her botanica one more time Corina was going to make *ebo* against them in her back yard. She didn't like to feed the spirits out of malice, because if you used your powers to harm people it might even tually come back on you. But Corina had begun to look at spell-making the way the NRA looked at handguns.

It came to her the day the phone solicitor called, probably on account of her being listed in the book as "the Rev. C. C. Youngblood III," which she thought made her sound more official and therefore more like a man and therefore more likely a potential new member of "America's largest voluntary organization dedicated to the Second Amendment of the United States Constitution." But if the NRA "friend" was surprised to be talking to a woman he hid it pretty well.

She listened because it was a slow day and she was bored. While the man talked, she tucked the phone between her shoulder and cheek and straightened up the votive candles on one of the sale racks. The man was saying something along the lines that as a minister and leader of her community and a *woman*, emphasizing gender now that he knew it, she should be especially concerned about criminals and liberals and gun control. About then is when it came to her—as if from the saints themselves. He didn't need to sell her. She already had a gun. Better than that. She had a *palo* pot.

As though the power of the revelation had burst from her very soul, Corina turned from the shelves, grabbed the phone in her right hand so hard the grip turned her fingers white, and began talking without even waiting for the NRA man to stop. Fast, almost breathless, she launched the tale of her own armaments—voodoo and *palo* and the *santos* and the power of Ogun and how maybe she'd get a .38 revolver from her sister Eddie and put it inside the pot for extra strength and deploy the pot and all that it contained against her enemies just like you'd point a Smith & Wesleyan (he didn't correct her) at a burglar coming into your house at night. She felt elated—like testifying. The man coughed a couple of times and said he could "see her point" and tried to get back to his speech but it was like he couldn't and then he sort of excused himself and got off the phone.

She was sorry. She wanted to thank him. He was only a strange white man from Maryland or somewhere calling on an 800 line but he had clarified things. How often had she preached to her congregation that the Spirit chose its own ways in its own time? What had the man said? "Concern"? As an ordained minister she was *very* concerned about criminals. About good and evil. About protection.

All this had been on her mind for some time now. But she had been unable to fuse a connection. You could never get to the bottom of the great conundrums, of course, or solve the riddle of good and evil or even clarify the basic human confusion, such knowledge being the way of the Lord and not of a preacher woman from the projects. No, you could not. God knew all. God was all. But He works in mysterious ways. Truth was, all manner of solutions and insights were open to a steadfast seeker and quick study and she wouldn't be where she was today if she was neither of those. So she was tired of messing with the Cubans.

They'd started out small, years ago, with a little Uptown grocery store mostly for the Spanish and then opened a small botanica across the river in Gretna, which was the first botanica Corina had ever been to. One thing you could say about the Delgado brothers—they knew about money and deals, which Corina hadn't learned as much about, coming up through the church and not being a man and therefore not let in on all the rules.

By last January Elroy and Julio Delgado had two more groceries and another botanica and then, to top it all, they built a brand new warehouse over in the east. Nobody was sure why until Elroy sent out word they were opening something called a SuperBotanica. And then maybe another one after that. A chain. They said it would be like "a Wal-Mart for spiritual supplies." They'd sell candles and incense and even iron pots for Ogun and metal crossbows for Ochosi and *orisha* statues so cheap they'd run all the other botanicas in town out of business. Then they were going to open SuperBotanicas all across the South, maybe even in Chicago and New Jersey.

Since Corina had once dated Elroy Delgado, before she knew what a waste of time that man was, even though now he was her *padrino*, she considered the entire SuperBotanica plan a personal attack. Also a kind of anti-black thing. It was her oldest boy, Jean-Pierre, first told her that. He taught social studies over in Metairie and was prone to overthinking everything, but there was more than a grain of truth in what he said.

When Elroy and Julio and the other Cubans had first come in, and set up their stores and their botanicas, they said their *santería* was a "real religion"—different from hoodoo and root doctors and the other sort of things Corina had grown up around. And Corina had gotten sucked into it, in a way. Until she'd seen the thing Jean-Pierre was talking about, that *santería* was for the Cubans and they were really just ripping off the Africans, who invented voodoo in the first place, which *santería* really was, and now the blacks in America were having to buy back their own damn religion. That was what Jean-Pierre said, and he'd studied on it. And that didn't even get into the thing about the *marielitos* in Miami selling coke out of their botanicas and feeding the *santos* to protect drug dealers. They'd go to hell for that. Corina knew it from the bottom of her soul. They couldn't twist the spirits that way.

Not that Corina's Cubans were selling drugs. What they were selling was what she sold, and they were going to drive her to ruin. They were going to take all her customers. They were going to dry her up. They would destroy her, her botanica, and her church, and never look back. She would disappear. She would never exist, nor anything of her works.

Corina made up her mind then and there, peering through the glass front door at the street full of rusty-butt children and old women in bonnets on porch stoops and at things only a minister and prophet could see, to fight the Cubans. They would take neither her botanica nor her basic rights as an American.

The hell with Elroy, she thought, and rebuked herself for swearing. And then said it again, smiling. Then she called her sister Eddie and asked her to bring the .38 by because she sort of owed it to the NRA and she knew both Ogun and the pot would like such a fine implement to savor.

Next time the Cubans cruised down Beauchamp Avenue in front of her store—they didn't even drive an American car, it was a big, new dark blue Nissan sedan—they'd see. Corina turned to her youngest son, Paulus, and told him to go down to market and get a goat, because the pot she was going to sink needed blood to start it up, and a goat was about the heaviest mammal you could get, at least in New Orleans, though she'd heard in Haiti and in Africa they used a bull for the most powerful *ju-ju.*

Then Corina said a silent prayer to Jesus, the Redeemer, to gird her loins in this battle but she wasn't going to use him for fixing the Cubans because there was a part of her that knew He wouldn't understand the fight the way she did, though she wasn't sure if it was because He was white or because He was a man.

2

G US HOUSTON hated the city when it rained, which gave him a bad attitudinal backdrop a good part of the year, rain being to New Orleans what snow is to Montana. On the other hand, rain allowed him a certain morose, even melancholy stance, which he occasionally indulged. He'd been indulging for about an hour, waiting for the sixth-period bell. He wasn't thinking big or deep thoughts, especially. Nagging, perhaps. He stared absently out the white-paned window in his office. Splat, splat, splat. Funny how rain seemed poetic coming down, until it was all the way down.

He glanced at the clock on the book shelf. Five more minutes till his first customer. He wondered if he should do anything special—get out a Bible, dust off the couch, fix his tie, something. But he wasn't wearing a tie, the couch wasn't dusty because he'd napped on it after lunch, and he'd forgotten to get a Bible from the library even though he'd made a Post-It note to himself to do so last Wednesday. All he could do was wait.

It was true that saying he had a year of seminary training in order to get a job teaching English at Miss Angelique's Academy for Young Ladies could, in some circumstances, be considered a falsehood. But last spring the long-term implications of lying had seemed irrelevant. What the school needed, according to the classifieds, was someone on very short notice to teach fiction and composition to New Orleans' "most exclusive" female teenagers.

What Gus needed was a paycheck. When Mrs. Hapsenfield, the owner and headmaster, had mentioned they were also looking for a part-time chaplain, Gus had just gone over the line. The funny thing was, it had taken less than a second. He'd barely even paused to catch a breath when the entire fabrication occurred to him. Having occurred, and having seemed dangerous and irresponsible, it was impossible to restrain.

Right there in Elizabeth Hapsenfield's office, toasty warm in the soft glow of bleached blond furniture and Santa Fe rugs, Gus had invented as he spoke a story of having dropped out of seminary training at St. Sebastian's Men's Bible College, a small church-run institution, now closed due to declining enrollment, in San Marcos, Texas. He left, he said, because he really didn't feel he could devote himself fully to the religious life. On the other hand, he said, he had come away from the experience with a true understanding of the human condition.

Then he kind of waved the whole episode off, as if to indicate it probably wouldn't be of any help to the Academy, but he had seen a gleam of a budgetary nature in Mrs. Hapsenfield's blue eyes. It matched the gleam of financial desperation in his own and he left the interview convinced he would be given the call. And though many were summoned—it being a time of recession across the land—he got the job.

Yet not until today had it occurred to (Acting) Chaplain Houston that the Academy could in any way be serious about *needing* a backup counselor for "our young ladies with particularly intractable problems," as Mrs. Hapsenfield had put it. Not until today had the semester "walk-in" sessions been reinstated. He could definitely expect visitors. The girls loved to go to Chaplain to get out of classes, which was why the Academy had discontinued the service last year, that and the Rev. Daniels's sudden decision to leave. Over the summer, the girls had pressured their parents to get Chaplain hours back. The headmistress had graciously acceded.

In the few weeks since school had started, Gus had become increasingly aware of the small part he was playing in a larger script. It wasn't that Elizabeth Hapsenfield had been gullible enough to believe his seminary story; she had been conniving enough to. If Gus were later found to be a fraud, it was his neck, not hers. And in the meantime it was he, not the Hapsenfields, who would have to listen to all the complaints, sad stories, freak-outs.

That aside, Miss Angelique's was pretty decent as jobs go, especially for somebody whose last meaningful employment had been night manager at a Tennessee theme park called the Garden of Dixie. And there was Mrs. Hapsenfield. The day she hired him, she'd been wearing a white silk blouse that came open at the third button. When she turned sideways, a little silken viewing tunnel opened to reveal a very robust cleavage neatly framed in a thin bra of ivory lace. She was a natural blond with a good tan. She liked to wear turquoise. Was it possible the brown rim of her aureole had inspired him to bear false resumé?

Perhaps that was poetic, too. Trying to get your head into being a phony man of God to minister unto the young by musing about your boss's bosom. A shrink, on the other hand, might say Gus at that moment was engaged in avoidance, or denial, or whatever it was shrinks liked to say. Bonita, the woman he loved, the woman he lived with, the woman who would kill him for straying, would have a simpler explanation. She believed most men "think with their dicks" and would fuck a tractor if they could find the parts.

Not to mention they are engineered to endure short attention spans. How affirmed would Bonita be to know that his thoughts were as of that very second no longer applied to the convex fullness of Nordic lace but to a lush Cajun triangle of thick, curly, black hair? That in the very throes of avoidance and denial, Gus's mind had stampeded to a fervent wish. At that moment he wished to be not at the school, in the school, nor anywhere having anything to do with the school, but in some faraway mountain lodge, on a goose down mattress, sweating buckets, looking up through the teacup breasts of his squirmy bartender, his life's love, fire of his loins, etc. Her taut thighs astraddle his pelvis. Him about to explode. He could see that image as clearly as its complement: Bonita standing over his dead, cheating body with a shotgun.

The sixth-period bell trilled, as it does in the finer schools. Gus emerged from escapist sex and settled in behind his huge antique desk. The mass of dark oak was like a moat, protecting him from invaders. Agon, Elizabeth's crane-like, blue-blood husband, had boasted that the desk and matching leather couch had once belonged to an Old Family on Henry Clay Street. The Academy had come into its possession after the Oil Bust, when priceless heirlooms often found new currency covering the tuitions of the daughters of proud gentry.

In the fraction of a second before the door opened, and with it the dread he had been awaiting—some young student thinking Gus was in any way competent to deal with her—the acting Chaplain had a comforting, though fleeting thought. Not a revelation. A revelation would be too Biblical, and Gus knew, if nothing else, he had to be secular, or at least ecumenical, in his approach if he were to fool anyone. His thought was that maybe his presence wasn't entirely without function after all, for when it came to counseling young women, or anyone else, about wrongdoing, who could be more qualified?

"Hi, Mr. Houston."

Gus recognized Angie Ballew, a tall, brunette senior. She was a medley of the times: jet-black jeans, black silk blouse, copious black eye-liner. "Can I come in?"

"You already are."

"Yepper."

Leaving the door ajar, as if it were not her custom to deal with such bothers, she half-slithered, half-bounced to an overstuffed vinyl armchair. A funny whump of rapidly compressing air escaped from the thick seat cushion as she dropped onto it. She sniggled somewhat gratuitously, and passed an official counselor's pass across to him. Since he hadn't given her one, he assumed she had stolen it. He looked it over, not unlike a blackjack player contemplating the first hit from a fresh deck.

"I guess you wanted to see me about sleeping with Mr. Hapsenfield."

Gus smiled back and got up to close the louvered glass door. Outside, the second bell had rung and 367 young women were moving noisily through the resonant, oak-floored hallways of the converted Greek Revival mansion. Angie fastened her dark-lined doe-eyes upon him with something very much like amusement—or possibly malice. Gus tried to imagine himself in a job interview with St. Augustine. "Maybe you'd better fill me in."

3

S HE KILLED the goat efficiently and without pain. Once across the throat with the white-handled *cuchillo*, then drip the blood over the shrines to Ogun on her back porch. A small amount she let run from the wound into a small salad bowl that had been in the family for years but not until recently used for this purpose. She and Paulus drank two or three mouthfuls of the warm liquid each. Then Corina praised Elegba and Ogun and Ochosi and all the *santos*.

Elroy said in Cuba they were called *orisha*. He said they actually called them "voodoo" over in Africa, which was why that name was over here, the slaves and all, but voodoo was a word Corina didn't like. Jean-Pierre called it voodoo anyway because he wouldn't use the Cuban names. But she had got used to calling the spirits *santos*, because she had learned from Elroy and even if she hated Elroy now that didn't mean he owned the names and she couldn't say whatever she wanted. Like she said SHANG-o while Elroy said CHANG-o and she said O-SHOON while he said O-CHOON, like he was sneezing. And the Africans spelled the *orisha* version of the names different than the Cubans did the *santo* version, Jean-Pierre had told her. Which she didn't care about either. Didn't any of the spirits or their names belong to anyone on this earth, any more than Jesus Christ himself did. Corina felt very strongly about that.

She could still taste the blood in her throat. It wasn't that bad—kind of salty and sluggish but lots of things tasted that way. Because it was still twilight, the neighbors couldn't see her or Paulus and what they were doing. Besides, a big wooden fence and the thick shrubs surrounded the back yard. It was a small house, not far off Elysian Fields toward the canal side—a better neighborhood than the projects where she'd grown up, though still a far cry from the fine old homes in the Garden District or the new ranch-styles up toward the lake.

When the last glint of the setting sun passed across her outstretched arms, holding the salad bowl red with the residue of goat blood, Corina felt the power that she had sought. She put the bowl down and thanked Jesus for the grace of life. While Paulus finished his praises in the African language they'd had to learn for initiation, which Elroy called the Yoruba, or sometimes the Lukumí, Corina slipped into a slight trance—not deep and uncharted, like the kind in church, but just enough to know that Jesus had heard her and was in communion.

Back inside they cut up the goat and baked some for supper that night and froze the rest in the new Amana one of Corina's clients had given her in gratitude for getting her son out of jail. Corina had gotten her El Dorado the same way. More or less. Back when she got on with the Cubans, Elroy Delgado had put her in touch with a rich man from Biscayne Bay and she'd flown out to give him a reading. He was only supposed to pick up her plane ticket and hotel and two hundred dollars for the reading plus another five hundred for the sacrifice. But he was so sundered by what she told him that he got all wrapped up in it and had her stay another whole week to read several of his friends and then, on a Sunday night when there was a half moon and the sticky heat was just fading into winter, he told her he wanted the *santo* for himself, too.

She went home to New Orleans to prepare and on her return to Florida hired all the drummers and priests and priestesses you need for that sort of thing and bought all the food and the crates of chickens and guinea fowl and the goats and she made him a child of Changó. Changó was the thunder god, and Cuban men especially wanted to be initiated to him. You didn't really have a choice in the matter, because the gods told you who would be your master, but it worked out for Humberto that it was Changó.

Later his air conditioning business tripled its earnings and he found a hot young Cubana to marry him and the stuff that Corina had warned him about in that first reading—unless he changed and got the *santo*—all that never came to pass. He cut back on the drinking and the cancer in his bowels went away. And he could get it up without *drogas*. He was a very happy man. One day, the El Dorado showed up in front of Corina's botanica. At precisely the same moment, she got a phone call from Humberto. As the delivery driver was giving her a set of keys, Humberto was in her ear long distance saying her she had given him what he wanted and he was showing his true thanks.

She had wanted to leap into the heavens with all the *santos*, but in truth she had to sit down on the curb for several minutes until she stopped feeling so faint. Surely this was some kind of proof of her powers and of the powers of the saints, too! It was just as she had told Humberto as he drank the blood on the first night of his ritual. The *santos* want praise, but they must also be fed. It follows that so must the priests of the *santos*; so, for that matter, she had said, must fortune itself never go hungry. Sacrifice was like offering money to Jesus in her church. It was a way of making faith real.

Phonies and hypocrites just talked: the real children of the Lord put blood on the altar or money in the bowl. The Cadillac meant Humberto was serious; accepting it meant she was awash in the blessings of powers so vast they sometimes scared her even though she was aware they inhabited every pore of her slender steeled body.

AFTER THE GOAT was put away and Paulus went back to his room to work on his algebra, Corina paced a little out in the yard until the mosquitoes drove her in. Normally by ten p.m. she was ready for bed. But tonight she was restless even before her head nestled into the foam pillow. Something wanted to break out of her brain, it felt like. She couldn't hardly think about anything, just a lot of different things so quickly none of them stuck long enough to seize any perspective on.

She turned on the TV and slumped into the gray-striped couch Grady had bought for a wedding present. The news was on. But it was white folks' news and didn't mean that much to her, other than to make her vaguely depressed. She thought about changing the channel but she was too tired to get up again. She wouldn't have paid attention to anything else, anyway. She slipped off her shoes and wriggled her toes on the worn carpeting. An airline stewardess who was a client told her that was a way to relax, and although Corina was far from sure that was true, she was still experimenting, for she had a strong disposition to continually seek out exactly what made the body tick. All such knowledge she could put into her work. But she had to be careful. Clients took what she said as gospel most of the time so if she recommended something, like wriggling your toes or hanging a pigeon upside down on your porch, she had to be sure it was tested and true. Corina was convinced that was why she was such a good spiritual advisor. She was very result-oriented.

She dug her toes hard, till the bones hurt, and she leaned forward so her head fell across her knees. She tried closing her eyes but they kept coming open and all she could see were her feet all veiny and cramped up and the brown carpet that hadn't been vacuumed in two weeks. She sat back up and rotated her neck until it cracked. Some time after the sacrifice the euphoria had given way to that bad familiar blue abyss. She'd hidden it from Paulus, and thought it would go away, but that wasn't the way of the funk. Now she was lowdown and trying very hard to shake the idea that she was in for another one of those nights. The weatherman came on and said it would rain but she didn't care because the only reason she was watching TV was so she wouldn't have to go into that bedroom.

Since Grady left, or more accurately since she threw him out, nights were so long she had nearly convinced herself time must stretch out in the dark somehow. Often she woke up three or four times. Back when they lived in the projects it was the noise and sometimes the gunshots that broke her dreams, but now it was just thinking all the time. If only Grady hadn't gotten so scared. He could have found another job sooner or later, because he was a very good mechanic when he wanted to be, but when Ford closed down the service department in Gretna he'd just never bounced back. The night he was fired he came in drunk, which he rarely did. "I put in fifteen years and they just threw me out on the street," he'd said to her, wadding up a severance pay stub and hurling it across the kitchen. "And you know something, Corina? Maybe I just stay there. Maybe I just stay there."

He didn't really mean it, but that's more or less what happened anyway. He started drinking all the time, and stopped going to church, and stopped talking. Then came the hitting. Corina took more than one hard shot to the jaw and the stomach before she accepted that he'd changed forever and he might really hurt her. Or Paulus or Jean-Pierre might find out and shoot him. So she told Grady he had to leave.

He did, and she got a lawyer to do the divorce, and Grady was gone and she was sleeping alone. She'd done it before, that was true. After her first husband, Louis Wayne, had died in a car wreck and left her with the boys she'd just disappeared for a while in her own mind. She worked double shifts at the sugar mill and didn't think about anything. For more than a year her children were more or less raised by her mother, who came to live in the house and helped some with the rent.

That was about when she met the Cubans and began learning about *santo* and saw that she might get some new power in her life. She was a Holy Redeemer all her life and believed in Jesus with all her soul but this was something to help with all that. Something extra, is how she usually explained it.

Louis Wayne's death was different than Grady's drinking, though. She could be sad for Louis Wayne, and she knew there was nothing to do about it. And it was just over and done. With Grady she'd felt it slipping away. Now, at forty-two, she wondered if she'd ever have a man again. She was still something to look at, maybe not as thin as when she'd met Louis Wayne but her booty was fine and firm and the rest of her was, too. Or so the men said all the time. People told her she had a nice face, too. It was caramel and oval and not lined yet.

People said she looked Nigerian, or that she resembled an actress on a TV show, a soap opera. But she'd never seen the show and didn't know who they were talking about. She didn't know any Nigerians either, except that one woman who worked at the bank, but she talked funny and seemed snooty. On the other hand Corina was always suspicious of foreigners. Furthermore, she had learned that people who said they were Africans always acted like they were superior to American people who were black, too. Even the Cuban black people did that. Nothing sent her over the line faster than somebody who thought they were better than she was.

She glanced across the room at a mirror near the hallway. Some man could want her, for sure. Question is, would she want him? Maybe sleeping alone could be gotten used to. Maybe her cat would just stay unused and she'd turn back into some kind of a virgin old lady. Anyway, there was more to it than just loneliness and sex. What she'd gotten most afraid of lately was just staying alive. Her nightmares and sleeplessness often as not were about money, in particular not having any.

After Grady and the lawyers she had used up everything old Humberto had given her. Except she still had the car. Each month was touch and go. Jean-Pierre helped, and Paulus had a part-time job at a drugstore, but she worried about money all the time. The botanica *had* to work. The people in her church were poor, like she was, and there just weren't enough of them in the pews. In truth, the readings and the botanica kept the church going, though she never really told anyone that. But the botanica had to work.

She got up abruptly and went into the kitchen. She took the wall phone from its cradle and dialed a number she had sworn to herself she'd never call again.

"That you, Elroy?" she snapped when a voice answered.

"Corina?"

"Yes, this is Reverend Youngblood." She turned so that her back flattened against the yellow wall next to the sink. Across the tile floor on the stove was a blackened metal tray with a few leftover goat ribs. Paulus was in the habit of late-night snacking.

"What can I do for you?"

Instantly she hated herself for calling. Right off, there was a friendliness in his voice. Her brow furrowed. It wasn't that. That lilting Cuban accent wasn't friendly—it was Elroy thinking she was calling to invite him over. It was him thinking about sex. She was furious and kicked the wall with her heel, which hurt, but got her mind back on the subject.

"Next time your boys come driving past my shop you better watch out," she said.

"Now, Corina. . ."

"You hearing me?"

He didn't say anything for a moment. "After all this time you just starting right in all over me." His voice had more than Cuba in it all right. Corina pursed her lips and rubbed her heel with her thumb and forefinger.

"That all done. What's now is you trying to put me out of business."

"Nobody's trying to do that. We just opening a new store, Corina."

"I heard all about that store. Your cousin Lupe say you want all the shops in town to close except yours and all the black people in the city buying everything from you and you probably trying to do all the spiritual work, too."

"Well, that's not what I'm thinking. That's Lupe talking. Maybe he don't know everything like he think he does."

"Well, I know, Elroy. I ain't stupid."

"No, you ain't that."

"Good. That settled, then. Now if I ain't stupid then don't be having those boys come by seeing what I might be up to at the shop. And they give us those snotty little grins when they go by."

"Sometimes they just like to cruise around. Maybe they just taking a short cut through your street."

"Did you hear what I just said?"

"What?"

"I said, I ain't stupid." She could feel her words grow thick, but her head was thick, too. This was a waste of time.

"I know you ain't stupid."

"Then don't be trying nothing on me, Elroy Delgado."

"I'm not trying nothing."

"You're trying to make me scared."

He was thinking again.

"Why don't I come over and we can talk?"

She laughed so hard she surprised herself. Kind of like something in her stomach burst out through her throat and thought it was funny for doing so. "The only thing we got to talk about is how you planning on taking away all my good customers."

"I got a right to have my own business, too."

"You know what I mean."

"I got *santo*, too."

"Yeah. And soon as the *santos* find out what you up to you gonna wish you never knew none of they names."

"Don't be talkin' to me that way, Corina."

"You better hope I keep talking. If I stop talking, I start doing."

He was silent a moment. "You shouldn't talk like that to your *padrino*."

Her eyes closed. "That's why I'm saying this. My *padrino* wouldn't do this to me."

"It's just business, Corina."

"You don't know nothing."

She hung up. Business was just a part of it all right. But the war was coming on a higher plane, too. She was going to have to break every bond with that damn Cuban, especially the one that scared her the most. But if she could divorce Grady, she could declare independence from her spiritual godfather. If he ever was even that, really.

She walked to the stove and picked up a cold rib and ate most of it. Last year, the doctors at Tulane Medical told her she had high blood pressure and had to change her diet. So she didn't usually eat meat, but sacrificed flesh was bidden to be consumed. The doctor had also given her some pills but she didn't take them all the time. She believed in doctors, and she knew when the doctors had to fill in for the work of the spirits and she always told her clients to go see a doctor unless it was clearly the work of an evil spell but she hated drugs, even aspirin, and she didn't take the pills. But her pressure had been getting better, and for lunch she almost always ate chocolate-covered granola bars instead of vienna sausages or cheeseburgers.

She went back into the front room and tried to watch a comedy show but it was all white people in California and it didn't mean anything and it also made her think of Lucy and Desi, which Elroy had often watched when they'd been not just *padrino* and initiate but also man and woman, side by side. Back when she'd trusted him. A stray thought from that time made her laugh again, and she turned off the TV and went to bed.

She only woke twice, but not out of fear. First, she was dreaming about being on the back of a giant dark bird over a reddened planet. The next time she was on the bird rising from a snowy volcano and soaring over all of the Lord's creation. What she felt in the dreams was so vast and powerful that both visions made her eyes pop open as though she'd been slapped.

In the morning, she felt rested for a change. Even though she had to get Paulus off to East Parish High and herself to the shop and tend to a day's worth of chores and duties she also felt, for the first time in a long while, that some big other thing waiting to happen was en route. She didn't know what, but it would be good.

While she was on the expressway driving towards her shop she remembered she had the .38 and while she was humming to the Gospel station she engineered an entire expedition in her head in which she sweet-talked Elroy into a stroll into the Quarter and when he wanted to kiss her she pulled the pistol from her handbag and stuck it up to Elroy's half-handsome brown face and made him sweat and then made him take his trousers down to his ankles and tied him like that to a lamppost on Canal Street and left him there for the tourists to walk past and the police to have a few questions for. That would be a pretty good way of telling him he wasn't her *padrino* anymore.

4

T HE CITY hadn't changed much since the last time Gus had seen it as a first lieutenant on leave. He'd taken two weeks off in celebration of orders sending him to Germany instead of some real shithole, or, worst of all, keeping him stateside. He thought the posting was great. Thought he'd see Europe on Uncle. So he went to the Big Easy for a week he could barely remember and then a week in the Big Apple he didn't want to remember and after that he found out why nobody back at Fort Hood thought Germany was all that good of duty. After a year, Gus would've taken a transfer to Beirut. But he faced no such choice. He was a three-year man, signed up as payback for college tuition and after Germany he was back in the World, and career-building. Strange, all that.

Strange, too, the World. Gus put down his cup of coffee and looked out the window of the little café on Jackson Square at the busload of Italian tourists staring up at St. Louis Cathedral. As often as possible on Saturday mornings, he liked to venture out of the little shell of gentility that was his new workplace in the Garden District and mix it up with the Quarter. He felt it kind of an obligation of a permanent resident of the city. Actually he didn't really come up with that, it was Bonita's idea. She really was from here, born in Thibodaux but had lived Uptown near the zoo since she ran away as a teenager. One night Gus had been drunk and confronted an altogether innocent man from Indiana in The Hellhole, the sort-of biker bar where now Bonita worked, demanding a "user fee" on behalf of maintenance of city streets and sanitation. Bonita had Wally, the bouncer, throw Gus out amid the street drunks.

Some hours after that, after he had talked and apologized his way back into the bar and they had ended up at her apartment, she had delivered him her "strong feelings on the subject." He couldn't remember all of it but the gist was that the only way the Quarter could be saved from the tourists and drag queens and reprobates and wiseguys was for the "real people" who lived in New Orleans to go down there as often as possible.

"It's empty space and anybody can fill it," she told him.

"Like your pussy," he replied. He remembered a terrible moment of silence.

"Just *like* that," she said, and hit him so hard with the palm of her hand he bit his tongue and couldn't drink anything hot or eat anything spicy for a week. It wasn't a religious experience, but it was memorable. And so on Saturday mornings he did penance at La Coupole. He drank coffee and read the *Times-Picayune* and watched the space fill up around him except for the part that he himself occupied. Bonita approved deeply, though she never said as much.

After coffee he walked around. With autumn, the mornings had gotten cooler, though it could still warm up enough in the afternoon to soak your shirt down to your waistband. Gus strolled across the square, past the jugglers and Italians and the rows of people trying to sell paintings or jewelry or ices. He felt benevolent, in good spirits, and even paused to take the photo of a man and his wife who needed someone to hold the camera while they posed. That was good of him, he thought. Not only a Space Occupier of the city but also a trusted guardian of its elite. He was very aware of being a teacher.

As he walked through the busy streets, past the restaurants and hotels and curio shops and always-open bars, past Napoleon's and then back toward Bourbon Street, past the oyster bar he favored, and aimlessly till he got to The Hellhole, he was filled with the kind of pride he'd observed among good German burghers. Responsibility. Sense of place. Sense of being at one with one's surroundings. He was not being ironical. He really felt like he was where he wanted to be and happy about it. He was glad to Occupy Space. It was a good and ennobling act and he would always love Bonita Rae Doucet for pounding the appreciation into his flesh. He had been adrift a long time. A decade, at least. Now he was thirty-nine. He needed an Occupation.

As he walked along, before he knew it, Gus was on Rampart Street, at the edge of the Quarter, and staring up at the Mortuary Church, the one where all the plague people were taken over a century ago. Past the church was Storyville, where jazz was born but which for some time had been a soulless Project that gave you the willies even in daylight. The cemetery was just down the street, too. Gus stood on the corner for several minutes, watching the buses shuttle down Rampart enveloped in blue fumes, listening to the particles of conversation of the people walking behind him. He sighed. Then he walked across the boulevard against the traffic and went into the church.

It was cool and dark, like something half-remembered from another life. Whatever had distracted him back on the corner was gone. Nor was he feeling burgher-like anymore. Something else had calmed him. He took a place in one of the rear pews.

Almost no one was inside. Three young black women up

front. A priest in robes walked along the front of the altar and exited a side door leading to the outside garden. Gus looked at the altar, and up at the statuary: St. Anne, the Virgin (for it was the Church of Our Lady of Guadalupe), St. Jude, St. Expedite. He knew that was the one they called the voodoo saint but he didn't know why. Over to the side of the altar was a large alcove filled with rows of burning candles. Gus wasn't a Catholic but he made his way down the aisle and put his quarters in the rack and took two small white candles and placed them on the rack with the others and lit them.

Returning to a pew in front, he made a place next to a young black woman. She was whispering her prayer. He heard: "Please let Mama get better and be out of the hospital. And if Frank won't help pay. . ." Gus turned his head away.

He didn't pray, not knowing how, but he offered a blessing. One for himself and one for Bonita. Then he got another candle and lit it and just sort of expressed a wish for things in general to work out. Which was what had hit him back on the corner, probably. Some little prick of a lie. Some little zap of electrical juice that said the world as he saw it had a crack in it and even being an Occupying Space couldn't fill it all up. But the zap passed fast, and with the candles and his offering he felt calm again.

Which, he thought later, is probably why he was able to see the vision. In calmness things can be revealed that hide from the mind of the perturbed soul. Amid the hundreds of calming, burning candles it had formed. It was quite clear. It was so plain he couldn't believe none of the other people saw it. Or maybe they did and they thought, as did he, they'd be crazy to mention it.

What he saw was a black rectangle, starting the size of a cigar box and expanding to fill the entire wall. And in the blackness a lightning storm of speckles of white gave way to a movie screen.

In the Mortuary Church, Gus Houston was watching "Star Trek." But instead of whoever they were in electron space the actual characters became Gus's friends, relatives, total strangers. Captain Kirk was a major he remembered from Germany and Mr. Spock was Bonita. They were trying to save a star from imploding by bombarding it with a special plasma particle bath. Twice, during the show, Gus glanced around to see if anyone was looking at him or if he was acting strangely or was in convulsions or anything medical but then he settled in for the matinee.

It was over in a few minutes. The screen just went black and imploded itself into the aura of one of the candles. When Gus rose to leave, forcing his eyes to look up from the floor where they wanted to hide, he bumped into pew after pew until he reached the back of the sanctuary. He turned back to see if the movie was on again but all he could see were the candles and the statues of the saints tending to the Virgin and the people at their places, beseeching their fortune.

He left the vestibule and walked back out into the late morning. The clouds had gone, and with them the cool, and he was sweating before he got a block. Gus considered himself a man of vision—who doesn't?—but not *Visions*. Had he seen one? Was it a TV show? Was he delirious? No, he wasn't that. He felt fine. It was his Saturday of Occupying Space. It was his day of personal definition in the city of eternal mystery. And in such frame of mind he proceeded on down Rampart Street, full of traffic and surrounded by decay, until he was at the gate of St. Louis Cemetery No. 1.

It was empty, except for the vaults of the dead. Nobody much ever visited the grounds, partly because of the bad location. But even inside the cemetery's stone walls, the tombs were protected from the eyes of the living by labyrinthine design. The walkways were so narrow and unmarked that the stonework of the dead rose around you like English hedgerows. They led to Marie Laveau.

He had developed the habit of visiting her from time to time, so that it wouldn't just be tourists and weirdos who dropped by, and so he wasn't really looking for anything. As usual, the base of the tomb was cluttered with half-burned candles, broken bottles, names etched in black ash. The chipped facade was covered with crosses of red brick dust, bits of balloons, dead flowers, coins stuck on with tape or wedged into cracks.

He stared a while, blankly, calmly. Zen and the art of voodoo. He didn't know why he kept watching. Then he realized he was waiting for the TV to come on. Then he thought he'd better leave. He turned to go, but he went the wrong way and had to make his way past vaults and statues of beauty and audacity that must have seemed right two hundred years earlier to the polyglot crew of misfits and geniuses who fed the city and brought it to life.

Now it all seemed over the top. Gus didn't want to be there then, in that moment, like some character in a French novel about to be driven mad by the sun and thus inspired to kill someone for no good reason. Not that you needed to be French or sunburnt for that. One time in Frankfurt Gus saw a gang of German kids beat a Turk to death for no reason and he'd had to run for his own life through the bar district to avoid the same fate. And now he didn't want to be in a cemetery. And he was quite hot, himself.

Outside among the living he crossed back over Rampart to Toulouse. He stopped in a café with awnings over the sidewalk, took a table, and ordered an iced tea. Just like a tourist would have, except he was not one and that was still the point.

SHE SEES THE FACE of Jesus but it's in a million dots, like something there and not there. She has seen it before but when she comes back into this world she can't put it together. Just the memory of the memory of it. It doesn't matter. She remembers that she was there and he was there and even if she can never describe his face she feels the vision all over her.

"Reverend? Reverend Youngblood?"

Corina comes back to the world. Arletta is staring at her across the small desk in the reading room. Although the room itself is filled with candles and the floor along the wall next to the outside door is covered with altars to the spirits, and though the room smells of the blood and flesh upon the altars, the desk is clean and simple. Just a white lace covering, a bowl of clean water, an oversized red-cloth Bible whose edges are darkened with the ceaseless labor of Corina's fingers over the years. Arletta is scared. She asks again, "Reverend? You all right?"

The dots of Jesus dissolve. Corina's black eyes regain focus. Arletta smiles nervously, but Corina doesn't, for she has seen into Arletta's being, just as Arletta knows she can. That is why she has taken the bus up from Elysian Fields to see the voodoo preacher lady, because she is a two-headed woman who can see into the past and the future—she has the second sight.

"When the last time you been with Charles?"

Arletta winces. She's been telling Corina six months, but she knows Corina knows it was so recent she still feels warm in her cat. She knows what happens when you lie to the two-headed preacher.

"You come in here asking for help getting that man back," Corina says. "But now you also saying you got pain in your side?" Her voice shifts to a mocking tone.

Arletta looks down at the water bowl.

"You think I'm stupid? You think the Spirits don't see you trying to make everybody think you not what you are?"

Arletta can barely breathe, let alone speak.

"You having a baby, girl. Only reason you want him back, since he ain't even left, is to get him in with you and make him think he the father. You been sleeping with him all along."

Arletta starts to protest but is cut short.

"Don't you lie to me. Don't you dare."

Arletta looks the preacher in the eyes. "It's true," she says. "I'm sorry, Reverend."

"More than that to be sorry about. He ain't the father, is he?"

It takes a few moments, but Arletta says, "No."

"And you want me to feed the spirits so he stay with you and think he the father?"

"Yes."

"Huh!" Corina snorts, moving back from the table. Her eyes close. Her head drops back. Whatever she sees, it isn't Jesus. Her eyes open again. "Spirit say they can help you but they say if you ask to trick someone you might end up tricking yourself. Spirit say they can do evil well as they can do good but if you poke into the evil side you get ready for whatever happen."

Arletta's jaw is tight and her eyes can't stop looking at the preacher lady's face, as though it were a fire and you just have to keep watching the flames. Then she begins to cry.

"I just don't know what to do."

"I say you got that right."

"I don't have no money to raise no child by myself."

"You a child yourself," Corina says, without sympathy.

Arletta wipes her eyes. "But Mama say you could help me."

"Mama don't know no *santos.*"

"All I wanted was for you to get Charles to stay—"

"And think you telling the truth when you say that his baby. Girl, you know who the daddy even is?"

Arletta nods. "It Lucius' baby."

"Where he?"

Arletta shrugs. "I think he went to Chicago. He don't even know about this."

"Who you love?"

Arletta cocks her head like a puppy. "Love?"

"I say, 'Which one of those boys you love?'"

"Charles, I guess. I don't know. Neither that much but Charles got a job at Sears and I know he like to be the daddy. He mostly good. Not wild and stupid like Lucius."

Corina sighs and looks at Arletta. It isn't like this is the first one of these she's heard. And she has a dilemma. The Spirit told her Arletta was pregnant and lying about it, but it also told her it was a toss-up whether Charles would really stay. And she wants to tell Arletta that, but Arletta's mama is in the church and Corina has to think about giving the child the kind of advice that her mama didn't seem to have done.

She closes her eyes again and thinks, praying to Jesus and the spirits, and when she has it clear in mind she takes Arletta's hand and tells her she'll do what she can. She tells the girl to go buy a crab at the market and bring it back and they'll make a plate for Yemonja. She is a great magic woman, Corina explains—she can at least tip the scales in Arletta's favor. It will cost another forty dollars but Corina doesn't feel there is any option. They pray for the baby and for Arletta.

Corina walks the girl to the front of the shop, around the display counter filled with candles and herbs, and sees her out the door. Across the street, Elroy Delgado sits in his Nissan. It looks as if he is studying some kind of paperwork. He smiles at Corina, but if he hopes to make light of it he's all wrong, and the fury in her returned scowl virtually cranks up the Japanese engine all by itself and drives the car away like a fresh-whipped hound.

Her eyes followed the car all the way down Beauchamp

Avenue, as far as Canal, to be sure it has left. Just before she goes back inside the botanica, her vision falls upon a lone white man ambling up sidewalks in front of the row houses as though he hadn't a care in the world or a lick of sense and for a moment she wonders what that might feel like.

Gus had gotten lost in the morning. He'd walked along the edge of the Quarter till he got to Canal and crossed over into downtown and walked some more and then turned lake side, up past Tulane Medical and found himself heading through narrow streets lined by shingled houses with porch stoops leading up to the front door like you'd see in Brooklyn or the Bronx. Most of the stoops were occupied. Old women, hair in braids, sat in the sun talking to their neighbors, and that was sweet, but then there were stoops full of young black men who often looked at Gus with what certainly appeared to be unkind intentions.

Gus detoured away a block. His general response to glances filled with unkind intentions was to move past them as quickly as possible, because like as not the unkindness was not without motive and also because in the city you learn the best way to survive is to stay out of survival situations. He had discovered in Germany and elsewhere it didn't really matter what Individual A might have in his heart, or in the coloration of his skin, if he was in the place where Individual A-type people were generally unappreciated. In those places people were beaten and killed. The pure of heart bled and groaned same as the vile and evil.

That was a lesson of great importance to Gus. It cut through a lot of philosophical conundrums about reality and illusion, mind and matter, and lesser fare like "visualizing peace." You could visualize the hell out of things and if you were on a street corner in the SachenStrasse at one a.m. and some Nazi-boys came along and had a different vision it really all came down to if your face was in the place of their boot at the wrong moment. Occupied Space went farther than Bonita and New Orleans. It was a world organizing principle.

"Look out, man!"

Gus reacted quickly enough to pull his leg back just as the blue Nissan flew past.

"Shit, you see that fool? He musta been doin' fifty. On this street full of kids. Shit, you can't even drive both lanes without sideswipin' somethin'."

Shaking slightly, Gus looked across the street. One of the burly teenagers he had figured to be menacing was shaking his head, still watching the car make its way through the narrow maze of parked cars and fast-moving pedestrians. Gus and the teenager looked at each other like strangers do when some idiot driver has done something beyond the pale. A moment of camaraderie based on mutual judgment. Actually very hypo-critical but deeply satisfying.

"Thanks," Gus called out. "I never saw him."

"He be comin' through here like that again I'm gonna find out who he is." The boy turned to look at the cross street. He shook his head. "My sister right over there on her bike."

"Takes all kinds." Gus thought about adding something else but the boy seemed to be getting angrier by the second. So he stayed on his side of the street and instead of crossing headed further up the block. The teenager lingered on the corner, talking to himself, and then, peeling off his shirt, he turned and walked slowly away in the direction of his sister.

Gus was hot, too. He thought if he kept going he'd come to a bigger street and find a Pac 'n Sak or something to get a root beer. Then he'd better get back home because Bonita would be awake before long and he wanted to see her before she went back to The Hellhole for the evening.

After three blocks he didn't see any Pac 'n Saks but he saw a couple of kids in baggy shorts and striped T-shirts coming out of a little store on a corner carrying cans of Shasta. When he got closer he could see a stenciled wooden sign hanging from an extended iron pole. It read:

ST. JUDE LAMB OF LIGHT BOTANICA
—RELIGIOUS SUPPLIES—

Fair enough. Gus had never heard of a botanica before he moved to New Orleans but now he thought of them as weird versions of the tobacconist shops he'd seen on street corners in London and Europe. The signs out front said they sold tobacco, but you could get almost anything you wanted in most of them.

It was the same with botanicas. In the Quarter, he'd even bought coffee and a package of Little Debbie's powdered sugar donuts from a botanica hosting an "Occult Sidewalk Special" of books, beads and assorted merchandise of the trade. One botanica with some Spanish name Gus couldn't remember was run by a white guy, a Cuban, maybe—Gus hadn't paid that much attention.

As he pushed open the dark-tinted glass front door at the Lamb of Light, he reached into his pocket to see if he had enough change. He'd drink a Mr. Pibb, he was so thirsty. The air-conditioner was full on. The cold air hit the sweat on his forehead and chest so fast he felt himself tremble. But the slim, toothsome woman talking on the phone on the other side of the entry counter didn't seem to notice. When she finally looked up at him it was with neither surprise nor interest, except that her eyes held his about a beat longer than Gus expected.

5

ELROY DELGADO got home so filled with funk he nosed his car into the Rubbermaid trash barrel at the front of the garage. Not only had he never done that, it was only last New Year's he'd yelled at Luz for doing the same thing after she drove them home from the party at Eduardo's. Damn Corina Youngblood. Why'd he let her get to him that way? She was nothing to him now. I mean, he dreamed about fucking her and she had that kind of hold on him but now this was business and she was being a pain, a real pain. He backed the car away, got out and buzzed down the automatic door.

Inside he went to the fridge and took out a cold Budweiser. He walked into the sun room next to the kitchen and settled into a soft chair and drank about half the beer. In a minute he'd look at the blueprints again, but for now it was best to relax. Staring up at the *superas* on the glass shelves along one of the sun room walls, he exhaled slowly and regained his composure. He didn't want to let Luz see him this way. Not because he would be embarrassed to be seen agitated—his whole personality easily fell within that sphere—but because he didn't want to talk to her about Corina.

He smiled reflexively and glanced at the front of his black trousers. Mother of Mary, his dick was hard. What a terrible thing to feel like a gushing schoolboy around the woman you were presently going to drive out of business. Even when he stopped to think about what might happen when the first SuperBotanica went online, not to mention the one along Chef Menteur Highway and who knew where else, he never thought of himself as harming Corina Youngblood. In his most reckless fantasies he envisioned marrying her and creating some kind of spiritual empire. Yeah, that could happen. If Luz didn't cut his balls off first and Corina whack off the rest of him sooner or later. Shit. Now his dick was soft again.

Elroy finished the beer and went back to the car for his briefcase. If they were going to break ground on the SuperBotanica by Christmas he had lots of deals and lots of paperwork and lots of lawyers to deal with. Back in the sun room, looking over the specs for what he and his brother Julio envisioned as a true revolution in the spiritual supply business, he kept wondering how long before Corina would find out where he planned to put up the flagship.

Hell, she'd be able to hit it from the sidewalk in front of her own shop with a .22 pistol. What could he say? Property was cheap along Ladeau Street. And who could say that she might not find employment with Delgado Bros., S.A., once things were geared up? Yeah, that could happen. Elroy glanced at his watch. It was only two p.m. but it was a weekend and what the hell. He liberated another Bud.

GUS GOT BACK to the upstairs apartment in the old house near the zoo not long after Bonita's alarm had gone off. It was a nice place—roomy, high ceilings, not too much furniture, just a whiff of Berlinish Bohemia via garage sales and Pier I Imports. It was hers, naturally. When they met he'd been living in a downtown hotel that had once been a Ramada until they thought it got too run down and sold it to some Arabs who now used it to cater to overnight flight crews from airlines you never heard of. It did serve an excellent $2.99 "American breakfast."

In the bedroom, Bonita was all twisted up in her speckled-egg sheets with her aqua sleeping mask still on. Gus pulled the mask down and kissed her big lips. She smelled like the house cabernet. He opened one of the blinds to let in just enough light to work on his life's love's central nervous system. It'd still be fifteen minutes before she managed to speak. It was difficult to imagine Bonita waking up in the morning. Four p.m. was taxing enough. Days off if she was up by noon she was in a bad mood till sundown. She took six years to get her degree from UNO because she wouldn't put morning classes in her schedule.

He walked out of the bedroom, flipped on the radio to a jazz station and opened the glass door onto the porch that looked towards Audubon Park. It was a nice afternoon. People were riding bikes, jogging, cruising the uptown streets and generally not doing anything remotely resembling what he'd been up to the past two hours.

Smiling to himself, he went back into the kitchen, switched on the ceiling fan, and brewed some Luzianne for Bonita. Then he sat at the kitchen table, going over it in his mind, waiting for Bonita to get out of the shower. When she did, and walked into the kitchen naked, toweling her short black hair, he forgot everything and they jumped in bed.

She drove him crazy. At five-six, she was a half-foot shorter than he but she was what you call curvy. He also liked it that her nose was a little too big and a little bent to one side and that she had a slight gap between her front teeth. He liked it that she had cut her hair. That really drove him crazy, glancing from her man's coiffure down to her breasts and back. Weird, a little. When they fucked he seemed to crawl high up inside her and was surrounded by her softness and wetness and buried nose deep into her brown nipples all at once.

She said she liked to feel him hard in her pussy, which was what she called it when they fucked but at no other time, an odd coyness for a bartender just turned thirty-three but he liked that about her, too. He was a little too thin and his dark hair was usually disheveled and people said he looked like a refugee from a Kafka novel, whatever that meant, but Bonita Rae Doucet liked him packed in tight as she could get him. She always tried to bite him and she always told him she loved him and he'd learned to tell her the same, though he wasn't that much of a biter.

WHEN BONITA LEFT for the evening shift, Gus hopped the trolley down St. Charles to Miss Angelique's. Weekends the place was mostly deserted. All but a few of the girls went home and those who stayed were either so timid they stayed in their rooms or so uncontrollable they had long since figured out how to sneak out the back gate and head for Tulane or the Quarter or the clubs down on Magazine Street that didn't look that closely at ID.

He made his way through the ornate, white-painted wrought iron fence and massive brass-topped gate into the rambling gingerbread building, soft now in the sunset glow. He walked quickly past the array of glass-walled offices (inner modernity to outward tradition, Elizabeth liked to say) and down the well-polished wooden-floored halls to his own spot. He liked coming in on weekends, especially now that he lived with Bonita, because it was one of the few times he could be on his own. Whatever the value of that was.

The door seemed stuck as he opened it but it was just a pile of papers and books somebody'd shoved through the mail slot. Gus kicked the pile over toward the small table where he kept his coffee pot and tossed his keys on his desk.

It was stuffy, so he turned on the fan. His basket was plentiful with ungraded papers. Parental notes and administrative memos were stacked next to his phone and his Mac. He had a motto about paperwork—all in good time. He leaned back in his chair but caught himself short of stretching his legs out to anchor on the desk. There wasn't much to look at in that direction, except photos of himself and friends he'd had framed to decorate the walls, so he twisted around to look through the window towards the long, hedge-flanked green field that spread back in a rectangle from the U-shaped interior courtyard of Miss Angelique's.

It was supposed to "be reminiscent of Versailles," according to the school recruitment brochure. To Gus it looked more like the parade grounds at Fort Leonard Wood, where he'd gone through basic training. Or the Olde Market, the shaded quadrangle where they sold fake rusticity to tourists at the Garden of Dixie.

In fact, the field was for playing soccer. Not that anyone played soccer on it. Miss Valthenough had left last Christmas and a new coach hadn't been recruited, and now the Hapsenfields were considering dropping the program because it was expensive and none of the girls played voluntarily anyway. Agon Hapsenfield had made it a part of the mandatory curriculum for juniors and seniors so that Miss Valthenough would have enough students and thus a job. Now that Eva was gone, Elizabeth Hapsenfield had gutted the soccer requirement from the curriculum and didn't seem to be in a hurry about finding a new coach.

Agon Hapsenfield's spirits, never all that high anyway, had plummeted, despite a new interest in crystal therapy, visits from the Rama Bam Doi at Easter, and, or so it was said, encounters with Angie Ballew. There was talk of a softball team, but nothing had materialized. Gazing through his office window across the "field of schemes," as some of the girls called it, Gus realized he was looking at a Space that might no longer be Occupied, at least not by athletic seventeen-year-olds and a busty blond coach who worked part-time as a TortureCize instructor at the Uptown Health Spa.

But the Space *was* Occupied.

Not particularly to his surprise—hadn't he just seen "Star Trek" in a church vestibule?—Gus found himself staring through the window panes at the face of Corina Youngblood. Which is to say a cartoon balloon image of that face, floating inward from midfield at about the speed of a looping penalty kick. The Corina face, its edges sharpening as it came closer, settled onto the panes of Gus's office window. The face bore the same expression as when he had first beheld it at the conclusion of his walk earlier that afternoon: a mixture of surprise, scorn and resignation.

"You sure you in the right place, honey?" she had asked. Now, in the replay filling the Space in his head, she was asking again and he was replying.

"I hope so. Depends on if you have any cold drinks."

And so, once again, Gus was coming in off the street, opening the door, walking into the botanica, shivering from the rush of air-conditioning, nothing between him and Corina but a plywood counter topped with jars brimful of bright candies and pickled pig's feet. Past the counter, along one of the white, freshly painted walls, Gus saw a long glass case filled with the standard votive candles, packets of herbs, and a few things Gus had never seen—strange and weird statues, metal implements, dried things, stoneware, porcelain tureens. The case stretched back to a rear wall filled with shelves full of similar items. To the other side, past the opening left by the plywood counter, two folding tables had been set up.

A teenage boy was sitting at one, reading a book. At the other was the woman who was speaking to him. Her skin was deep caramel, virtually glowing, as smooth as any skin Gus had ever seen. Her hair was pulled back and bunned, and she wore golden earrings and a turtle-green cotton dress. She was older than he was, probably, but she was still one of those women who froze men's minds on initial sight.

"Paulus, get up and get the man a Pepsi," she said. "That'll be sixty cents."

The young man rose and went to a refrigerator wedged next to the bookcase. Gus noticed that there was a half-open door in back, and he could see into something dark and shadowy. The woman caught him looking.

"I said, you know where you are?" she asked, leaning forward in her chair.

"Is the correct answer 'a botanica'?"

She cocked her head. "You a smart boy, then."

"I get around some. But really, I was just out walking and looking for a Coke—" Paulus brusquely handed him an icy can— "or a Pepsi is fine."

"Paulus a Michael Jackson fan."

Gus nodded, popped the top, and drank about a third in one draft. He was about to say something when he heard a noise from the back. A sinewy black woman of about thirty-five, dressed in jeans and a red T-shirt that said "Mardi Gras" on the front, came out, followed by the strong smell of incense. She went directly to the woman at the table and, surreptitiously glancing at Gus, put some folded up money near a small metal box.

"I wish I had more, Reverend. Some day I might."

"You get more, and when you do, I know you'll be back and not forget Reverend Youngblood."

Then the T-shirted woman walked toward the door, brushing

past Gus as though he weren't there. Gus noticed she had two parallel streaks of blood on her forehead. And that her eyes were fixed on some spot far beyond the moment.

"She a client. Now you know where you are?"

Gus drank some more Pepsi.

"Where you from?" the reverend asked.

"I live here."

"I know that. I mean where here. What you do? You look weird for a white man."

"I'm a schoolteacher."

"Uh-huh." She was looking him over much more intently than he liked. In some way he didn't know. Merchandise, maybe.

"There my rates," she said, and pointed to a placard on the wall. Gus read it, only partly distracted by the rotten bananas hanging suspended by a purple ribbon from the ceiling.

REV. CORINA YOUNGBLOOD
AFRICAN SPIRITUAL CHURCH OF MERCY
DAUGHTER OF OGUN
SPIRITUAL ADVICE AND COUNSELING
$30 AND UP
APPOINTMENTS AND WALK-INS
NO CHECKS

Gus finished his drink and put the empty can on the counter. He read the sign again, then looked up at the bananas. Then he noticed, in a corner at the front of the store, near the door, a metal tray filled with ash, fruit, a mortar and pestle, and an odd-looking stone cone with eyes fashioned from seashells.

"So if I had thirty dollars you could give me some advice?"

She laughed. "Honey, advice ain't nothing. I give spiritual advice. It ain't me gives it. It's the Spirit. That's what it say on the sign, don't it? If it said advice I wouldn't have put 'Spiritual' advice, would I?"

"I guess not."

"So you want a reading?"

"Reading?"

"That what we call it, too. A reading. Spirit read you like a book."

"I see." Gus felt his back pocket to be sure he had his wallet.

"It's okay. White people come in here, too. I get all kinds."

"Well, that makes me feel better."

"You got that smart mouth, I can tell you that no charge."

He looked at her. The boy had gone back to the table. He was reading Huckleberry Finn. Gus started to offer a literary perspective but she interrupted him.

"Paulus my youngest. He want to go to college like his brother Jean-Pierre, the school teacher." Paulus looked up momentarily. "He got his nose in a book all the time. Myself, I don't like 'em. Except the one book."

"Huckleberry Finn?"

She shot him a look. "I don't joke about the Bible. I don't joke about Jesus."

"Sorry."

She leaned to within a few inches of his face. She studied him. Then she moved back and, looking at Paulus, motioned with her head toward the back room. The boy put the book down and disappeared through the door, closing it behind him.

"OK," she said. "I'll read you. Now you sit down in that chair over there in the corner next to Elegba and Paulus will come back for you in a minute. When you come in bring your thirty dollars, fold it up, and give it to me."

With that she exited to the rear. Gus walked back a few steps to the metal folding chair she'd indicated and sat down. That must be

Elegba there on the metal tray, he guessed. He decided not to ponder it too long and instead flexed his neck and shoulders and tried to relax. He wasn't sure if he were about to enter a carney sideshow and get fleeced or get himself good and scared by something about which he knew absolutely nothing. Before he could figure it out Paulus had slipped up next to him. He was a thin, quiet boy, almost girlish in his prettiness.

"How's life on the river?" Gus asked.

"They make us read it. Don't mean I like it."

Gus reassessed the boy. There was a timbre in his voice. And something otherworldly. And, Gus noticed, a row of three scars on both cheeks. "Go back there. She be just inside." Then Paulus went back to his table. Gus didn't know whether he felt abandoned or relieved.

A very short hallway led past a small storage area with a gas water heater and some other things and then directly to a medium-sized room at the nether end of which waited Corina Youngblood. He went in. The walls were white, with no adornments save a large framed likeness of the Black Madonna and a white Jesus. But at the base of the walls were plate after plate filled with candles, fruits, and all manner of dead creatures—pigeons, crabs, the head of a goat. It might have smelled awful except for the thick, semisweet incense.

She was alone at a small table covered with white lace. A candle burned next to a clear bowl of water. Most of the surface of the table was covered with a huge, red Bible. She had draped herself with a white shawl, cascading around her head and over her shoulders. She motioned for him to come forward. She seemed different, he thought.

"You should give me the money now," she said as he sat down.

He'd folded it tight and had been clutching it in his hand and passed it across the table. She touched the bills to her lips and seemed to offer a prayer, then placed them on the table next to the candle. "That to give you prosperity."

Gus nodded. He couldn't stop staring at her.

She gave him a piece of paper and a pencil. "Write down a word, any word you like. And then write down a book from the Bible."

He accepted the task like a child. "Any name?"

"Any you want."

He wrote: "Candide."

He didn't know too many Bible books, so he wrote, "John."

"I never heard this first name."

"It just came to me."

"That okay. Okay." She looked at both words and then placed the paper in the Bible. She closed her eyes and let her finger rummage the pages. Then she opened it. It was "Judges." She seemed to be pleased.

Then she ran her fingers along the text of the open book, eyes closed, and her finger eventually stopped. Gus could see her unpainted nail rested along a capital "C."

She looked at the letter, then closed her eyes again. Gus had no idea what she was doing. She didn't open her eyes for more than a minute. It was as if something had startled her. When she looked at him, she seemed on the verge of saying something, then changed her mind.

She started speaking about ordinary matters. She asked him about his job, and how long he'd lived in the city. Then her tone shifted. More distant, same as her eyes. Like a litany of his life, she read him his past: that his parents were dead, and that one had died in a freak accident, she didn't know what—it was a boating accident—but she knew it had been unusual and violent. She knew he'd been in the Army and she even knew he'd had a job "in some fun place, but you didn't have fun yourself," which pretty much described the years at the Garden of Dixie. It was all eerily on the mark, and Gus felt himself getting into it despite his doubts.

Then, just as he was really enjoying his chance indulgence in the occult, she stopped talking. She stared at him for a few seconds. In a still different, much throatier voice, she said, "Children. Spirit say you about to have children."

Gus thought he misheard at first. Then he smirked. He looked at the glass bowl, the Bible, the piece of paper sticking out of Judges. She was way off the beam. Way off. So it was a carney ride after all. That other stuff, maybe she guessed. Maybe she was just intuitive. Maybe a little psychic. But this—this was stupid. Having felt pleasant, he downshifted to disappointed.

"Not very likely," he said.

She looked at him with either harshness or pity. "Spirit not interested in what you think is likely." He returned her gaze. It didn't faze her. "You got a girlfriend?"

He nodded.

"She make you feel good?"

"You mean—"

"You know what I mean."

"Yeah."

"Spirit know that. Spirit say she gonna give you baby."

"Yeah, well."

"Hup!" She threw her head back. Her eyes fluttered white, then the lids closed. Her mouth hung open. He wasn't sure if she was breathing. In a moment, her mouth began to move.

"You ever been in a foreign land? Somewhere, someplace cold?"

Gus nodded cautiously, staring at her.

Her head shook violently. Two, three times.

"You kill a man—no—you with a man killed?"

He answered slowly.

"Hup!" She fazed out again for a few moments. Gus felt his facial muscles go slack.

"You could've saved that man—Spirit say."

Gus looked at her. His hands were sweating despite the air conditioning. "I don't think so."

"Spirit say he know you couldn't save him either but—Hup!—Spirit say you think you could. You blame yourself. Hup! Spirit say man name Kadur. He Turk man."

"I don't know—maybe. I don't remember—"

"Spirit say that make you sick. Spirit say you got a shadow on you. Or you already got a shadow and it getting bigger. You feel like you in a shadow?"

"I don't know. Maybe."

"You know. Inside you do. Spirit say you come here because you being sick inside. Spirit say new child come out from you to make you well."

Gus said nothing. He didn't move.

Presently, the Reverend Youngblood opened her eyes. She looked around as if just awakening and needing to remind herself where she was. Then she slumped back slightly in her chair, as if exhausted. More silence. Then she was in the present again with him. Her eyes seemed dilated and her face had softened. She touched his hand.

"You know where you are now, don't you?"

He said he did.

Then she talked to him a little more, in what he would later understand as the epilogue of a reading. She imparted sound advice: what he should eat (less meat, less beer, more "salty food"); what he should wear ("nothing purple").

She told him, too, that his spirit was hungry for something and that it wanted out. She chided him for never going to church. She told him he needed to be cleaned to rid the bad spirit. She said that would mean a sacrifice but she said he would have to come back because she didn't have time. In the meantime he should go have sex with his woman and buy an orange and rub it all over his body to *start the cleaning and then throw the orange away because it would be full of evil. And then the session was over and he left. Paulus watched him all the way out the door.*

The movie was over.

GUS GOT UP and pressed his face to the glass panes. It was dusk. Shadows faded into the blue night. When he had told Bonita about the child thing, just before she left for work, she had smiled but he didn't know what that meant. They didn't talk about it. Kids just hadn't come up much with them. The part about the dead Turk he didn't mention.

Gus realized he had unfinished business. Opening his door, pausing a moment to listen for stray students or janitors, he moved silently down the halls to the kitchen. It was clean, deserted. It was full of pots and pans suspended on hooks over butcher-block cutting boards and stainless steel prep counters. He looked quickly through the huge wooden cupboards until he found what he wanted—sacks full of Florida oranges. Miss Angelique's didn't skimp on fresh juice because that was the sort of thing it was important for properly trained young women to be able to distinguish.

He took one of the oranges, then returned to his office. In the encroaching darkness he took off all his clothes and rubbed the fruit over his body, head to toe, squeezing it so hard the skin began to break. He allowed the leakage to course over him and he wasn't quite sure where his mind was traveling. He shivered a little, though it wasn't really cold.

When he had finished he set the orange down on his desk. He wasn't sure how long he remained there by the window until he was aware that he was standing naked in his office with sticky streaks of orange on him because that's what a voodoo woman he had just met told him to do. But he did become aware of that, and when he did he got dressed.

Outside the school gates, he figured to go down the Quarter to drink. He was still clutching the orange, now full of the evil shadow of his soul. She hadn't told him exactly what to do with such cargo, so after about a block he hurled the mashed and unwanted thing as far as he could towards a lot overgrown with weeds and full of debris.

CORINA FINISHED THE DAY by going over the numbers in her book and sorting the cash. Normally, Paulus or Jean-Pierre took care of that but Jean-Pierre was gone down to Houma for the weekend to play organ and Paulus had left early to meet some friends. Then she put the cinnamon buns in the refrigerator so the roaches wouldn't get them and swept the entryway and went back to her reading room. It had been a slow afternoon after that strange white man and she hadn't really wanted to return to the room. But she had to see that it was clean and ready for the next day.

All the altars were well fed, though she knew she'd have to get rid of the plate of crabs left for Ochosi, to help Mrs. Brown's boy Tom get out of Angola in one piece. Even with the air conditioning, the fishy funk was starting to get thick. Turning to straighten her Bible, Corina suddenly stopped. It was as if she couldn't move. She sat down. She cradled the edges of the Bible with both her hands, as if it were a fragile sheet of ice, and she looked beyond it, into something on the white lace.

It was the same thing she'd seen when that man, Houston, was there. It was the thing she couldn't tell him. It was true, Spirit said he would have children but it wasn't a firm thing, just something she had felt was probably true and because the Spirit had told her about some fire-woman who loved him. So she had said the first thing she could think of that started with a "C", like the letter from the word he'd written down for her—Candy or whatever it was.

But when she was with Houston it was something else that started with a "C" came to her. It was a phrase. It had appeared in the lace on the table right in front of him. If she'd ever seen it in the Bible before or knew what it meant or hadn't been startled by what it said she would have told him because it was his reading and so it must have been words for him. But it wasn't.

Corina knew it was really words for her. She was afraid it was for both of them, and she wanted it to be for him, but she believed it was words for her. And now she saw the words again, and she stared at them perhaps a half hour, until her right forearm began to ache from holding the Bible with the strength with which you would firmly hold an egg not wanting to break it but not to drop it either. The words said:

"Come Ye to the Trough of God."

At home, she was not comforted and slept badly. About two a.m. she awoke in a sweat. She sat up and blinked several times, trying to focus. There was slight pain beneath her temples. The room was half-lit by the street lamp seeping through the blinds.

She got it. Even though it was late and she was groggy from bad sleep and she was wearing a shabby yellow nightgown she got out of bed, knelt and crossed herself.

"Praise Jesus!" she said in a hoarse whisper. Then, louder, "*Praise Jesus!* Thank you, Jesus! Thank you, Spirit!"

She let her head fall against the percale sheets and smiled. Later, with sunrise streaming in, she awoke again. She was curled up on the floor, a quilt half pulled down to cover her legs. She was not sweating, and she felt calm.

6

DELGADO BROS., S.A., started off as a P.O. box and a gray military surplus desk in the spare bedroom of Elroy and Luz's old place in Gretna, but the success of their first venture, Botanica of the Bayou, had propelled them directly into the spaciousness of commerce, including the half-dozen little corner groceries that now settled around them like the clouds of the gods themselves.

Elroy did not think the comparison to the heavens unjust. The corporation's new sky-blue warehouse out Airline Highway was admittedly made of prefab corrugated tin on a concrete slab and bore little outward resemblance to anything divine, but considered as the manifestation of a *marielito* and his family who had shucked off the shame of their arrival in America and done exactly what the Dream had intimated, the fifty-thousand square foot enclosure had at least as much beauty as the finest cathedral or skyscraper, considered against either of their respective struggles.

Julio, who had read much poetry, said beauty was truth. So this warehouse was the truth of the Delgados. Since the priests had always told him truth was God, then Elroy knew he was on safe theological ground considering his warehouse a temple. And his business to be God's work.

Elroy called out to Corvette, his secretary, to see when was the appointment with the architects.

"Tomorrow, at eleven. I told you to mark that down."

He leaned across the papers on his desk to the flip calendar next to the phone and jotted down what she said. "I did," he called back. "Here it is. I see it right here." She was a good secretary and, as anyone in business knows, it is better that you pluck out your eye with a letter opener than lose a good secretary. He accepted attitude from her the way a baseball manager might cut some slack for a twenty-game winner.

Elroy was anxious to see the architects' plans. He wanted ground-breaking moved up if possible. Word about the big new store had gotten around, too much so. People like Corina were mad as hell. There weren't that many rival shops—six or seven real botanicas in the city, and that was stretching it—but it was no secret what Elroy would do to them.

Certainly not to Corina.

What really galled him, though, was that she was also trying to make it a black-brown thing and an American-Cuban thing. Elroy thought that unfair. Except for Corina, all the other botanicas were run by Cubans. Nor did Elroy think he was attacking the blacks. Elroy himself had African blood. Corina knew that. How did she think he heard about the *santos* in the first place? Not from the Catholic fathers back in La Habana. It was from his great-uncle, Elfego, a priest of Ochosi.

From the age of seven or eight, Elroy had been to the parties they called *bimbés* at Tío Elfego's apartment in one of the housing projects of the Revolution. He had seen the *cuchillo* cut the throat of a goat—the first sacrifice he had ever witnessed—on a Friday night as the adults around him danced and sang and made strange prayers and drank the blood from the animal's throat. He had not been allowed to drink—not then. But by his thirteenth year he had taken the way of the *santos,* lost himself in the wonders of Changó, whom he thought the greatest and most powerful of all the spirits, except for Olofí, the greatest of all— God himself. And now this black woman who had never even set foot outside her own country was telling him he was attacking African people. Well, they would see.

He pushed back from his desk and walked out to the balcony railing. His office, and Corvette's, and a few other cubicles, really just boxes created by plexiglass partitions, were perched on a small platform at the front end of the warehouse. From the catwalk railing, Elroy could look down on the vast space. A half-dozen workers with front-loaders moved about, shifting pallets of boxes here and there.

It was a good system. Elroy had seen how Wal-Mart did it, and Federal Express, and he wasn't that sophisticated yet, with conveyor belts and computers, but he and Julio had set up a system in which supplies were routed by content and destination. Each of the three Delgado Bros., S.A., botanicas had a special area, color-coded because many of the workers had trouble reading. But the biggest area, so large it consisted of aisles full of boxes of candles and oils and statues and sacramental clothing, and of course Bibles and cassette tapes—"No Need of the Spirit Left Untended," as the motto went—was for the SuperBotanica.

Even Elroy was sometimes astonished at the stockpile. It hadn't been easy, setting up contracts in New York, Miami, Oakland, La Habana (very difficult), Chicago, even Minneapolis. And most of the people he dealt with were crooks. That's what he tried to tell Corina as well. He wasn't just going to change the scope of the botanica business in America, he was going to reform it. Volume would speak. Prices would go down. The crooks and hustlers would be driven out of business. That was his dream.

As he dreamed, he noticed Julio down on the floor, talking to one of the front-loader drivers, jotting something down on his clipboard. He was wearing a yellow hard hat. That was his color. By some weird fate, Julio had been given to Ochún as a child. Normally that was a woman's god but not always. Tío Elfego said it was because Julio was a poet and Ochún was the best spirit for that. And anyway, like all the *santos,* Ochún could be man or woman. Same as with Ogun and Corina. Ogun was a war god, usually for men, but Ogun suited Corina fine. The *santos* always seemed to know in whom they should dwell.

As Elroy always told Julio, even his own god, Changó, could switch sexes, so it wasn't that big a deal. For example Tanya was a daughter of Changó. She had those long, cylindrical breasts, which at first Elroy didn't like but then later he did. She was a beast in bed. She said it was because they were both Changós and so it was like fucking yourself and someone else at the same time and therefore had to be intense, and, being so intense, had to eventually eat itself up, which it did, and they had a huge fight and then it was over.

That was all when he was twenty and she was twenty-five. She had stayed behind in La Habana when he took the *marielito* express. She was a schoolteacher and, like her parents, would never leave the Revolution. That was her nature. A fighter. Elroy believed he was, too. He fought here, in America, and she there, in Cuba.

Elroy smiled. He was sounding like Julio, making stuff sound a lot grander than it was. He was a businessman. Simple.

"Half an hour," he called down to Julio, and pointed to the watch on his wrist.

Julio looked up, at first as if he didn't understand because of all the noise of the warehouse, but then waved to say he did and make an OK sign with his fingers. Thin and wiry, he was three years younger and two inches taller than Elroy. His left ear had a notch in it the size and shape of the pointed end of a beer can opener, from a strange childhood accident. He also had a splotch of freckles across his nose. Like Elroy, his skin was white and his appearance Spanish, despite the blood from the Lukumí.

People said he looked like the dead actor Montgomery Clift, which he resented, because Clift was gay and it was bad enough sometimes dealing with the Ochún image, and the poet image. On the other hand, people said Elroy looked like Carlos Fuentes, especially when he wore glasses, and Fuentes looked like a jowly version of Floyd the barber in the old "Andy Griffith" television show, which they used to watch sometimes on Miami stations when they weren't jammed. So Julio was the better-looking, it was commonly agreed. Except for the ear.

Elroy looked out at the warehouse again and went back into his office. He studied the construction schedule again and was clear in his mind that the time was right. He was clear that things couldn't wait and that the best way to avoid trouble would be just to tell Corina right off the bat, before the grapevine picked it up, exactly what would happen and when. That way she could get mad now and have time to get over it and then things could settle down and the project could begin.

Sooner construction began, sooner the store would open. Sooner the store would open, sooner the battle would start. Sooner started, sooner finished. Elroy felt it would be better for all just to get on with it. He thought if you couldn't avoid something, best to get through it and go on. And best if you could minimize the duration of the fight with a little thought up front.

So that was his plan. He'd decided to stop having his people drive by Corina's botanica on Eldora Street so much, but he would make at least one more trip himself. He and Julio would drop by and tell Corina exactly what was coming down. Not for her benefit, but for their own.

SHE WAS ON a roll. Good thing, since three clients were already waiting for her at the botanica when she got there at eight and four more had come in before noon. But the spirit was in her and she pulled through the vortex swiftly and effortlessly like a strong sailor lifting up shipwrecked passengers from a lifeboat to the deck of an ocean liner.

Lateesha needed to take better care of her son, to keep him away from the gangs in the projects, and a pigeon to Ogun bolstered her strength in the battle. Clyde required more of a scolding—he was back for the third time from his drinking. Corina didn't need a spirit to tell her what was wrong. She told him not to come back till he hadn't had a drink in a week and she thought maybe he was scared enough to do it this time.

Miz Odetta was still upset about her sister dying and leaving her in the big house off Simon Bolivar by herself. Corina told her to burn a candle to St. Jude and promised to visit the cemetery and make an offering at Wylotta's grave, but she didn't tell Miz Odetta what it would be because although she was in Corina's congregation at the African Spiritual Church of Mercy, she wasn't voodoo and didn't approve of it. Or at least didn't want to say she did.

And so on. By noon, Corina had run through all her clients and was so hungry she sent Paulus out for a cheeseburger and Dr. Pepper, cholesterol and high blood pressure and the doctors be damned. She felt good. Very good and ready for an afternoon full of twice as many clients. It was the Lord's day, she thought, still stoked from the confusion and then the clarity after the strange message last weekend in her reading with the white man, Houston.

When she heard the tinkle of the bells over the front door she looked up with a smile, expecting Paulus with nourishment for the hours ahead.

She got Elroy.

It took less than a second for the blood to drain completely from her head, then pump back at twice the volume, and for her smile to twist into something that could best be described as not of this earth.

"Good afternoon, Reverend."

Nor was he alone.

"Afternoon, Mrs. Youngblood," said the scarecrow behind him.

"I know it must be July outside," Corina said. "'Cause I know I wouldn't be seeing Elroy and Julio Delgado in my store unless Hell was frozen over and it be snowing in New Orleans on a hot day." Standing next to a shelf filled with Ogun pots and *superas*, she made no move to greet them. Nor did her crossed arms and deepening scowl offer encouragement.

Elroy wasn't fazed. He walked up to the counter, smiled, and laid down a stack of papers. Julio was less felicitous, waiting back near the doorway, studying the hanging bananas, Elegba altar, and, over by the corner refrigerator, a large iron kettle filled with sticks. "*Mayombera*," he said under his breath to his brother, who heard it and nodded, as if it meant nothing. It did and didn't. Elroy knew Corina had studied the ways of *palo*, which was like *santería* but without the saints. It was a cult of the dead from the heart of the Congo. Elroy knew the rituals himself but Julio had never liked *palo*.

Corina heard Julio and saw his anxiety. She liked it. She

smiled at Elroy to show him both things.

"Now, Corina," Elroy began. "Don't be mad. We have come here out of respect for you because we have business to talk about."

"Huh," she snorted. "Monkey business if it from you."

Elroy forced himself to keep smiling. He forced himself not to think about the shape of her breasts. What perfect fits for his mouth. She was amazing and never ceased to move him. Fortunately he didn't get a hard-on.

He began to unfold a large sheet of paper. "I know you don't like the store we want to open, *querida*—"

"Don't be talking that Latin shit to me—"

"—and I can understand. That's why Julio and I have come down here today."

"Unless it's to tell me you're moving back to Fidel, I don't want to hear it."

Elroy sighed. Maybe this was an idiotic idea after all, as Julio had been arguing all the way in the car. "Tell your competitor your business plans?" he had said. "Are you totally insane, Elroy?" And like that.

Elroy unfolded the paper all the way. Corina could see that it was a map of the city. A big one. Like you could get at City Hall. She saw Elroy catch her looking and immediately averted her gaze.

"Okay, I'll get to the point. Because you are my friend, because we are, or maybe were—" he looked at her.

She said nothing.

"—Because we were good friends" —he smiled, again without reaction from Corina—"and because I am your *padrino,* and because I want to prove to you I am not trying to destroy you, that I only want to start a business, I am going to tell you my plans in person, now. So you won't hear them on the street and so you won't be able to say I was doing things behind your back."

Elroy looked around to Julio, who came up to join him at the counter.

"This is the map of all the botanicas in town," he said. "Please," he said, extending his hand, palm up, to her, "please come here. It is important and I only have so much graciousness in me, even for you."

Corina studied his face. It was true. The smile's edges were hardening into a mask. Pursing her lips, leading with her hips, she stepped forward. When she reached the counter, she drew back slightly, as if to say she wasn't to be touched.

As Elroy's finger moved from one red circle to another on the map—each site a botanica—she could see the pattern. Two were over across the river in Algiers and nobody went over there anyway. Two more were in the Quarter and were phoney—just for the tourists. A fifth was hers, just lake side of the Quarter. And the other three, Uptown, lake side toward Gentilly and over near Xavier University, were all run by the Delgados. Most of the business was in a cluster more or less cradled by the river, and about halfway up towards City Park. That made sense—more people, more traffic. It was one of the reasons she'd chosen her own site off North Canal.

Then she saw another red dot. A bigger one. With an X in the center.

Her eyes shot up to meet Elroy's.

"I don't believe it," she said.

"That's why I'm here."

She looked at the dot again to be sure. It hadn't moved.

"But there's an old washateria on that corner."

"Won't be after next week."

She stepped back from the map. She was trembling but didn't want him to see so she held her hands behind her back, tightly.

"It was the best place," he said.

"We looked all over," Julio added. "But this lot had been vacant a long time and it was a repo. The bank wanted to get rid of it."

"I never did hear nothing about it for sale."

"It just came open," said Elroy. "And that's the truth. We were looking at a place more over toward Elysian Fields, up in there, because it's not so poor even though it's all black in the neighborhood—"

"—And the agent we were using phoned and said Delta National had to get rid of some property fast to take care of some government loans and we should come look—" said Julio.

"—And we saw it and it's perfect, that's the truth," Elroy resumed. "Most of that block on Ladeau is empty, except for that laundry, and it's the right size for us and the price was right and we took it."

"And it didn't matter it's only five blocks from where I stand right now hearing all this."

"That's not true. It mattered."

"But it was a good price," Julio added.

"And a good location—you have to admit that."

She looked at them both. She looked at the red dots on the map. Her daddy had said that once—people do anything when it comes to money. "Nothin' mean nothing' when it come to money, except money." She thought about her *palo* pot. She thought about the .38 her sister Eddie had given her and how it was in that pot.

"Only thing I have to admit is you got some nerve comin' in here to tell me all this."

Elroy sighed and began folding the map. "Maybe it wasn't a good idea." He glanced at Julio. "I just thought—"

"Get out."

"Damn it all, Corina. Why don't you close this up like I'm going to do my other ones, or if you'd rather just sell it to me and come work for us? You could make more money—" He turned his face quickly, just enough to avoid an ashtray spinning past the bridge of his nose.

"I told you she was crazy," Julio said.

Elroy and Corina looked at each other a long moment. Megabytes of data were exchanged; an entire world lived and died. Children were born, families reared, generations bequeathed unto others. Love made, wrinkles earned, diseases faced, conquered, succumbed to. Landscapes changed from swamp to concrete, back to swamp. Snakes curled upon lambs. Children grew vipers from their dreadlocks and great swords descended from the heavens to smite enemies of the Lord. Unity, calm, destruction, rebirth, peace.

But Corina left Eddie's .38 be.

"We're done," Elroy said, and turned to leave.

And it would have been a strong exit. But as Julio opened the door, Paulus came in, trying to balance a cardboard tray holding two Diet Cokes and a bag of cheeseburgers and fries from Jack-in-the-Box. Not expecting Julio, Paulus collided with him, and, trying not to drop anything, fell backwards onto the sidewalk. The drinks spattered on the concrete and on him.

He banged his head, hard.

Spooked, Julio pushed the door all the way open and rushed outside. A quick half-skip at the last possible instant allowed him to clear Paulus's extended legs. Landing near the boy's upper torso, he steadied himself, dropped down on one knee, and reached out towards Paulus's head. His intention was to see if the boy was okay. Paulus batted Julio's hand away, mumbling, "Get off me you Cuban faggot," or something to that effect.

Elroy reacted quickly, too. Gathering up his papers, scrunching the map into a wad, he followed Julio out the door.

Corina waited a moment. From her position, she couldn't see Paulus stretched out on the sidewalk and thought he had merely stumbled because of the stupidity of Julio and random chance—accidents happen.

But when Elroy bolted, she moved, too.

As she got to the door, she saw Paulus on his back looking up at the two Cubans, who were jabbering at each other in Spanish—Elroy seemed to be angry at Julio, who seemed defensive. Now raised to a sitting position, Paulus touched the back of his head, bringing back a smudge of blood on his fingertips. "Baby—" said Corina.

But as she stepped forward, thinking maybe to get the .38 after all, everything turned upside down again. In a trice, she was slam down on her own butt, not hurt, but heedful that her skirt was now up around her cat for anyone to see. Which was, at that moment, Julio, who was face down on the sidewalk between her ankles.

She shook her head and sat up. Julio, his face scraped and rosy, got up quickly, averting his eyes. She had been wearing light blue panties.

Paulus, who had been spared the latest barrage, sat hands in lap in a kind of stupor. Just behind him, near the curb, Elroy was draped around the frame of a bicycle. The rider was a few feet away, on the hot asphalt of the street. Spread all around them both were dozens of ice cream sandwiches and popsicles.

"I be God blessed!" exclaimed Corina, in a rare lapse of language. "You been hit by your own people."

Moaning and clutching his left arm, Elroy dragged himself to his feet, just as did the unfortunate who had been on the bicycle. Not a bicycle, really. More a tricycle. The driver was a Mexican man of about forty, in a vendor outfit of white shirt and blue slacks. Mounted on the back of the trike was a heavy, insulated trunk which said, *"Helados Delgados."*

"It your ice cream man." Corina began to laugh.

Elroy glared at the driver. "Don't you use your bell?" was all he could think to say.

"*Sí, pero*—"

"Oh, shut up," Elroy interrupted. Then he sat down again in pain. It was too awful to even think about. They hadn't even planned to get into the ice cream route trade except they thought it was a way to eventually advertise for the SuperBotanica. They made money off it but—*shit.* His arm really hurt.

He couldn't think. All he could do was observe this goddam Mexican standing in front of him looking like he was going to be in big trouble, which was true, true, true, and then Corina laughing and Paulus getting up and neither laughing nor frowning—some weird in-between expression—and Julio having about the same dog-face as the Mexican.

"I need to go to the hospital," Elroy said to his brother. Then, to the Mexican, "Get this out of here."

Then, to Corina, "I shouldn't have come."

"No, honey, I guess not. " She laughed. He hated her voice when it was that way. Loud, street-like. She was an American nigger when she was like that and he didn't even like thinking that way but his arm hurt and she was laughing and now it was going to be war.

He bent down and retrieved his papers. Julio tried once more to touch Paulus to see if he was okay but the boy glowered at him so intensely he backed away toward the car.

THEY WENT TO THE ER at Tulane, because it was closest.

Hairline fracture. Six weeks in a cast. For Julio's face, some antiseptic cream but no stitches.

Julio dropped Elroy off at his home up near the University of New Orleans, and, without it needing to be said, drove over to Delgado's #1, the small grocery from which the ice cream tricycles were supplied. He quickly found the driver, Mr. González. In fact, the man had used his bell to warn Elroy, because Julio had heard it and had moved aside, but there wasn't much point telling Elroy anything about the afternoon other than that it was over. Which it was. Julio gave Mr. González two weeks' severance.

All considered, it was strange that Julio was smiling later as he drove down Broad Street toward his own modest, but immaculately refurbished bungalow near City Park. He knew he was smiling when he glanced in the rearview mirror to inspect the abrasions on his cheek. He fumbled in the dash pocket for a *meringue* tape.

In the armories of siblings, nothing is so powerful, nor so long-lasting, as the unspoken I-told-you-so. But Julio said it aloud to himself anyway: "Damn it, Elroy, I told you so."

What was so crazy about that? People speak prayers when no one is around. Last rites fall upon the silent ears of the dying. Cannot filial comeuppance find a place amid the dance-beat of the congas?

"*Santa . . . Santa Maria*," began the singer for the Wilfrido Vargas band. "*Madre de Diós . . .*"

7

FTER THREE LONG counseling sessions, Gus wasn't really up for number four, Stephanie Daedaleux, but there was no way to get out of it. He had become possessed of a thorough understanding of his situation. He knew exactly why Reverend Daniels had resigned to take a job at a small church in the Florida panhandle. He knew exactly why Elizabeth Hapsenfield no longer made any pretense of looking for a replacement for Daniels. He had a full appreciation of the downside of the overall venality of the pact into which he and Elizabeth had entered, and through which, he further understood, his downside was but her line item personnel reduction.

Each new visit to the chaplain was thus but a fresh astringent to Gus's wound. Self-inflicted, to be sure, but painful nonetheless. And being used was only the half of it. Had he not misrepresented himself in one of the more profound ways possible?

As he watched Stephanie shake her handsome, patrician head just enough to send the blond page boy into a double-reverse gyration with flow-back lock—twice to one side, twice back, then back to exactly the same place as it had started—Gus felt all his chickens roosting in his brain. Flapping around. Pecking. Doing nasty chicken things. It was awful. One of his greatest aversions in life was listening to somebody else's petty problems. Now that was his job every afternoon of the week. It wasn't even Biblical. It was bigger than that. Olympian, maybe. Cosmic. Certainly advanced jurisprudence: punishment *during* the crime.

Or maybe he was judging himself too harshly. He was hardly in the ranks of the Great Pretenders—no Elmer Gantry he; not even a Jimmy Swaggart. Looking alternately at Stephanie's robin's egg-blue eyes and five-thousand-dollar Chiclet teeth, Gus reflected how he could scarcely even claim to be a faker.

You could be a de facto Man of God in the Army, ad-libbing a prayer for a young man in your command hit by a tank during a snowstorm, bleeding in your arms with his ribs sticking out of his chest, without having so much as a fake diploma from the PTL Club. It was simply that you chose to minister. That's all Gus was doing. He was choosing to minister. He was choosing to have a job, to be employed, to be an upstanding citizen of the finest city in all of the South, if not the North American continent. He was a Presence. He was—

"—but now it's been three weeks and I don't know and I just can't tell anyone and. . ." Stephanie stopped speaking. She wasn't crying, but her face, normally as healthy as you would expect from a girl of her breeding, seemed filled with grayness.

Before Gus could anticipate what was about to happen, the young woman leaned forward and a spew of the day's lunch—pasta Florentine and Caesar salad—shot across the top of his desk and directly into his chest. Since it was more a spray than a stream, the expulsion also speckled his face, his trousers, and a good part of the white-paned window overlooking the dormant soccer field.

Stephanie's head dropped onto a stack of absentee reports and turned slightly to one side. For a moment, she looked like a chicken waiting for the mercy of the hatchet. In reality, she was the possible salutatorian of the senior class. In further reality, she was breathing from the corner of her mouth into a green-brown pile of half-digested lunch. Her dark blue T-shirt was damp and wet down to breast level, and her hair was thick with her own misfortune.

Gus sagged against the leather head rest on his chair, thoroughly splatted. Like someone shot but not yet ready to accept the reality of the bullet, he enjoyed an instant of denial. Pell-mell in his head, compressed into one of those moments which constitute infinity, came a cascade of conflicting insights. The proof of his theory about the value of punishment during the criminal act was one of them. That was quickly followed or superseded or overlaid by an escapist path of thought—this time, not of sex—in which he was back in the Tennessee hills worrying about attendance figures at the Garden of Dixie and whether the log plume scaffolding needed a safety inspection. *I.e.*, Gus was not here, in the aching, pungent Present.

He snapped to right away. He had promised Bonita he would stop wishing he were somewhere else. He had promised to Occupy Space. That space was now. "Oh, shit," he said, and got up.

Stephanie was sick. Completely. She was sick in his office. She was sick all over herself. She was sick all over him. She was sick all over his Mac. She was sick over portions of the walls. And it was an excellent bet she was pregnant.

"Ohhh . . . ohhh . . ."

Now up from his chair, with but a cursory flick of his hand to dispatch some of the larger chunks, Gus was around the desk and gently lifting her, then maneuvering her back to the couch. She slumped back, moaning low.

Gus locked the office door. The shade already was pulled, as was the courtesy during chaplain hours.

"Don't move. Don't get up."

"Ohh. . ."

He gathered a stack of paper towels next to the coffee pot and knelt in front of the girl, wiping her as clean as possible. That wasn't much. Looking around, he saw a bottle of mineral water Jackie Numann had left and used it to dampen more cloths and so eventually wipe the worst of it from Stephanie's face and hair.

She seemed to have nearly passed out but as Gus ministered to her, the blood returned to her face. Then her eyelids opened and she was looking at him. He had a terrible, terrible thought. She was quite pretty. But the thought passed—no more of a thought than the kind which comes on an accidental glimpse of exposed thigh on a stranger in a restaurant, or church pew.

"I'm so sorry—"

"It's okay. Don't worry." He gave her a cup of water.

"I need to go to the bathroom."

"I know."

She started to get up, but fell back again. She shivered an instant, and then began to sob so deeply Gus thought she might be choking. The sobs became more regular. She cried a long time. Somewhere in there, she said, "I know I'm pregnant," and then cried again.

Gus held her hand, then cradled her.

When she stopped, they sat silent for some time. Footsteps and voices came from the hallway and at least once person knocked but that was in another world and Gus and this young woman were in a place all too familiar to some and all too terrible if you weren't wanting to be there.

He had no idea what to do. He had decided very early on in the counseling game that he would not divulge confessions. It was Angie Ballew's admission about sleeping with Agon Hapsenfield that enlightened him in that regard. The sanctity of the confessional was good for all parties concerned, not least the confessor. Gus had learned plenty in two months on the front lines of young women's hearts. They trusted him—even the wild ones like Angie who mostly liked to see if they could shock him, and often did.

Essentially, they were correct. Gus could be trusted. He could keep his mouth shut. And yet, that same Gus-within-a-Gus, the Shadow Gus, the Gus known to Corina Youngblood and possibly to Bonita, the Gus which dared him to lie in order to get a job and had even perhaps sent him South to seek his fortune was also capable of who knew what when in possession of the secrets of the daughters of the rich and powerful? Gus did not like this about himself and often swore to maintain a high ethical posture. The philosophers would say: What is that? Gus knew— anyone does. But did not St. Peter himself succumb to weakness in what should have been his finest moment?

Gus poured fresh water on another towel and wiped Stephanie's brow and lips, where a slight, unsightly crust had formed. "Why do you think so?"

Her mouth crinkled again but she set it firmly. After a moment, she answered, "You know." Her eyes fastened on him as if they were in some kind of primordial understanding.

Gus moved back. "You don't have to talk about it."

She shrugged and sniffled. "It was stupid," she said, and began to cry.

Gus stood, pulled over a chair from the other side of the desk, sat down, and watched her.

"My parents will kill me."

"Well—"

"They *will*. Oh, God—"

It went on like that for a quarter hour. Mostly crying. Fear of Family. In that time, the obvious occurred to Gus. Stephanie was telling him all this because she had no one else to talk to. No one else to trust.

He felt like his spine had been plugged into the wall socket.

She was totally dependent on him.

She thought he was a Man of God.

Quickly reviewing his qualifications, he reached the expected conclusion. Well, he could talk to her as a wise uncle, maybe.

He inched his chair closer and took her left hand, pressing it between his own. It was cool, damp. Scared. "Let me just ask you, are you sure this could have happened?"

"Yes."

He took a breath. "Why do you think that?"

"Because he did it to me."

"Sex, you mean. Made love."

"Yes."

"And this was without a condom or anything."

"Well it wasn't like we planned on doing it. We just did it. We didn't—"

"Okay. I'm just trying to be sure." In fact, he was trying to buy time. He couldn't tell anyone in the school, and he couldn't tell Christopher Daedaleux, and the Hapsenfields weren't on the list at all. But what could he do?

"Have you been to a doctor?"

She stared up at him. "You mean a doctor?"

"Yes. A gynecologist, something like that."

She looked down and attempted to corkscrew into the couch. In a very quiet voice, she said, "No."

"How about a test? Have you used one of those tests like on TV?"

She shook her head. She continued to avoid his eyes.

"But you think it's true? That you're pregnant?"

She nodded.

"Have you told the boy?"

Her eyes shot up in a flash, held his. He looked away.

"Have you told anyone?"

She shook her head.

He nodded and sat back. "More water?"

"Yes, please."

He took her glass and went over to the bookcase to fill it up with Evian. As he poured the glass, late afternoon light drifted across the room and into the glass and the glass grew rosy yellow in one of the fullnesses of physics that interfaces with our consciousness and translates as beauty. Then the light was blocked—a cloud, unaware of its aesthetic sundering. The refraction ended and the glass was as glass: clear and full in his hand. And his head was possessed of a bizarre idea.

Gus carried the water to Stephanie, standing like some kind of shy waiter, as she drank. When she had finished he sat back down. Moving the glass aside, he took her hand again.

"I have to tell you the truth. I'm a little new at this, and I'm a man. I think I'd like to have you talk to a friend of mine. A woman. She might be able to help you decide what to do."

Stephanie's eyes narrowed slightly. "Someone here?"

"No," he shook his head vigorously. "Definitely not. No, not at all. I had in mind someone no one here knows. But someone I find, well, insightful."

"I just don't know what to do."

"I know. But I think Reverend Youngblood could help you."

"A preacher?"

"Yes, a minister."

Stephanie's eyes softened again. "I'm Catholic. I should go to a priest, if anyone."

"Sure, of course."

She looked at him carefully. He could tell she was weighing it. "But I can't—I mean I don't want to—I don't like them."

"She's black."

Stephanie's head cocked slightly.

"Does that bother you?"

"Well—" Weirdly, he could tell it didn't, but that she was waiting to see if he wanted it to bother her. Rather than pursue all those implications, he dropped the line of inquiry altogether.

"She's very good." He pressed Stephanie's hand in reassurance, even enthusiasm. "I go to her on occasion with my own problems."

Stephanie seemed to come to full attention. He had the feeling she was suddenly trying to peer inside him. He wouldn't let her.

"What kind of problems do you have?" In her shift of topic, he knew she had consented to go. It was the way of Southern women, sidling up to that which was too demanding face-on.

"I don't want you to worry about that. So you'll go?"

She looked away. "I guess, if you say." Then she fastened her eyes on him again. "Can I go soon?"

"I'll call her now if you wish."

She nodded.

He went back to his desk and dialed information. St. Jude Lamb of Light had a working number. He smiled at Stephanie as he wrote it down. Then he called. The reverend answered. Yes, she remembered him. Why hadn't he come back? He had "unfinished business," she said.

He told her about the girl, and lied only slightly in saying he was her teacher. He didn't want to get into the chaplain saga in front of his referral. Referral? How easily it rolled from his tongue. The reverend said she would be more than happy to read the girl—did she want to come on over? Could she make it before nine?

"Want to go now?" Gus asked Stephanie.

She nodded. "But I have to clean up."

He relayed the agreement and said the girl would be over in an hour or so. The matter of a fee came up. Gus said he'd take care of it, but, not wanting to discuss details in front of Stephanie, listened to the terms, saying only "yes" or "yeah, don't worry" or "I will." The agreement was that Reverend Youngblood would take the referral and Gus would pay when he came by, which was to be no later than Monday.

It was now well after school hours and the halls were silent. Stephanie arose. She could say she'd spilled something on herself if anyone caught her before she got to her room and the shower. She was worried about the smell and Gus didn't have anything so he sprayed her with Lysol, which transformed vomit to lilac with far more success than either of them expected. She thanked him and promised to call him at home after she got back. He gave her cab fare and the address.

8

G US'S BROW furrowed as he tried to take in what Corina was telling him. He unsnagged a kink in the cord and carried the phone into the kitchen.

"What you mean, pregnant? You some kind of fool?"

"You mean—"

"She got flu. Ain't nothin' in her. My mind, never was."

"But how can you be sure? She said she was."

"Men."

"What do you mean, 'men'?"

"I mean what you don't know about women I could write a book about and I can't even write."

"Maybe. But I still wonder how you know."

"That's what I do. I know things. Spirit tell me and I know. And I know this. That child no way pregnant. She very sick, and she got a boyfriend and she late with her time but she is not pregnant. I don't even say she even done it with that boy."

Gus listened. He felt relief. He felt exasperation. He felt in way over his head.

"How long ago did she leave?"

"Leave? She still here. The fruit bath take another hour to be finished."

"She's there at the botanica?"

"Well, not now. She lying down in the church. I let her go in there to stretch out on a bench because the cot in here all piled up with junk Paulus was supposed to put on the shelves today."

Gus looked quickly at the clock. Seven-thirty p.m. Getting dark. Seventeen-year-old blond student in his direct care over in a part of the city whites had long ago abandoned—but that was another story. This one was about Stephanie. It was about his stewardship with his charges. About the salutatorian at Miss Angelique's Academy for Young Ladies holed up in a voodoo church next door to a botanica. Having a fruit bath. With the flu. He'd never even make it to jail. He'd be lynched from a lamp post on St. Charles.

"And she believes what you've told me? That she's not pregnant."

"Of course she does. Spirit don't lie. The Bible don't lie. And anyway, she'll start by tomorrow."

"Her period?"

"Yes, child, of course her period. Lord have mercy!" Gus could hear laughter through the receiver.

"Well, then. I guess I was wrong."

"I guess to Jesus you were."

Gus leaned against the kitchen cabinet. Bonita was already gone to work. "Look. I'll come over and pick her up. Tell her not to take a cab."

"That's a very good idea. And when you come over, you and me have us a talk."

"A talk?"

"That's right, Mr. Candy Man. I want to know how it is you have yourself a job telling these young girls what's what when you don't have the slightest idea what you talking about."

"Candy man?"

"You know, that name you tell me. Candy. Paulus call you Candy Man."

"Candide."

"What I said."

"Not Candy—Candide. It was the name of a famous book."

Silence. "Well, you Candy Man to Paulus."

"It doesn't matter."

"So, you want to talk to me?"

"You mean about my job?"

"Not your job. About how you do your job."

"What do you mean?"

"I mean, you could use some help."

A rush of exhalation spewed from Gus's lips before he could stop it—like the old spit-takes on TV, except he had nothing to spit. What came out was nothing more than breath.

"Amen to that."

"Don't you take the Lord in vain."

"No—I mean it. I mean, you're right."

"I'm always right."

"I'll be right over," he said. "Tell Stephanie for me."

"I'm letting her rest. I'll tell her when you get here."

"See you soon."

Before he left, he opened a beer and drank it while he watched the new orange tabby bounce around on Bonita's wicker sofa. His true love was down at The Hellhole serving the first of many Jägermeister shots to guys with tattoos on their earlobes and women with rings through their nipples. Or the other way around. So what would Mr. Doucet, her daddy, say about that if the ol' boy were still alive? Would he rather his baby girl were wet with spiritual fruit in a church pew over near Broad Street? No, he would rather she be among bikers than niggers, fine ol' Cajun tool pusher from Thibodaux that he had been.

As for Gus? Well, he liked where Stephanie was just fine. He liked that she wasn't pregnant. And he liked that preacher. He just hoped that if what he thought was about to happen actually did happen, that the Reverend Youngblood liked him, too. Because this was going to be her show.

He walked downstairs and started up the K-car, which was actually a used Mustang Gus had gotten for almost nothing from the Garden of Dixie fleet. Bonita called anything made in Detroit a K-car. She drove a Honda, which her father called Jap Crap, and may have had a lot to do with why she bought it, but Gus wasn't thinking about cars or the Doucets. He was headed down Magazine Street, through the Irish Channel, across the trolley tracks, and up around the haggard uptown side of the business district. The city was all lit up. The streets were full of people entirely too disoriented, or desperate, or drunk, or detoured from Des Moines, or all of that, for him to have had any reasonable chance of explaining to them exactly what he was doing, impersonating a chaplain and flirting with the gods.

IT WAS NOT a good week for Elroy. His arm hurt and business was slow and the architects were giving him a hard time and now there was some question that an underground gasoline storage tank at the site of the SuperBotanica had leaked into the ground back from when a Tiger Oil station had been there and construction might have to be delayed until the Spring.

He was eating cornflakes and watching a morning news show on TV, trying to figure out if he could bribe anyone at City Hall about the gas tank. Shit—who knew about things like that? Nobody could even remember how long since the gas station had been there. Nobody at the bank or the washateria had said anything about a gas station at all.

And anyway, so what if something had spilled? Who cared? It

was all under the ground. Mother of God, he was getting ready to concrete over the top of the whole damn block and put up a fifty-thousand-square-foot store so what chance was there anybody could be harmed by a couple of gallons of premium that might've "leached out," the little *maricón* inspectors from the city said, thirty years ago? Fucking city. Fucking whoever.

"BEEF! BEEF! BEEF!"

It was a dog's voice, or a pretend dog's voice, on the TV, with the dog's lips moving like he was talking, and his words in little balloons over his head—how they do that stuff in the movies with the talking horses and whatever. It was a commercial for dog food.

Elroy had seen the commercial before but it had never quite hit him this way. This dog, the hound dog kind you'd get at the pound and call Ralph or whatever was jumping around in the kitchen of some *gringo* house while a thirty-year-old woman with a pony tail was holding a bowl of the dog food up so Ralph'd go crazy with anticipation. There they were again—balloons coming out of his head saying, "BEEF! BEEF! BEEF!" and he was woofing like that, too.

"... Sooo good he'll think it's BEEF—but it's NOT!" exclaimed some announcer's voice, with some kind of glee, or sense of triumph—some bragging feel to it that just like that dug into Elroy's skin and twisted. The woman put the bowl on the linoleum floor and Ralph dug in, jowls slobbering, tail wagging to beat the band, the woman smiling like she'd pulled another one on him.

Elroy slammed his spoon down on the table. He was by himself so no one saw him, which was probably good, given the way he'd been acting of late. With his mouth full of cornflakes, he said to the TV:

"Now what kind of goddam sick person would fool his own

dog? What kind of goddam sick yankee sadistic bastard would go to all the trouble to buy something just to *fool a dumb animal?* What—"

Elroy stopped himself short. He picked up the remote and clicked the TV to another channel. A movie star was being interviewed by Bryant Gumbel. Elroy, who didn't like Bryant but did like his brother Greg, the sportscaster, watched in silence, crunching away the rest of the flakes.

One damn thing, no forgotten gas tank that pops up out of nowhere was going to stop his first SuperBotanica. Nothing was. Fuck all these surprises, these little City Hall pricks telling him what he could do and couldn't and how it would cost twenty-five thousand dollars at least to clean the thing up. Fuck that. This was New Orleans. Nobody needed that kind of shit.

He clicked off the TV and wiped droplets of milk off the cast on his arm. For some reason he had remembered something far back in his head, remembered a name, a connection, somebody political, that he could call. Someone he'd done a favor for with the *santos*. Someone who would be glad to help Elroy and who also wouldn't want it to get around that he had once been mixed up with *santería* and curses on enemies.

Elroy beamed. Shit, he knew a politician.

THING WAS, he only stopped by to settle Stephanie's bill—sixty dollars, including reading and treatment, which turned out to be far less than the hundred and forty-eight dollars the school's on-call GP would have charged for antibiotics and a five-minute exam. Next thing he knew he was explaining about being the school chaplain and she was scolding him about "responsibility for people no matter who they think you are." Now he and the Reverend Youngblood were agreeing to the terms of future visits. She said bills from then on should be paid on the spot.

That was fine. Most of Gus's charges at Miss Angelique's carried plenty of pocket money.

He should've left it at that. But for some reason—same kind of feeling he'd had during his interview with Elizabeth Hapsenfield—Gus volunteered a completely unnecessary backup plan. He said if the girls wanted to get a reading but couldn't pay, he could arrange to bill their parents for "consulting therapy." He said he could forward her the payment, if she'd extend the credit.

She smiled like someone who'd just received a windfall of grace. "I be happy to work with you, Mr. Gus Houston," she said, taking his hand, pumping it with an enthusiasm that was almost embarrassing in its vulnerability. "I be happy to help all those little girls who got all those problems can't nobody fix." Then she had winked warmly. "Especially you, I guess. And I promise you this. Each one you send to see Reverend Youngblood, or you can call me Corina, I give you back twenty percent. That what we all do in the business around here."

"Oh, I don't really want anything back out of this." Even before he had finished the sentence he tried to pull it back in but it was too late. Her smile disappeared. Her lips pressed tightly where her teeth had been clean and glistening.

"What you mean you don't want nothing *back*?" she half-whispered, quietly, deliberately, as if the sinking in were still not finished; as if something that had opened and filled her with glory had snapped shut and left her doubled over in pain. "You don't think you earning it?"

"Well, not exactly," he said, evading, trying, as in conversations with Bonita, to find a space to figure out how it was he had erred.

She was two feet from his face, hands gripped in fists at her side. It was one of the fastest boil-overs he'd ever seen.

"So you don't think I'm earning it either?"

"I didn't say that."

"What you did say, then? I'm some kind of joke? You don't want to do business with me?"

"I never said that at all."

She put a finger in the center of his chest. Later, he would find a bruise. "Let me tell you the facts of life. What I do *help* people, and I got a right to charge for it. And if I don't then I got no right to do spiritual work at all because I give people something with a value on it and if it have a value then they got to give a value back to me."

"I—"

"Plus you telling me you don't want to be in business with me after I sit here and say I cut you in as a partner. Huh!" Wheeling abruptly, she stalked off to lean against the refrigerator. "You insulting the Spirit every time you let people get something for nothing. It make them think the Spirit cheap. Or that they don't have to sacrifice something to get help. It mean they get something for nothing and that be the problem with half the people come to see me anyway, that attitude. I say they work for what they want and they put something into their prayers."

"Hey, I wasn't trying to insult you." He rubbed his chest.

"Don't matter what you *trying*," she said, coming his way again, stopping just outside arm's reach. "Matter what you *doing*. Look here, Candy Man, I do what it take to keep my church going. Why you think I got this botanica? Cause I like to get up early and drive through all that traffic and stay late and never have no life of my own? I got lots of *santos* to feed and people to look after, too. What your problem anyway? I was just asking you for business is all."

"And I told you I'd send you some." Gus realized his voice had begun to rise.

"Yeah, you give me some business like people who put a dime in the collection plate give the church an offering. That ain't giving, it *looking* like giving. But it ain't doing shit—Jesus forgive me. Now you got me cursing. Well you don't be *looking* like you with me if you *with* me. The Lord say that and Reverend Youngblood say that, too: In or out. You in business with me, you in. You out, get out. You treat me with respect. I ain't to be treated like no nigger you too good to do business with. And this ain't no hobby, Candy Man. You get that?"

Gus crossed his arms and stared tight-jawed at the linoleum floor. The "get out" option sounded just fine just at that moment. And he almost took it. Except that one of those milliseconds of perception that he sometimes experienced and that were probably responsible for keeping him Going, instead of Not-Going, flushed up through his neck and turned his face scarlet. He could see that Corina saw. What she saw was that he knew she was right.

She was good. Barely knowing him, she had picked him off at his best move. On a different occasion, Bonita had gotten him like that too, and just as quickly. "You're *not* too good for me, you selfish shit," she had screamed one night not longer after they'd met when for no reason he had risen from the bed and thought to go away, maybe forever. When he had told her, "That's stupid, of course I don't think that," she had raced across the room and caught his jaw full-on with her elbow—definitely hitters, the Doucets. But he had deserved it, and did not leave.

To Corina, he threw up his hands in peace. "Okay," he said. "Okay."

They looked at each other a while. Her face looked like it had gone a little red, too.

Eventually she spoke. "You got to be honest with yourself, Houston. Then we don't have no problems."

"I suppose."

"So be honest. Why you came down here today?"

"I came down to pay you for Stephanie."

"I said don't lie to me."

"I'm not lying. That's why I came. To give you sixty dollars. Why else would I come?"

"What you think?"

"What do *you* think?"

"I don't think nothing. I know what the Spirit tell me."

"Which is?"

"Which is you came down here to do business with me. Flat truth."

"The Spirit told you I was coming to do business with you?"

"What you think I just said?"

That was, in fact, what Gus thought she had said.

Then she told him about her vision. They got Shastas out of the fridge and opened a package of Kountry Krisps, which Gus paid for. When she came to the phrase, "Come Ye to the Trough of God," she spoke with uncharacteristic shyness. She asked if he knew what the words meant. He said he didn't know much about the Bible.

She considered that a long moment, then let it go.

9

THE WEIRD THING WAS, it was working like a charm. Walking through the dark streets of the Quarter to visit The Hellhole, Gus laughed aloud. Tourists moved aside. Gus didn't care. They'd laugh, too, if they'd known. My god, he thought, in me lurks the soul of a supply sergeant. Three weeks after sending Stephanie Daedaleux to Corina Youngblood, Gus Houston was hip-deep in a business not even the spirits could have foreseen. Actually, Corina said they had and that's why she was "working with" Gus at all. Gus laughed again. He tried to be a Sky-Cam and view himself moving along Decatur Street. He was one of the people he himself usually avoided.

Already he'd sent three students, not counting Stephanie, over to St. Jude Lamb of Light. Every one of them came back to him so appreciative he thought they were going to cry. Amber Burleson, for example—the first post-Stephanie referral. Amber said she suffered severe muscle cramps after P.E. but the doctor hadn't found any physical cause and so she had been sent to Gus. His personal opinion was that Amber didn't want to go to P.E. class and was looking for him to give her the coveted chaplain's release. Corina's verdict: a pigeon to the altar of Ochosi, the hunter-god, to get the cramps from the legs. And a little female chat.

So entranced had Amber been about her visit (Gus always made sure the girls he sent had just the right touch of weirdness to accommodate the experience) that she'd completely given up on getting out of gym class. She was convinced her legs really had been seized by an evil spirit. She told Gus she was going to try out for the soccer team, which no longer existed, so she would volunteer for cross-country. And she wanted to go back to Corina—a good piece of information for Gus to find out. He said he'd let her, but only if she promised not to tell anyone, a condition he decided to impose on everyone. And he could enforce it. He heard things. He knew things.

His thoughts were interrupted just outside The Hellhole by a hirsute man the size of Utah who seemed to pop out the saloon-style doors like a cork from a Champagne bottle. Slamming into an iron light pole, the man stopped, backed off a few feet. He looked at the handbill-festooned pole, which must have appeared to have looked back, and raised his hand as if to strike.

But then he shook his head, extended both massive arms skyward and yelled, so loudly you could hear it over the Zeppelin inside the bar, "Excuuuse me, lady. Excuse the fuck out of me." Then he laughed and walked on, stopping about twenty feet on to examine his bare feet. He said, "It's them damn socks," and proceeded into the night. Nobody said a word to him. The only thing he wore was a black gimme cap and a pair of boxer shorts with interlocking candy hearts on the back.

Gus went inside. Bonita nodded hello. "Thurgood's probation was over yesterday."

Gus took a seat where the dark cypress bar curved into the wall. Bonita chinged the cash register toting somebody's tab. To Gus's surprise, The Hellhole was nearly empty. In one corner, two white guys in dirty striped shirts cut off at the sleeves, probably from the oil patch or maybe some city street crew. Old

Clyde, a retired truck driver who had adopted the bar as his nightly home fifteen years ago when it was called Toppy's and was mostly jazz and who stayed at it even after its metamorphosis into a biker hangout—especially weird because Clyde was black—was at the opposite end, on his usual stool, bent over his Dixie beer and doodling on a beer coaster. People said Clyde had bounced on the interstates too long but Gus liked him and Bonita wouldn't hear a bad word about him.

But that was about it. Except that the juke box was real loud, and now playing Rush. Along the front of the bar, at the base of the stools, was a discarded pair of huge, grease-stained jeans, a Harley-Davidson T-shirt, some black boots, beer-soaked gray socks, and a skinning knife. Also a watch, a set of keys on a chain, and a crumpled assortment of envelopes, letters and a catalog, that, when Gus leaned closer, was seen to be from Victoria's Secret. On the counter directly above all this was a row of beer cans of several different varieties, and a pyramid of perhaps a dozen shot glasses.

Bonita scooped up the dead soldiers and put them in the washing rack, then wiped the bourbon soup that had accumulated underneath them. When she was done she came over to Gus. He was looking at a big crack in the wall near the hall to the bathrooms, and a scattering of all the framed photos of biker patrons on the floor. "He danced right into the wall. Half-naked. Just stuck there, too, for a minute, like he'd been glued." She shook her head and attempted not to laugh, thinking it unprofessional, even for Thurgood.

"That's right. That's sure enough right." Clyde nodded his head and continued his doodling.

Bonita ducked under the waiter's entry leaf next to the register and carried over two fresh bottles to the oil patch boys. They said something to her and laughed, and she came back to the bar. She dug into the cooler and got Gus a Dixie.

"And how are *your* crazy people doing?" she asked, half-watching a couple of Tulane students who had just entered. They liked to drop in time to time to breathe the air of the defiant. She always had to check their ID.

Gus followed her almond eyes, then returned to gaze upon her petite person. He had never stopped thinking she looked out of place in The Hellhole. For that matter, so did he. But to her it was just a job and, as she frequently pointed out, macho guys were usually big tippers.

"Not bad."

She nodded. Gus thought he saw her jaw set slightly. It was still far from settled about his "scam," as she insisted on calling it, with Corina Youngblood.

She left the counter to carry a tray of neat vodkas to the students. Gus knew she just didn't see it yet. Not the whole Big Picture. She thought it was a money thing. But that was Little Picture stuff. There was a Picture so Big even Gus himself hadn't quite taken in all its dimensions. Though he was working on it. From the shadows.

He adjusted on his stool and grabbed the *Times-Picayune* from the corner. Thinking of Corina, Gus smiled involuntarily, though he tried to hide his expression from Bonita, because unexplained facial smirks were one of the things that sent her into protracted inquisitions.

"To the Garden of Dixie," he said, raising his beer mug. No one except Bonita had any idea what the toast meant, although one of the Tulane students yelled over the jukebox, "Whoa, that place sucks—we went there last summer."

Flipping through the paper, Gus began reading a feature story about how city officials were already planning for Jazzfest, the two-week outdoor music extravaganza at the Fairgrounds every spring. When Bonita had a moment to talk to him again he folded up the paper and pitched it aside. Jazzfest wasn't her favorite event. Two years ago, walking back to her car after one of the shows, she'd been mugged and robbed. Three young white guys broke her nose and took her purse. It might've been worse, but some people had come along and the muggers had run away. Never got caught. Last year Bonita hadn't gone. She was even starting not to like Mardi Gras. Things with big uncontrollable crowds. But she didn't mind working in the Quarter.

She took a drink from his mug and touched the top of his hand with her fingertips.

"Corina's good for the girls. She understands them."

"That's good," Bonita replied. She withdrew her hand. "One of you needs to."

"I thought we talked about this."

"We did. I just didn't think you'd keep doing it. Don't give me that look—you know what I mean. You could get fired for that shit. I think we talked about that, too."

"For a bartender you worry a lot."

"You tend bar you see a lot to worry on."

Gus held her eyes a moment, then decided not to ruin the evening. A bar was no place to pick a fight. "I'm just having fun. Keeping the game interesting is all."

She glared at him.

"I'm sort of drawn to it, okay?"

"I'm glad." She walked over to the tap to pull a beer for the oil patch boys. To Gus's amazement, the golden-brown stream from the spigot froze in midair.

AT SIX-FEET-ONE, a hundred and ninety pounds, and with a full head of only slightly gray-flecked brown hair, Joe Dell Prince would have been handsome except for the way his dark brown eyes seemed to leak evil into the universe. Neither flaw was Elroy's concern, though it did make him wonder how this white man had made a career in state politics instead of something considerably more mundane. Julio always said Joe Dell should be selling shoes at the mall, but the back half of the joke was that they had to agree he would probably sell more shoes than anyone in town and eventually have his own shoe empire and go into politics anyway.

Today, the *gabacho* was uncharacteristically casual: navy blue golfing shirt and khakis, which made sense, because after breakfast, Joe Dell was on his way to play eighteen holes at the Metairie Country Club, which most everyone in town called Club Met.

He was alone, which also was unusual. He normally traveled in bunches. A bunch of assistants, or aides, or secretaries, or good ol' boys. The senator was always going somewhere, doing something. Elroy didn't really like him. As Julio said, it was hard to like someone who thought of you as a member of the "mud races," and had got elected promising to send you back to Africa or Mexico, or Cuba, if it were ever free again. Which was also on the senator's agenda.

But Elroy didn't have to like Joe Dell Prince. Eight years ago, when the senator was nothing but a Metairie ambulance chaser who got publicity because he was some big honcho with the Knights of the Aryan Swords, he had come to Elroy with a request that probably changed his life. And Elroy's, for that matter, if the business at hand today worked out.

Joe Dell Prince had been running for his first term in the Louisiana legislature. He was up against a black building contractor who carried a lot of weight with his own people. His name was Charles Davis, but everyone called him "Hindfoot" because he'd been a track star at Loyola. There was something else about Hindfoot—he was very superstitious about hoodoo. To Elroy, hoodoo was a mishmash of African and Indian and Cracker weirdness—amateur stuff. Corina hadn't been much beyond hoodoo and Bible prophesying when Elroy had met her, and had led her to the *santos,* but in Elroy's experience most of the black people he knew in New Orleans had some kind of hoodoo thing. Hindfoot Davis, for example, grew up drinking root tea for colds and burning cotton in an iron bucket for the fumes to take away the pain from broken bones. He also grew up believing in fixes.

During the campaign, Joe Dell had learned how Hindfoot still went to hoodoo women and root doctors and kept a pot of herbs in his house to keep away evil spirits and so on. It came to candidate Prince that this was a very damaging trait of character for a politician to have in a district that had recently been redrawn to favor the middle- and upper-middle-class white conservatives as opposed to the previous, mostly poor and black constituency.

What led Joe Dell to Elroy was Robbo, of Robbo's Airline Highway Grill, the small pancake and steak house where they were meeting today. Robbo was part Mexican but out and out hated black people and he and Joe Dell occasionally raised their blood pressure over coffee and sausages denouncing welfare and Spike Lee and that kind of thing.

Make a long story short, Joe Dell mentioned to Robbo how he'd found out about "Hindfoot's" interest in hoodoo, and they got to talking some more, and Robbo later on talked to Lupe, his produce jobber, who was also Elroy's cousin, and bingo, late one evening there was the candidate at Delgado's #1, the grocery where the ice cream routes now ran out of.

The candidate said he knew Elroy was a *santero* priest and that he was interested in spiritual matters and needed to talk to him in the utmost confidence. So Elroy closed the grocery to talk. They sat in the back on cardboard boxes of Northern tissue.

Not knowing much about Louisiana politics at the time, Elroy had agreed to help with what seemed a routine bit of spirit work. Just a small "fix" was all Joe Dell wanted. Elroy explained that a *santería* priest like himself didn't do fixes but Joe Dell had said fixes was all the Hindfoot guy would understand and that it was important to do it in order to stop "that dangerous man" from getting into office. Joe Dell had added that Hindfoot hated Cubans and was pro-Castro, which sent Elroy's blood boiling. Turned out Joe Dell was lying—but Elroy didn't know that at the time.

They agreed on three thousand dollars. It was high, and Elroy expected to have to come down, but Joe Dell didn't balk. Within a day Elroy had his plan—a cow's tongue on the front porch. The message was that people who talked too much might lose their own. Or worse. Joe Dell thought it was a "wonderful idea even if it was kinda sick." He wanted to go with Elroy to see it done, which was normally a strange request, but he was paying premium, and to be frank, Elroy didn't care about either Joe Dell or the man he didn't want in office. He didn't even consider this to be real spirit work.

But Joe Dell had obviously considered the fix very important. Late that very Thursday night, Elroy had no more than nailed the swollen blue-gray tongue—which he got from the butcher who supplied his grocery store—to the eave over Hindfoot's porch and gotten back to his car up the street than he heard someone yell, "Hey nigger, come on out."

Startled and angry, Elroy got in his car ready to peel away. But his intuition—or the *santos,* if they were having any part of this— stopped him. Instead of cranking the ignition, he hunched down so he could just see over the steering wheel. He hadn't taken time to notice, but now he could see it was a nice, middle-class house. Ranch-style, red brick, with a white porch surrounded by thick shrubbery. Elroy thought how he wouldn't mind living in such a house. But mostly he wondered what was happening.

There was another shout, then quiet. Elroy thought it best to stay put, that driving away now would only expose him. So he did nothing. Five minutes passed and he decided that maybe it would be best to leave after all, but then the porch light came on. Through the rim of the steering wheel, Elroy saw a tall, black man of about fifty emerge from the front door. At first the man didn't see it. Then he did. Then he seemed to explode in lights.

Strobe lights, they were called, illuminating him so brightly you could see the moment of terror in his eyes as, having clearly beheld the curse, he was transfixed by it. Really, it was only a moment, but had the terror not been so intense, had the anger of being summoned out and startled not taken so long to supersede the shock of that terrible torn flesh no more than a foot from his face, maybe things would have been different. But what came out was a photo of a black man with eyes popping from his head. To Elroy, it looked like a cartoon character. A black guy gaping at a bloody tongue hanging from his own house. Those were the photos that everybody saw in the newspaper and on TV. They were so awful even Elroy felt kind of bad about it even though he himself had been deceived.

Hindfoot never lived it down. No amount of talk, not even a police investigation, which didn't amount to much because no one but Joe Dell and Elroy knew about it and weren't talking— nothing ever changed the gut reaction in the white voters when all the publicity got out.

Joe Dell won big. He was now in his third term. People said he wanted to go to Washington or be governor next. He didn't talk much about the Aryan Knights anymore, and nobody even remembered the primary from eight years ago. But Elroy did. He

knew exactly how the *gabacho* senator had earned his first land-
slide.

WHILE ROBBO POURED a fresh round of coffee, Elroy explained
his problem. He outlined the SuperBotanica plan. He tossed off
demographic profiles and marketing projections. He exuded
success. He could see how the Senator (who had decided "white"
Cubans, whom he thought Elroy was, were acceptable) was
impressed. In fact, the Senator mentioned that he might consider investing a little himself in such a "drugstore for your kind
of people" if he could come up with the cash.

Elroy said such an investment could be arranged—maybe a
loan of some kind. He also wondered if the Senator could help
with these city environmental *maricón* shitheads and their gasoline tank rules. Then everyone's share in the enterprise would be
worth just that much more. They agreed it could all work out.

They parted in the parking lot next to the café, shaking hands,
generally effusing that extra bonhomie that sometimes erupts
between men who basically dislike each other but don't want
their feelings to interfere with their respective goals.

Watching the Senator drive away in his LeBaron to his golf
game, Elroy smiled. At exactly the same moment, he felt his
stomach knot up like it was full of uncooked dough. In the world
of the *santos,* Elroy knew, you never knew what was what. A thing
could be its opposite. Nothing was ever settled, and Elegba could
come in and shake up the best-laid plans on a whim and hurt you
for fun and make you like it. That was the way of the *santos.* But
what was the way of the world Elroy was now trying to enter?

10

CHRISTMAS SLIPPED BY, and then it was New Year's Eve, and that seemed to leave only Mardi Gras before Elroy could have his dream, even with the delays. Now, though, it had gotten on to March. By Jazzfest in May, for sure, Delgado Bros. SuperBotanica would open for business and become the only thing of its kind in the South. In anywhere. Not in Lagos was there such a store, not in Port-au-Prince, definitely not in La Habana, and nowhere at all in North America although LA was a definite possibility sometime in the future. But right now, nowhere did such a giant discount warehouse for the gods exist.

Elroy was overwhelmed by the transcendental nature of the venture almost as much as by his own marketing genius in thinking it up. The yankees, whether black or white or English or Spanish or Protestant or Catholic had never understood the *santos* or their following and so none of the corporations or the guys like Sam Walton had ever thought about getting into a market that would never go dry. Elroy couldn't help smiling to himself. It was better than selling food, even, because people could go without food, or eat cheap food, but they never went without their faith and it was well known that even the poorest soul would find a way to bring gold to the altar.

And that was just the Christians. The followers of the *santos* had a need to feed their gods that the preachers and the bishops could only dream about. And Elroy was the middleman, the one who would show them a way to nourish their spirits even more often than they had imagined, because no longer would the faithful have to shop at tiny, out-of-the-way botanicas likely as not to charge twenty times what something was worth, and thus screwing the faithful to the wall. Elroy would give them bargains. He would give them volume. He would give them selection. He would make it easy. He would give them an 800 line.

Elroy was aware that he was a businessman and wanted to make huge amounts of money off his SuperBotanicas but he also felt he would do for *santería,* even for voodoo and hoodoo and those other half-assed American things, what Henry Ford had done for the automobile. Once upon a time, nobody even knew what a car was; now there was one in every garage. Because the cars became cheap and everyone could have one.

Santería would be affordable, it would be competitive, it would be completely out in the open. People would go to the SuperBotanicas like they went to BizMart and Computer Universe. This Elroy would do. He would make a change. It would be a change that counted and he would be remembered for it.

Thinking along those lines made it almost impossibly difficult to wait on Senator Prince to finish the business with City Hall. Elroy had told him to get it done during Christmas because nobody would know, but Joe Dell had said wait till Mardi Gras when everything's a mess anyway and nobody knows what deals get done.

And they had. And Elroy had been right and Joe Dell wrong.

Elroy still wasn't sure how it happened, although Corina and that asshole *gabacho* teacher Houston were at the bottom of the shit, but just as some city inspector who got way too fucking much money for it was going to clear the permit to start construction a story about the SuperBotanica and the gasoline tank had popped up on the TV news. Now the city *maricónes* couldn't let it all go. Now the media who ought to have better things to do knew about the plans for the SuperBotanica, which that TV bitch called the "Voodoo Mart." And now the whole city knew.

It was a nightmare top to bottom, and if it didn't get worked out soon, Elroy was afraid he'd lose his option on the property from the bank, not to mention sales for every month the stupid delay dragged on. Not to mention kill the *gabacho* and maybe Corina himself—Elroy caught himself. He'd been drawing lines on a note pad on his desk and saw that the pen had dug so deeply the pad looked like he'd taken a razor to it.

He glanced up to see if Corvette had seen him through the office window. Shit. She was looking right at him. She gave him one of those eyebrow arches that was supposed to imply he was doing something that she found pathetic. Fuck her, too. He stared back until her expression changed from contempt to boredom and she swiveled her chair back around to her computer screen. He looked back at the shredded pad. He felt a rush of heat and realized blood had drained from his face. But he was a Changó and anger came to him easily.

Julio said, "Patience will prevail," but Julio was of different stuff and anyway Julio didn't wake up nights with his gut turning the shit inside it to water so often Elroy had started to wonder if Corina had managed to get some of her *palo* poison in him somehow. But he killed three chickens and threw the *obi* and knew that the battle had not reached that level yet and that it was his own fear and anger that were, literally, eating him. Thus had Yemonja the sorcerer told him. And that to pull out of his sickness he must act—Ogun had appeared to him and said this, too. These were strong spirits and Changó could only agree with them.

Elroy then bought six young roosters and fed them to the spirits and slept an entire night with their blood on his abdomen and head. It did not keep away his anger, but instead of turning it against himself, all that terrible power coursing through his dreams and his gut as he slept, he now welcomed the anger and knew it would transform him as it had led Changó to so many victories over his enemies in the dawn of time. Things would happen.

If he could just get going, get the *maricónes* to give him the permit, even if it had to be legal and through the courts, the land could be cleared and the building could be up in sixty days, maybe less, and stocked out and open in another thirty. Maybe in time for Jazzfest after all. Hell, everything was planned down to what went on which shelves, they'd had so much time to work out the details. Elroy felt like the SuperBotanica was some big explosion waiting that would burst into being like the sun if only he could get the thing ignited.

He was calm again. He looked at the pad and laughed, for he realized it was not he who had raked it with the point of the pen but *Los Guerreros,* and Changó, who were girding for battle. Like any of the spirits, they could pop out of their human servant at will, at whatever time they chose, and that was one of the things about the life of a *santero,* and if Corvette didn't know that she was stupid because if she held Elroy in contempt she was defying the *santos* and one day she would find her life as ripped apart as the yellow legal pad Elroy tossed into the trash can. And he didn't want to hear another damned word about Paulus Youngblood.

Elroy stood and smoothed his red Polo shirt and black slacks. He looked out at the business in the warehouse. Then he reached across his desk for the phone and punched in the automatic dial for Senator Joe Dell Prince. Patience was not the way of a son of Changó. An environmental permit was not an obstacle to the greatest botanica in all the world and in all of history.

11

THE EVENING had been cool so Paulus had gone around to open all the windows in the sanctuary, but with all the people crowded into the pews he wished he'd turned on the air conditioner. Even sitting at the door, watching outside to be sure the streets were safe, he felt his back drenched in sweat, so he couldn't imagine how hot it must be up where his mother, in her black robes, was leading the singing. He couldn't stay up there too close anyway until his nose got better. The incense smelled as glorious as it always had—all his life Paulus had thought incense smelled like his mother's hands and it always made him feel safe and good to be around it—but the smoke got inside his nostrils and made the sutures itch so much it almost hurt.

His mother was clapping now and they were at the end of the chorus, so the hymn was almost done. *"Get right with the Lord, Get right with Jesus"*—it was something Jean-Pierre had written and it always made Paulus want to sing, which he couldn't do at the moment because of the wire in his jaw bone, but the sisters up at the front were loud and clear in his stead.

Still, Paulus could tell his mother wasn't happy yet with the tone of the service, or the pace—that it hadn't reached that thunder that she wanted of it. He knew because she clapped more when she was trying to fire people up, and because Jean-Pierre had moved the beat up on the electronic keyboard and had added more volume to the drum on the synthesizer. But they weren't even to the prophesying yet. Paulus knew his mother, and her powers, and he knew that by the time the amen "power" chorus and the trancing began that it would be a night for God and all the Spirits to look upon with favor.

In the distance, Paulus could hear a MAC-10 popping off rounds. Probably in the air. The gangbangers usually just shot into the sky. He thought they were stupid but not especially threatening unless you were in the drug business or crossed them for some reason. They shot up the night just to talk to each other, brag, like having guns was something to get worked up about. Paulus didn't like guns, but he wasn't afraid of hearing them go off. Anyway, gangbanger sounds weren't the sounds Paulus was listening for. The ones he would hear, if they came, would be close in and normal: the sounds of men walking up the streets in creaky leather shoes, of synthetic shirt cloth rustling. Of low murmurs in Spanish.

His mother and Jean-Pierre said he should try not to think about that night too much, that thinking on it would make it bigger than it was, but he couldn't control his thoughts that easily. Now, by the door, watching the people in the church rise and sing and sit and rise again to pray, like waves along the beach, like wheat flowing in a field—he had never seen such fields, except in movies—and him so close to the dark of the evening, the eternal hunger of the New Orleans streets, the ongoing promise of sudden evil that he now knew and would never, ever forget—with all this he could not stop his mind from rolling back. And then a waft of incense was seeking the open door, as the laws of physics he had studied demanded that air currents must. The inside of his nose began to throb and he was there again and he could not stop it.

"I SAID YOU a little far from your mama, ain't you?"

At first, Paulus didn't even turn, not taking the hoarse words to be directed at him, but then the question came louder, tagged with a "Yes, I talkin' to you, sweet boy." A half-turn of his head gave Paulus a view of a short, dark-complected man moving out from the edges of a Mardi Gras crowd that had spilled out of the Quarter where Esplanade met Rampart.

Instinctively, Paulus kept walking. Probably a drunk or maybe one of those queers who'd moved into the Quarter trying to pick up a black boy. He was Mexican, Paulus thought, from the accent, or maybe a Cajun. Not black. Paulus moved faster—he was already too far behind Orwell and Kareem, who were taking him to a Wild Tchoupitoulas party somewhere on Frenchmen Street.

A half block later he heard the voice again. "Say, little boy. You know where is your mama?" He said it like a Cuban that time and Paulus turned his head to look again. The man was waving at him. He wasn't a big man, but he looked all smooth in the face and mean. He had on a short-sleeved brown shirt and green trousers and paint or something on his face.

Paulus picked up his step, but didn't break. It wasn't good to run until you had to. He thought he had seen one or two other Cuban-looking men in the crowd as well, although with everyone in costume or painted up it was hard to tell in the dark. Later, Paulus realized he had known at once that this was not an accident, that the men intended him harm, and that it was not going to be his fate to escape. But he had clung to the idea of freedom. They shouldn't be acting like this around here. Some of the brothers will take care of them. Too many people around for anyone to try anything.

But they kept following him.

At Dauphine Street he got in front of three white couples drinking and waving Champagne glasses and darted off Esplanade. He figured that would lose them and he could hurry ahead a few blocks, then double back and still get down to Frenchmen and run into his friends. He only wished more people were there on the side street like there were out on Esplanade, which was so full of tourists the cars couldn't even get down the boulevard.

He felt a pop on the back of his head.

It burned and he was on his knees, blinking, and had forgotten where he was going or why. It was as if he had been transported to another world in an instant and although he knew he hurt somewhere he was mostly surprised and confused.

"What the matter, church boy? You lose your way?"

He heard the voices but he couldn't see, exactly. Now his head was starting to hurt more. He blinked, rose to his feet, sagged back against the wall of an apartment building. It was three of them, all right. The little guy in the brown shirt and two others. They were saying things to each other in Spanish. "Mierda"—he knew that word, it meant shit.

"Why you do that?" Paulus asked. He could smell the alcohol from them, saw them laughing and one handing another a bottle. He watched the bottle closely. He hoped it wouldn't be used on him. For the first time he was scared.

"Who said niggers could come into Mardi Gras?" one of the men said, his words slurred. He wore a red tank-top. Paulus didn't say anything. He was looking to see if anyone was around. A loud group of young men in women's hula skirts passed on the other side of the street but they didn't stop.

"Come back—" Paulus began, stopped when a small board appeared out of the darkness behind the red tank-top and fell full across his face. Paulus sunk against the wall.

"Fuck him up," said the hoarse voice. In what might have been a few seconds or time beyond noting, Paulus felt a foot hit his throat, then something else on the top of his head, and the board again against his cheek, and feet in his ribs and one in his groin, though it just missed his balls.

"Leave him," said a voice.

"We ain't finished," said the hoarse one.

"Orale, people comin', let's go."

Then there was another kick. And then they were gone.

Paulus opened his eyes and as he did a bottle wheeled out of the dark and broke on the wall just above his head, which was good, but as he crumpled lower onto the sidewalk, he couldn't keep from resting his broken and bloody face on the amber shards and breathing in the fermented fumes.

Probably one of those had cut open his right nostril. When the two young white men had put him on the stretcher and loaded him into the back of the ambulance, they had thought he'd been drinking and gotten into a fight and hadn't been all that compassionate, considering. He remembered hearing one of them say, "He'll be lucky to eat again," and another saying, "I wonder if his mama will recognize him."

She did, of course, at Tulane Medical, and cried for him but mostly a calm quiet. After he got out, and even though the doctors had sewn him up so that you could barely see any scars, except for the three African spirit marks on his cheeks from his initiation, she didn't like to talk about it. When she did, she got that smooth-face expression that seemed so cold it almost made him think she was mad at him, not at whoever had done it. Jean-Pierre told him it was best not to bring it up, and that was mostly the reason for trying not to think about it. But he had to think about it. And he knew his mother did, too. He knew she thought about it a lot.

He knew she had killed a goat and spent most of the night under

the moon in some kind of trance and that no one would go near her
all the next day and that whenever she saw Cubans in the neighbor-
hood she went silent and cold in that same way and that something
was on her mind and in her soul and that there would be revenge.
Revenge no one even wanted to talk about. And that Aunt Eddie's
Smith & Wesson from the palo *pot, which had never before been*
loaded, now had six shiny cartridges in the cylinder.

"I KNOW SOME OF YOU think you know Jesus, think you know the
Bible, think you good Christians." Corina paused. Her mouth
curled in a sneer. Her face fell into the surrounding blackness of
her full-length cotton robes, offset only by a white lace caplet and
shawl. As she stared out at her congregation, swollen with a half-
dozen visitors, including Gus Houston and Bonita Rae Doucet,
the membership in turn stared back.

They were like donkeys about to get beaten. Not because they
deserved it, but because it was their fate and because in some way
perhaps they did deserve it. The African Spiritual Church of
Mercy, newly affiliated with the Jerusalem Church of the Holy
Redemption, which everyone in town called the Holy Redeem-
ers, was not given to deep theological analysis, and so few were
those who dwelt long on the question of why the reverend could
turn on them so fast in the name of the Lord.

It wouldn't have done much good. The Reverend Youngblood
would have found them in their philosophical redoubts and
dragged them out by the scruff of the neck and cudgeled them all
the more for ducking the issue. The issue was faith. The sermon
was that you could never have too much of it. That you could
never be sure of what you did have. And so you had to be on
guard against your own sloth at all times.

Put simply, you were never good enough for God, as the
Reverend Youngblood saw it. Her job was to make you aware of

that deficiency every conscious moment of your life, and in that awareness of the foolishness of your supplication to the Almighty to possibly—if you were lucky and so devout it hurt—possibly secure Grace.

For a while, Corina was silent, staring out over the tops of the heads of the worshipers. When she looked up from her trance of Holy Bible, not an eye met hers, and none hoped to. But not all could be lucky.

"You think you know Jesus, Sister?" Corina was looking at Estella Bourgeois. A stout, fiftyish night supervisor at Tulane Medical, she was to devotion as granite is to solid. Nor was she timid. She had raised six children, none gone bad, except one killed at a stoplight when a cokehead trying to become a carjacker shot him in the face. She had gotten the supervisor spot moving past three white women. She lived by the Bible and didn't skimp in the collection plate. She said, "Yes, Reverend, I do know Him."

Corina nodded. She looked off to one side of the sanctuary, where Jean-Pierre sat as quietly as possible at the keyboard. She looked to the other side, where Paulus fidgeted near the open door and she saw the dark, steamy street outside sucking incense out of the building. Then her gaze shifted across toward a porcelain statue of Blackhawk, the Indian spirit, and to a wooden likeness of St. Jude carved by one of the deacons who had a year ago tried to gain Corina's affections. He had carved St. Jude as an African.

Corina wasn't sure about that at first, but since she also hung portraits of the Black Madonna and a black Jesus (also a white one) in the church, it seemed to fit. All the members liked it and one time a weekly black newspaper had come to her church to write a feature story about it, which had brought in a half dozen new members, and so Corina liked the statue even more.

Her vision snapped back to Estella Bourgeois.

"That good, that very good." Corina addressed the rest of the congregation. "Here a woman who know the Lord Jesus Christ." She smiled. "She know him well." She laughed. "Why, she know him so well I don't even know what I be doing up here—ain't that right?

"Reverend, I never said that—"

"What you say? You say you know *Jesus?* You know the *Lord?*" Corina paused a moment. "You know what I say? I say, 'Ha!'"

Estella looked at the preacher. She said nothing. She knew she'd already said too much.

"Well, that's just fine," Corina said, moving up to the front so that Estella was only one pew away. "I guess a fine lady like you that got such a good family and such a wonderful job and such a nice, fine house and a nice, fine car naturally think she know Jesus." Corina laughed viciously. "Why, Miz Bourgeois, I expect you be having Jesus over for supper this very night!"

No one in the small, smoky room moved. Bonita shot Gus a glance, almost certainly of disfavor, but Gus didn't hold the look long enough to respond.

"Reverend, you got no call to be saying this to me."

Corina leaned across the pew, through two semi-frozen schoolgirls of twelve, until she was inches from Estella's rocklike, coal-black face. Then the preacher lurched back as if she'd been grabbed by the nape of the neck. Stumbling, spinning with her arms stretched out like some kind of prehistoric bird of prey, she retreated to the front wall, just under a gold-plated metal crucifix.

"You know who you *know*, Miz Bourgeois? It ain't Jesus. Who you know ain't even the devil." She laughed, her eyes flashing. "All you know is yourself and your puny little pride, and all you know for knowing that is you ain't even in this church."

Estella cocked her head.

"You heard me. I said get out. Get out of this church right now."

The woman's face turned gray, her arms began to quiver slightly. Looking to her daughter on her right, and then back to Corina, she seemed paralyzed.

"What you waiting on? I said get out of this church, proud woman that know Jesus all to herself, probably on the phone to God and Mary all night, too."

"Mama—" said the daughter on the right.

Estella had started to cry.

"I never said it the way you say."

"Oh, I see. I must have got that wrong. When I said, 'Do you know Jesus?' and you say, 'Yes,' what you mean? 'No'?"

"I didn't never mean the way you say is all. I just say I know I love Him in my heart. I don't mean nothing else than that."

"You love Him in your *heart*? Now what you doing with Him? Having Him over to stay with you?"

"Stop," the woman whispered.

"What that?" Corina said, still against the wall at the crucifix, her ferocity all but flesh and blood of its own.

"She said, 'stop,'" said the daughter on the right, Willie, holding her mother around the shoulders.

Corina laughed. "Maybe I ask Jesus to stop. Maybe I say, 'Lord, please stop making this woman think she so high and mighty she know You, cause if she know You that well she don't need to be in church and she don't need to pray and she don't even need to try to have much more to do with You on account of she so familiar with You and all. Just give her a bus pass to heaven right now, Lord, and let us poor sinners get on with our singing.' That what you want me to say?"

"You a mean woman, Reverend."

"Or maybe I should get the Holy Ghost to come down and just take Miz Estella out of here right now like I said before. Didn't I say that clear enough? Didn't I say get out of my church you proud woman? So be going."

Corina straightened up and marched to the door. She pointed outside. "Get."

Estella Bourgeois rolled her head side to side, then picked up her purse and, shaking off Willie's arm, moved out of the pew into the center aisle. She was almost to the door when her knees stopped working. For a moment she seemed suspended in the air, like some big building a millisecond after the demolition dynamite has gone off. And then she was down, first on her side, then on her back. Faster than a cat, Corina was next to her, kneeling low. No one in the church moved.

"Tell me, Sister."

"You killing me, Reverend."

"Tell me, Sister."

"I—" she began to sob uncontrollably.

Willie tried to get out of the pew, but one look from Corina held her in check. Then Corina bent her head directly over Estella. "Who are you in the eyes of the Lord?"

"I ain't nothing, Reverend. I never meant to say I was anything."

"Then say that to Jesus. Tell Him."

She sobbed more. The silence around her was too much. Jean-Pierre began a soft chord progression.

Five minutes may have passed. Corina was crouched over her charge like a battlefield nurse. Waiting. The difference was that she would not mend the wound.

The crying continued as the organ music became more fluid,

less mournful. Corina waited. She would not intervene.

"Tell Him," she said when there were no more sobs.

Estella looked up into the preacher's face. She saw something. No one ever knew what but it stopped the contorted expression. Very softly, she said, looking upward, "I don't know You, Lord."

"No, you don't."

"I want to."

"But you don't."

"No."

"Then why you say you do?"

"I thought I knew You."

"But you don't, do you?"

"No."

"And how you think you going to?"

Estella's eyes were like huge brown oceans into which anything could have been poured.

"I don't know."

"You don't know? Then what you do?"

"I don't know, Reverend. I don't know."

Many would have taken pity on those eyes. But pity was not the way of a true preacher, or of a daughter of Ogun.

"Then I guess you better find out."

"I don't know how."

"You don't?"

"No, Reverend, I—Reverend, I don't know what you want me to say?"

"It ain't me want you to say anything."

"What the Lord want me to say, then?"

Corina touched the woman's cheek. Then she placed her other hand on the other cheek. Then, close enough to feel her breath, she squeezed Estella's face so hard the cheekbones began to hurt her palms. Then she stood up and looked down.

"What I say is you pray and you tell Jesus you nothing on this earth unless He make you something. That what I say. What He say is what He saying to you right now. "

Corina stepped back and folded her arms tight across her chest, then she whirled around, extended one arm toward Jean-Pierre, and turned to face the congregation, arms crossed again. The music came up. She nodded once and Willie came to help her mother off the floor and back to the pew.

"Bring Me not your pride nor your riches nor your deeds," said Corina, in a voice difficult to recognize. "Bring Me nothing for ye are nothing and to nothing ye shall return and none shall pass save through Me and through faith in Me."

Then the iron-like expression in her own face seemed to slip off. She let out a short, audible sigh.

"Sing with me, children." Jean-Pierre brought up both the organ and the synthesized drumbeat. But Corina did not sing with them. She retreated to her hard-backed chair and sat with her head bent down, her shawl pulled tightly and knotted up in one hand, her red Bible in the other.

Gus felt Bonita's hand in his, her nails dug into his flesh. She was singing from the hymnal but something in her voice made him uncomfortable. Even an hour later, after the service, after the prophecies, after Corina called Estella Bourgeois forward and covered her face with Florida water and then bathed her feet with it, Bonita seemed stiff and wired. When Gus tried to talk about the service she changed the conversation. For the time being he let it drop. His intuition wasn't always correct, but Gus didn't think Bonita was repelled by what she had witnessed.

12

T HE IDEA didn't come to Gus all at once, but once in there
it rooted like cypress in a swamp and it had to be
accommodated. Or some other metaphor. The point is
that one fairly normal morning it came to Gus Houston that the
state of things being what they were, he should create and enter
a girls' choir from Miss Angelique's in the Gospel Tent at Jazzfest.
In that moment of clarity, he considered the idea an inspired, so
to speak, synthesis of a number of paired entities: black and
white New Orleans; the St. Jude Lamb of Light Botanica and the
chaplaincy; elite and street; and, not least, his future and pretty
much everything going on in his life at that moment in time, as
the special counsel to the White House had so often phrased it.

The moment of clarity occurred on the sun deck of Bonita's
apartment, gazing out at the park and sipping iced tea with
lemon, nursing a mild hangover on a Saturday morning. Funny
how ideas worked, he mused. You can spend years stuck on a
knot of a problem and never cut through and on the other hand
you can achieve diamond clarity in a thought-tableau of pristine
logic and permutation within the space of what, seconds?

Gus plucked the lemon from the glass and sucked on it. He

had read of Chinese monks who had spent all their lives transfixed by such simplicity, which of course was also a weird way to deal with enlightenment. Gus's take on the issue was that *satori* came in stages, rather than all at once, but that no matter when and how you got it, you didn't need to devote a lot of rituals to keeping it. It wasn't a barter deal with the gods.

This had become more difficult to assess in the months with Corina. She was of the daily reminder school of thinking— continual payback. They'd never really arrived at a consensus on the issue of faith and enlightenment, though he had to admit he had come closer to seeing her point of view than he thought he might. She was very impressive on matters of the spirit, and her insistence on Absolute Loyalty to God was intimidating, almost catching.

Gus had told Bonita that's why the people in Corina's church were so devout. They were like permanent recruits with the toughest drill sergeant in the world. They didn't dare fuck up and she wouldn't let them because it would be hard on all of them, eventually, should any fall.

As a former military man, or at least a person who had served his time to pay off a graduate English degree that now, like the Garden of Dixie and sundry other items on his *vita*, seemed at least digressive, Gus found the logic of responsibility compelling. He didn't know what Bonita felt. But she had made him attend Saturday night services at the African Mercy church for the last seven weeks in a row. On all but one of those weeks she had gone to Mass the following Sunday evening before she went to work. But she never talked about it, and rarely spoke to Corina after church.

Corina had asked Gus about Bonita several times, but he'd just said that was the way she was. Corina said, "She look at me like a child look at the river the first time. Don't you know what that mean?" To which Gus had said no, to which Corina had said, "I tell you someday when you ready." Then he thought he heard her say something *sotto voce* about "men" but on that afternoon he was in a rush picking up Trudi Harrelson after a reading and had let it go.

The idea of the choir at Jazzfest, though, was unquestionably enlightenment, not faith. It was not something in which to believe, but something to know. He could see it and that made it a vision instead of an act of faith. He made the distinction because seeing it made it real, at the very least a function of will. Believing in it would have made it a function of something he didn't have.

In his mind's eye the singers appeared in the hot exuberance of the big striped Gospel Tent on the Fairgrounds not in Academy white but in the electric blue gowns favored by real Gospel groups. There were at least ten of them, fresh-scrubbed and virginal to the point of lust, amid a sea of the blackness of the South, a sea corrupted and intercorrupted by the commerce of the vile trade routes over the Atlantic but now in the way of the cosmos flipped into an *opposite* blackness of the South, the sea now triumphant and cleansed in real human blood not anything on any white man's cross. In this opposing sea of reality would appear these children of fiction and in such debutante drama would they themselves be transformed and the final surrender of evil into good would occur in the kind of port city in which it all started. *Viz.,* the old slave market now an overpriced tourist restaurant.

A true vision wasn't anything you thought through, but rather something that thought through you. At least he'd learned that. In Hollywood and Madison Avenue they called a vision a Big Idea. Except in those places all they'd see in a vision was the theater. What Gus saw was the soul. But wouldn't it make a damn fine show, too? White girls in the Gospel tent, bringing the house down? Maybe some of them would find Jesus with a black preacher. Maybe—

No, it would be a damn fine show. The talk of the town. And somewhere in that talk would come the inquiry, "Who put up this fine show? Who had this fine idea?" And Gus, being interviewed by reporters on the veranda of his fine apartment overlooking the park, could say, "Well, it came to me one day as I was sitting right here . . ."

Which was how Gus's vision started to go bad.

JEAN-PIERRE HAD READ one time that you never get mad, you get even. He tried to concentrate on that ever since Paulus got beat up and he wanted evenness really bad. He and his mother had quarreled hard—always out of the hearing of Paulus. Jean-Pierre was not a violent man but after he had left the hospital and seen Paulus that way all he could think about was blowing Elroy Delgado's head off.

But he knew Elroy hadn't been the one who smashed Paulus's nose and ribs, even if Elroy had somehow been behind it. That knowledge had squelched Jean-Pierre's vengeful rage. It was a strange, abstract kind of rationale, but one he seemed powerless to discount. He was thinking about doing exactly what he spent hours each week counseling his students not to do. And so he left off the idea of getting a gun and thought all through the night. He drank brandy and listened to Percy Sledge and Sam Cooke and Al Green then most of his Gospel tapes until dawn. And he did not kill anyone.

Now he sat at his kitchen table listening to his answering machine. It was that Houston man, wanting him to call back. Strange cat, that man. He was a teacher, too, but nothing like Jean-Pierre's version of the profession. All Houston taught were rich white girls and Jean-Pierre suspected he didn't even have a teaching certificate, but you didn't need one at a private school.

And then all that shit between his mother and Houston. It bothered Jean-Pierre. He was a very religious man but had not taken the *santos* like Paulus. He thought of himself as a kind of scholar; certainly a man of reason. His efforts went into working with the gangbangers and sometimes helping with the marches and rallies and whatever when the black politicians needed to turn out the people. Even if it often seemed little more than a charade, Jean-Pierre did his bit. He had read Sartre on that and believed "the being was in the doing," which was the phrase he came up with to explain it to teenagers.

Jean-Pierre listened to the other messages and decided which to return and which to let go. Suddenly it hit him. One voice among the half-dozen on the tape. Paulus had said it was hoarse, like the guy had a cold, and definitely Cuban. Jean-Pierre's teeth ground together. It had been in there, in his head, in his knowledge, all that time but it had not been manifest. Now it was—brought out among the voices on the machine.

13

J ULIO SET UP the meeting with Joe Dell. They had exactly
forty-five days if they wanted to hold the grand opening on
May 1, the start of Jazzfest, and draw from the big out-of-
state crowds. Some people thought Mardi Gras was the biggest
retail time for the city, but in Julio's experience in the spiritual
trade, two weeks of Jazzfest generally proved equal to it or better.
Maybe there were more black people involved, or maybe the
people who came were less likely to be drunks and more likely to
be interested in the festival itself.

Elroy was unwavering about it, insisting on being open for
business during Jazzfest to "announce our presence to the world,"
as he had taken to saying. Julio was not exactly worried about his
older brother, for Changós were prone to such melodramatic
statements, but the rush to start up the "flagship SuperBotanica"
had been troubling Julio ever since that day outside Corina
Youngblood's.

And then the business with Paulus had contaminated everything. More was bound to come from it. No one knew what, and
not even Elroy would talk about it. He was pretending nothing
had happened and that he didn't know Ocho or Ramón or
Elusário even though all of them worked in the warehouse. Elroy

just didn't want to deal with it. He wouldn't even fire them because that would be to acknowledge that something had happened.

The only good side to the boy getting beat up, Julio thought, was that at least Elroy never talked to that damn woman anymore. Though he would confess it to no one, Julio was afraid of her. He knew Elroy was, too, even if Elroy would not confess it even to himself, not least because he had been her *padrino* and if anything it was she should be afraid of him. But Elroy was also sex-crazy about her, even now, and it made a bad mix. Julio tried to think that maybe Ochún and the other *orisha* had allowed the beating, or even moved those three drunken assholes to it, as a way of keeping Corina and Elroy, and their *santos,* apart. That was what he tried to think and it might be true but it was troubling.

Another upside of the bad blood was that Elroy had been much more able to concentrate on the building site and the permit and to put his anger where it needed to be, on Joe Dell Prince. Julio hated the man. He did not fear him; he hated him. He was the kind of gringo *gabacho* you thought about when you thought about the worst kind of American. All that mud race shit and his golf clothes and he always had bad breath. It made Julio's flesh crawl just to be around the man.

Once, Julio had told one of Prince's bootsuck buddies, a guy named Finnester, to go to hell. Finnester had said Julio and Elroy were "acting like a couple of pushy beaners." Julio actually had put his hands around Finnester's skinny throat as they stood outside a car waiting for Elroy and Joe Dell to finish arguing about something. Julio could have hurt the man. Partly to overcome his pretty boy image he'd studied tae-kwon-do for a while, gotten a brown belt. But Finnester more or less apologized, even though it was only to get Julio's hands off his windpipe, and the moment passed. Funny— until then, Julio hadn't thought the bad attitude had gotten into him, too. He thought he was above it, not a hothead like his brother. But it was in him all right; that, too, troubled him. He was starting to have dreams.

Still, today might be a good meeting. The media had finally gotten off Elroy's case and the little pricks down at the city were saying they would go ahead and process the waiver for construction for five thousand dollars. Joe Dell was taking credit, saying it would have been fifty thousand or more, normally, and might not have been granted at all, except for his influence. So he was asking five thousand for himself and another five thousand for the city supervisor. Elroy and Julio had agreed to pay—on condition everything would be finished by Friday and construction could start Monday. The contractor said that should give them time to set the foundation and throw up the shell and at least allow the place to open up, even if everything wasn't completely finished, before Jazzfest started.

Julio hoped Elroy would be on time. If not, Julio would have to pass the time at the Denny's with Joe Dell and probably Finnester, too. They'd decided to stop meeting at Robbo's after all the media stuff because one time a TV cameraman hiding outside in a car had taken footage of Joe Dell and Elroy together. Robbo had gotten so mad he hit the cameraman's zoom lens with a big soup spoon and knocked it to the ground. But the videotape didn't break and Robbo was on the evening news, too. It was a terrible experience over weeks and weeks. No matter where Elroy went, it was like the reporters knew and kept dogging him. People said he was like Joe Dell—a racist. That was about when Elroy started drinking too much.

One day Elroy had been so furious he came into the warehouse drunk and told all the workers he wished Corina Youngblood's botanica never existed and not her either or any of her friends or family and that God and the *santos* had cursed him, Elroy, for ever having fucked her in the first place and now the *santos* should take the curse off because he was doing their work and making it possible for more people to worship them and why didn't something happen?

Everybody knew Elroy was drunk, although not until then did everybody know he'd fucked Corina Youngblood (Luz found out, too, and there was hell for a while). Julio wouldn't have probably even remembered that day except it was some-time in late January and it was only a couple weeks later at Mardi Gras that Ocho and the others had run into Paulus and almost killed him. They were pigs. They were real *marielitos*, the kind that gave the others a bad name—petty crooks, what the government called *lumpen* in Cuba because they were like a professional breed of no-goods. Fidel had been only too happy to send them to Florida to live with the *gusanos*. And they had done a bad thing in the family name.

Julio looked out the window toward the traffic on Airline Highway. Sometimes it calmed him to see cars just going back and forth and you never knew where or why. He sipped his second cup of coffee and glanced at his watch. He would kill Elroy if he was late, which it was looking like. Then it occurred to Julio that Joe Dell would probably be late, too, so maybe it would even out and he wouldn't have to talk polite for long.

Four o'clock came and went and then 4:15. Julio switched to decaf and glanced again at the folder of construction plans and permits and financial papers he'd brought. Elroy had been be-having so erratically since Mardi Gras that Julio had become the brother who kept up the documents. He could finish everything with Joe Dell, for that matter, but Elroy was still the oldest and it was really his company and the SuperBotanica was his idea and Julio wasn't really an ambitious man and not really that competitive. He liked having Elroy be the front.

"Bastards not here yet?"

Julio looked up from his haze of thoughts. It was Elroy after all. Julio hadn't even seen his car pull up. He shot his brother a look of disapproval and slid over in the booth. "You're lucky they're later than you."

"Fuck that. I wanted to make 'em wait on me."

"Yeah? Well why didn't you tell me that? Fuck you, Elroy."

Elroy shrugged and signaled to the waitress to bring another cup of coffee. "Don't worry about it." After a moment, "Did you bring the papers?"

"I'd tell you if I didn't?"

"Hey, next time you can be late, OK?"

"I ain't meetin' this asshole any next time. It's over after this or we're wasting our time."

Elroy looked at Julio carefully. "You think I like the guy?"

"I think you're spending way too much time with him. And me, too."

"Fuck you."

"You know what's going around."

"Yeah, but not from my own little brother."

"I'm just saying—"

"I'm just saying we got to do what we got to do. We got to get open and if I got to play with this *gabacho* a little that's what we do." The waitress slid the cup across the tabletop, backing away slightly at the sound of muffled anger in the voices of the two middle-aged Cuban men huddled together like spies.

"And I'm saying I'm tired of it—shit, there he is."

They looked out the plate glass at a black Oldsmobile pulling up to park. Joe Dell Prince and Finnester got out. En route to the door Joe Dell said something in what Julio construed as a furtive demeanor. And then they were inside. Joe Dell waved at Elroy like a good buddy—what the American rednecks called each other—and then came over and slid in across the booth. Finnester was right next to him, across from Julio. Julio was satisfied to see that Finnester acted nervous and wouldn't look him in the eye.

"My friend," said Joe Dell, "this is a good day for both of us." He opened a thick brown folder, pulled out an official looking form, glanced at it as if to certify that it was authentic, and then passed it across to Elroy. It was from the Department of Environmental Safety. Julio didn't need to read it. He knew what it said. It said it was okay to build. It said the underground gasoline storage tank had "minimal leachage" and could be removed without further contamination and so on. It was probably a lie; Julio didn't care. It covered the city and it covered Elroy.

"The thing is, you've got to pull that tank out right away—I mean today or tomorrow—so nobody can do any more testing."

"No problem. We been ready since Thanksgiving."

"Maybe do it real early in the morning or something."

"No problem." Elroy looked at Julio, who made a note in his appointment book to call Geronimo Casey at Delta Construction and get the damn tank out at five in the morning.

"Then all you have to do is sign this and Albert will take care of the rest," Joe Dell grinned. So did Elroy. Even Julio. It occurred to them all at once that this was it.

"Sometimes these things are harder than they look like they'd be," the senator said. "But eventually they get taken care of."

"Anyway, it's done," said Elroy.

"Say, Albert," said Joe Dell, making a show of looking at his watch, "it's getting late. Go call Olsen and tell him you'll be by this afternoon and for him to wait for you in the office."

Finnester's brow furrowed, then he shrugged and got up. "Fucking bureaucrats leave at the stroke of five," Joe Dell said to him as he walked away.

As soon as Finnester was gone, Elroy took a plain white envelope from his trouser pocket. He looked at it the way Joe Dell had looked at the form, then pushed it around his coffee cup until it rested next to the salt and pepper holder at the edge of the table. Joe Dell eased it to the brown folder he was holding. Then he put the folder inside his jacket pocket. Julio noticed that the transaction only took about ten seconds and that Joe Dell seemed as fast and quiet as a blackjack dealer.

Then it really was done.

"We got to be going," the senator said. He leaned slightly toward Elroy. "We sort of even now, wouldn't you say, son?"

It was funny, Julio observed, the way the senator responded to what his brother said next. Probably he had expected something else. But Elroy said, "We'll be even when I get open."

Joe Dell's eyes narrowed, just a flash of the real feeling he had toward mud races. But it passed. "Then you just get open. Nothing to stop you now."

The senator slid out of the booth and started to walk away. He stopped, turned, and extended his hand. "I'm sure we'll see each other again, Elroy."

Elroy shook the hand. He nodded and smiled. The two men looked at each other and Joe Dell cocked his head as if in some sort of agreement. Then he walked past the cash register to the door, where Finnester caught up with him.

Elroy and Julio sat in silence until the Oldsmobile was gone.

"I'll be damned," Elroy said, and laughed.

"He didn't leave a tip," said Julio.

BONITA RARELY let things eat on her. It wouldn't have been good in her family. Her brother let things eat on him and was dead. Her mother let things eat on her, too. But in a different way. Her mother let things be. She allowed them to occur. She didn't throw Bonita's father out of the house. Bonita would never be like that. She feared no man. She never really planned on loving one, either—Gus caught her so by surprise she didn't really have time to throw up defenses. Something about his smart mouth made her laugh a split second after it pissed her off and that made her feel vulnerable and in the vulnerability she had an ability to love. Mindful of mama, she kept close watch on that tendency, but it seemed the only way a man was going to get to her. Not a straight route at all; on the other hand who was in charge of these journeys?

What was eating her wasn't Gus so much as it was Corina Youngblood. At first, Bonita had merely objected to what she saw as Gus's foolishness, putting a good job on the line by sending girls over to a hoodoo woman. It was plain crazy. Stupid. It had made her mad, because it was the smart mouth gone over the line. It made him funny to a point but then after that point she wondered about the man she'd fallen for just like they said— first sight, no real time to catch herself.

But now there was something different. Bonita had started to like Corina—much against her better judgment. The woman was a tough cookie. She'd seen how Gus behaved around her— like he was buffaloed, like Corina knew something he didn't. The thought of that made Bonita further uncomfortable because it was close to the way she thought of Gus. So if Gus himself was buffaloed, then such a woman must hold an extra thing over Gus's woman. Bonita felt twice-hooked.

Walking through Audubon Park, she tried to get the thing to stop eating her. It had been inside her for weeks and she was tired of it. The problem was that if she actually did go see Corina for a reading, Gus might have even more on her, not to mention what the hoodoo preacher herself would then have. So Bonita was torn. Something told her she had to go through Corina to find out something important. And something told her that if she did, she might as well take off her clothes and walk down Canal Street at noon as far as being exposed went.

A young man on a bicycle sped past her on the path. As he did, he checked her out. She curled her mouth at his staring and thought about flipping him off but then he turned around and she let it go.

The preaching was probably what had done it. She wasn't a regular at Mass, but she did believe in the Church and she knew something was funny about the one Gus took her to that first Saturday night. Gus said she was a typical Cajun racist, which pissed the hell out of her. She knew all about racists and she wasn't one. What she felt had nothing to do with Corina being black: it was all the talk about *"santos"* and the strange statues along the walls, and the incense, and just the general feeling of being in the weirdest place to call on the name of Jesus she could ever have imagined. It made her feel like she would go to Hell for being there.

That first night at these strange services, she had gotten so mad at Gus she made him stop the car on the way home. It was a very cold night in January but she got out next to an all-night drugstore on Canal and told Gus to leave her alone. He wouldn't leave but there was a lighted pay phone on the wall outside the drug store and she called a cab. When it arrived, Gus drove off and she went down to The Hellhole. She took a busman's holiday. After an hour she was drunk enough to stop thinking about Hell and Desecration. She called another cab and went home.

That was one of the nights she made Gus sleep on the couch. It wasn't fair; it wasn't like he was an evil man, but she felt like he had made her witness an evil rite and she wasn't sure if she ever wanted to be with him again.

In the morning, watching him asleep on the couch, she had seen no evil in his face. Stupid smart-mouth gullibility maybe but nothing bad, and then she thought maybe she had reacted too much to the church, or whatever it was. Hoodoo never scared her growing up; everybody in Thibodaux got into it somehow sooner or later, or at least knew about it.

But no.

Something else was in that church. She didn't like anyone having anything on her, and there was something down at that Mercy Church that she didn't understand more than she didn't like.

LOST IN THOUGHT, she had actually begun her second circle along the walking path. She was at the top of the pond again, where the lily pads grew. An older couple sat on a flat cropping of reddish rock, watching the birds. She watched them. They were talking about something that seemed serious, for she was looking at him intently and he was looking at her, then away.

Bonita kept walking. Around her the park was alive with the coming of spring. It wasn't that hot yet, nor steamy, and her spirits rose. She walked faster, to finish the extra loop and cut across the meadow to get back to her apartment. She could make it before Gus was out of school. If she wanted to tell him later, that what she most wanted to know, she wanted to know from Corina Youngblood, she could. If not—that would give him a vulnerability to match her own.

14

L IFE AT Miss Angelique's had settled into as much a routine as Gus could have expected, and even that was like a
lead weight to him. The consulting therapy had gone so
well he thought maybe it was going too well; his chief fear was
that sooner or later Elizabeth or Agon would find out and,
finding out, not like it. At the same time, he thought maybe they
already knew and kept it to themselves because if all went well,
the morale of the girls would stay high, and if there were a screw-
up, then Gus could be blamed. The more Gus knew of the
Hapsenfields, the more he leaned to the latter. He even kind of
admired them for it.

Today was his last day of lunch monitor. The job was easy,
because the school cafeteria served lunches so tasty Gus didn't
mind eating them himself, and because no matter what was
served, half the girls ditched anyway in favor of the junk food
places up on St. Charles. And the ones who stayed were not the
troublemakers. So lunch monitor meant little more than nouvelle
cuisine three days out of six (Saturday was included). Or Cajun.
Or, at worst, "Hi-Pro-Teen," which despite what it implied was
usually just poached fish or tender roast beef.

The only weird part about the duty was eating with Elizabeth. She had made a habit of sitting with Gus every Tuesday and Thursday. At first, Gus enjoyed the visits, including the familiar sight of her blouse half-buttoned. He hated having a thing about her breasts but there it was. He didn't even try to hide his looks anymore, and she didn't discourage him.

But it was just that, and after a while Gus had found the game mostly stupid. Probably a good thing, since he had begun to realize that the major purpose of her visits was not to show off her figure, but to draw information out of him about the girls, about himself, or, most of all, about any activities involving Agon. Gus figured she was looking for ammunition for a favorable divorce settlement. Without Miss Valthenough, or sufficient documentation of what had happened between her and Agon, Elizabeth needed something else on Ichabod Crane, as the girls called him.

Gus could have told her plenty. But he didn't. He wished his circumspection owed to his choosing not to become involved in sordid games, but that would have been a half-truth even Gus couldn't abide. It was more that the timing was premature. During his rookie year, Gus, at least the Shadow Gus, had come to see the Academy as a way to advance himself. He also knew the real currency in a social town like New Orleans was gossip. So he had no intention of giving Elizabeth something he might need for hard cash some rainy day hence.

Of such thinking doubtless did the purity of his vision for Jazzfest devolve into the thing it was becoming. As soon as classes were over today, he planned on getting over to Metairie to meet Jean-Pierre Youngblood and try to hook him the way Jean-Pierre's mother had hooked Gus. That was not true. Corina seemed to be mostly after a good business arrangement. What had crept into Gus's soul, had distorted his vision, was nothing so straightforward. What had created his admiration for the Hapsenfields' manipulations—including using him—was altering him, changing him, in ways he could neither control nor resist. He did not feel cynicism; it was a grander kind of feeling, as though his grasp could finally be measured by his reach.

Bonita had begun to remark on his behavior of late. She said he was acting like he'd come out of one of those wormholes in the sci-fi shows on TV he watched late at night waiting for her to get off work. It had become a term of definition between them. When they argued about sending the girls to Corina, when he talked about "making his mark on this town," she said he was in his wormhole again and she wouldn't talk to him.

Yet he would persevere. In the wormhole was the Shadow Gus, and it didn't mind not having to discuss sensitive or moral issues. What he had in mind might or might not be an idea whose time had come, but now that it had arrived, it was more or less just a matter of seeing it through. Gus tried to remember the way Hamlet had put it, about the readiness being all, but the lunch room had gotten noisy and he was distracted. Also, Elizabeth had come in unexpectedly—it was a Wednesday—and was walking toward him carrying an aluminum tray with a Caesar's salad perched on top next to a glass of Evian. She wore a light blue cotton turtleneck. Her cheeks were flushed, but Gus wasn't sure if she had just had sex or was just about to.

"Not many girls today," she said, winking. "Are you being as strict as you should be about passes?"

"Oh, about the same."

Elizabeth walked past slowly. He could see her nipples under the cloth. She sat at an empty table next to where he leaned against a decorative column.

She was acting coy, he thought. Usually she was brazen. He was confused, and therefore attracted. He pulled out a chair at her table. "You seem awfully . . . relaxed."

She looked at him as she tore a sliver of lettuce with her teeth. She licked her lips. "The Academy is doing very well this quarter. We just finished the taxes and things worked out very well."

Gus smiled.

"I was going to take Agon out for lunch but he—" she paused just enough— "but he went out for the afternoon."

Gus looked at her. She looked at him.

Fifth and sixth periods passed in the school as they normally did. In the back half of the first floor, where the Hapsenfields kept their on-site apartment, the door was locked and the answering machine on. Inside the apartment, in a door that could have been broached at any time by a man who had the key, *i.e.*, the missing husband, the smell of sex was thick and strong. The husband was emitting odors elsewhere, was the thing.

She was more gorgeous than Gus ever could have imagined, not just the breasts like grapefruits but the softness of the skin, the curve around the hip bones, the gluteus that just filled out his hand and was firm as the bosom. She sucked him first, until he was ready to come, and then pushed him away so that he wondered what he had done. Then she was on him again with her mouth, and pulled away once more. He was miserable and incoherent.

She slid to the edge of the bed, a sad, king-sized affair that had been covered in cream-colored sheets and Navajo blankets when they had come in, in the minutes before they had pulled each other's clothing off and without talking gotten into this thing. Then she had pulled his legs to the edge of the bed and rubbed his cock inside her breasts and then she was on top of him again, this time with her pussy on his mouth so he had no choice but to taste her and lick her and in less than a minute she came so much his face was wet and sticky.

He looked up and her eyes were closed tight and her mouth in a grimace. Then she opened her eyes, and they kind of smiled at him and frightened him in the same moment, then she slid down along the length of her body until he was inside her, fucking her, fucking her, rolling over and all around the bed then, wondering how long he could keep from coming and then he did and she held him much more tightly than he had expected. When he was done and could breathe and see again, she kissed him, then pushed him off.

"I guess you always wanted to fuck the principal."

She laughed at her joke, then got up to get some water. He noticed she still had on the white socks she had been wearing. It made her legs look longer and more brown. He drank from the glass she brought back and kissed her and then began to idly stroke her nipples and to his amazement everything came back on line and they were doing it again. That time they fucked for a half hour. That was what kicked up the stink of what they were doing and wafted it throughout the apartment and left it there so that even when Agon returned that evening and almost had to have smelled it, he didn't say anything, and neither did Elizabeth. It had gotten that way with them.

It had not gotten much of any way with Gus. Elizabeth had told him, "Maybe we'll never do this again, you know?" He had said, "Maybe that's a good idea," and she thought he had seemed sad and realized he probably gave more of a shit than he let on. Not about her. About someone else.

So she wasn't sure if that made her want to fuck him again or not. But she was glad for that afternoon. She let Agon know the score and she had something else on Chaplain Houston if it should happen she'd need further help in the divorce she was planning. Fuck Agon. Let anyone who wanted to fuck Agon fuck Agon. A year from now he'd be looking for another batch of teenagers to make him feel young and maybe he'd have another wife to use as cover.

THE FIRST THING Gus did was to call Bonita to tell her he had to run out to Target after school to pick up some supplies but she was gone and he left a message on her machine. Then he secured himself in his office as well as possible, meeting with three girls from the freshman class who were upset because the other girls on their end of the hall were teasing them for studying the Bible together.

The girls were all from a small town in the rural northern part of the state. Two of them, Rhonda and Ellise, had come because their mothers, alumni of the Academy, made them. The third, Helen, more or less joined them so as not to be left behind in farm country. They all dressed Bobbie Brooks-ish and were always quiet and cute, and generally seemed appalled at the behavior of the other girls. They had expected the Academy to be more conservative, more religious, and more tame. In response, they held Bible-reading sessions several nights a week. This had incurred the opprobrium of the other girls.

Gus could understand the problem from all sides. He could understand the disorientation of the girls, and he could understand why their classmates thought they were such little geeks. But he was the chaplain and they had come to him. Moreover, he was a man of God in the outside world, with vast connections to the Spirit and to the holiness of the cosmos. He was a man to whom young girls could turn for guidance. He was a hell of a guy who had to wait to go home until the woman he loved had left for work because he couldn't face her so soon after betraying her.

"Rhonda," he said, "did you girls ever visit any of the Holy Redeemer churches in Grambling when you were growing up?"

Jean-Pierre dawdled at his beer and peanuts. He didn't drink very much, not least because of his mother, but he was having one now because Houston made him nervous. It wasn't even happy hour yet, and the small bar next to the Westside Inn was so empty Jean-Pierre could hear the nuts crunch between his teeth as he nibbled. It was an okay place—light and lots of windows, instead of dark and hostile to the day as were most of the places downtown or in the Quarter. Actually, it was one of those chains, O'Kerrigan's. It was the only place they'd both been able to think of on the spur of the moment. It was easy to find and it was unlikely they'd run across anyone they knew. Not that they were doing anything secretive, probably. All Jean-Pierre knew was that it was "an idea so good I can't even tell you about it over the phone."

Even if Houston hadn't been a friend of his mother's, and therefore ipso facto a problem child, Jean-Pierre might have begged off without thinking twice. Instead of meeting. Houston was okay, and he could be funny, but there was something around his edges. It was like some kind of faint bluish glow, Jean-Pierre had told his mother. She had said there was no such thing, although she agreed Houston was "strange for a white man." But Jean-Pierre had seen the glow. He wasn't sure if it bothered him or not; probably it did.

He believed he had the gift of prophecy, even though he had not taken the way of the *santos,* and he believed he could see things beyond the flesh. He knew he could. What he didn't know was how to interpret these things. When he prayed for guidance, he came up with nothing. So he had decided perhaps this was his soul's mission, to see these things that others could not and to try to find their meanings.

He knew his mother knew this about him, and that for some reason she kept a distance from it. She was very spooky about spirits; if she sensed something she could not understand or conquer she gave it wide berth. So whether or not she knew Jean-Pierre had seen the aura, she didn't let on to him. That was another reason Jean-Pierre thought his mission to be a private one, for his own soul. That was another reason he was waiting in O'Kerrigan's for Gus Houston. Something wanted him to.

The bartender, probably a UNO student, reached up to a tape deck behind the bar and put in another cassette. It was Miles Davis. Jean-Pierre glanced over. He wondered if the tape was for him, the only customer, or if the bartender, a white guy, was into jazz himself. You never knew. Jean-Pierre had refused to believe Clint Eastwood liked jazz, and when it turned out to be true, it made him rethink his own position on it. But it was African whether Clint Eastwood liked "Bird" or not.

Jean-Pierre considered that an important lesson in the maturation of his own taste, and he used that example of Eastwood many times in his classes at Metairie High to tell students that art is not dependent on the beholder, but on the artist. If it were the other way around, artists could never create, because they would live in terror of encouraging evil, or of comforting it.

Gus waved from across the lounge as he came up. Jean-Pierre glanced at his watch. Houston wasn't late; he was right on time. That was good. It showed respect. Jean-Pierre made respect a fulcrum of his pedagogy and of his life.

"Have any trouble getting a table?"

Jean-Pierre laughed in spite of himself. "I had to wait for this window, though."

Houston sat opposite him and signaled to the bartender to bring a beer.

"I appreciate your coming."

"No problem."

"Talk to your mother lately?"

"She called me early this morning to ask me to help her with some insurance forms for Paulus."

Houston looked at him, then up at a satellite soccer game on the TV mounted over the bar. He nodded and shook his head. "He seems to be pretty much healed up, considering."

"Considering they damn near killed him."

"Yeah, considering that."

There was a silence.

"Your mother says it was the Delgados."

"She says right."

The bartender came over and put the beer down. Jean-Pierre covered the top of his glass with his hand. The bartender smiled and moved off. Miles was gliding into trumpet sex.

"So what's this big idea?" Jean-Pierre leaned back in his chair.

Houston took the cue to change the subject. He looked at Jean-Pierre, smirked a little, as if talking to himself, and then spread his palms open before him. "You might think this is crazy, but I want to put a choir from Miss Angelique's in the Gospel Tent at Jazzfest."

Jean-Pierre's face didn't move, but one of his eyebrows arched.

"Yeah. And I want you to help me set it up."

Jean-Pierre crossed his arms. Eyebrow still raised.

"Also, I want you to be the choir director. And train them. You'd be paid well."

Jean-Pierre nodded slowly. "Anything else?"

"That's a pretty good start."

Jean-Pierre uncrossed his arms and reached for his beer. He heard himself laugh softly. It was an odd instant. He realized he was simultaneously slightly offended, intrigued, and even excited.

He grasped Houston's idea thoroughly. It was big. It was

crazy. It was also pretty close to brilliant. Where this white man with the vague past was coming from with this idea was open to wildly contradictory interpretations, but if Jean-Pierre's mother saw something in him other than a blue aura, maybe Jean-Pierre could give him the benefit of the doubt, too.

Jean-Pierre laughed—a full baritone, his church voice laugh. Although he was shorter than his rangy, dark-haired companion, he was stockier and probably stronger. When he laughed, the volume filled up any room he was in, and when he sang, as he had done in almost every major church choir in town in the last decade, he could see the power in his voice in the faces of everyone within his sight. He could see the glow above the audiences as he pushed the melody up the mountain like a giant moving a boulder as though it were a pebble.

Sometimes he thought he could sing like Miles Davis could play, though that was vanity and he was quick to suppress such thoughts. As a choir director to many of the churches in which he had sung, he had learned to push his energies and his ambitions and his ego through the voices of others. In that, he had felt closer to God than in using his own voice. He didn't know why, but it was true. He was a good and natural teacher, and that also was his soul's mission. All these were. He was laughing so loud the bartender turned to look.

"You're right," he said at last to Houston, who had been watching him with a quizzical expression and pursed lips. "You are crazy."

"I knew you couldn't resist," Houston said, turning suddenly to look over his shoulder, which is where Jean-Pierre's gaze seemed to be directed. But no one was there.

15

ONITA HAD SEEN St. Jude's Lamb of God from the outside many times on her way to Corina's church services
next door, but today was the first time she'd stepped
inside. Although the March norther was bitter, the inside of the
little store was so warm it nearly choked her. Gus always said
Corina's thermostat was 180 degrees different from everyone
else's. Bonita unbuttoned her old Navy pea coat at once. Oddly,
it made her shiver to feel the warmth.

"My mother say have a seat, she be right out." Bonita recognized the boy Paulus from church.

"No hurry." Looking at the boy's still discolored face, she felt
she had to say more. "How you feelin'?"

"I feel pretty good." He looked down in what she realized was
a kind of male shyness. She realized he was looking at the way her
breasts swelled in her red sweater. She'd seen the look three or
four million times a night at The Hellhole, and rarely thought
about it. But Paulus's look was not rapacious. Lustful, but in a
curious, innocent way. She did not mind, and was sorry he felt
self-conscious.

"Well, that's something that takes a long time to get better.

One time my brother got his jaw broke in a car wreck and he looked all black and blue from his neck to the top of his head for weeks, but then it all faded out and you'd never have known it ever happened."

"I've been able to eat again. That's the main thing."

"Well, your face won't be that way much longer." She caught herself. "I mean it's already gotten a lot better since the last time I saw you."

He shrugged and looked over his shoulder. The door in the small hallway in the rear was open. Wisps of incense floated out. Paulus left the counter and went back to the room. After looking in, he came forward again. "She say she ready now."

Bonita picked up her jacket and walked around the counter, following Paulus. He stopped short of the door and bade her continue. He smiled again, shyly, as she passed.

When she reached the open door, she stopped for far too long. It was very plain, very white, except for pictures on the wall and plates full of dead things along the baseboards. The woman she knew as the Reverend Youngblood was sitting behind a small desk, watching her closely. Bonita knew she had to go on inside. Then she heard a quiet laugh.

"You in the right place, darlin'. Come here and sit."

Bonita felt her feet move forward. The incense filled her lungs. It did not make her cough. It made her feel like she was in space. She sat in a chair to one side of the desk. Reverend Youngblood was explaining something about the "spirits" and "feeding" them and why crabs were on one of the plates and the heads of some kind of bird on another.

Bonita was glad the incense was so strong. A Bible was open on the table, next to a clear goblet of water. The reverend wore a simple blue dress—nothing weird or strange, except maybe the white lace shawl around her head and neck.

"You nervous, child. Relax. You never been in a reading before, and you from Louisiana?"

Bonita looked into the eyes of the woman across the desk. Those eyes were very dark. But to Bonita's surprise, they were not the eyes of evil. She felt herself breathe for the first time. "You have to excuse me, Reverend," she said. "I've been to palm readers and like that but I don't believe I've ever seen anything like this."

"This is the room of the Spirits, and of the Lord," the reverend said. "I use all the help I can get to help people. These are the *santos,*" she said, indicating some iron pots and other statues Bonita had never seen before. "That one there the one belong to me—Ogun. A very powerful spirit."

Bonita nodded. "It's just that I was raised a Catholic—"

"I know that, child. You don't got nothing to fear. Half the people come in here good Catholics, too, and Baptists, Pentecostals. I get everyone."

"But we were told not to be around hoodoo."

The reverend's face seemed to tighten slightly. "I don't be doing no hoodoo in this place."

"Well, I guess I thought that's what this was."

"It ain't no hoodoo. This is the *santos.* They the one and only Spirits from Africa, come to America with the slaves. And now the children of the slaves finding the Spirits again. That's what this is. Those old ladies in the church and most white people all they see is hoodoo but the *santos* is different. *Santos* the power of the Lord. Don't you see this Bible in front of me?"

Bonita nodded.

"You think I be letting anything in my church or my body don't work with the Lord Jesus Christ? *Santos* all work together. Jesus is above all of them but they all part of the Lord." She looked at Bonita. "You understand that?"

Bonita glanced around the room, then at the Bible, then at the Reverend Corina Youngblood. She was breathing quite normally again, and though her face was still flushed, it was from the excessive heating and not from the fear that had inflamed it before. She hated herself for being such a priss. She had seen things in her life she'd bet even this preacher would have trouble digesting. It had caught her off-balance, is all.

"I didn't mean to be that way."

"Spirit brought you here, no point fighting with it."

"I guess I know that."

"Good. Now we get started. You got your money?"

Almost eagerly, Bonita pulled thirty-five dollars from the pocket of her black jeans. Gus had told her about the fee. She had wanted to be prepared and not look like a fool about money, same as in a dope deal.

"No," said Corina, pushing her extended hand back. "Hold the money in your right hand and make a fist." Bonita did. Corina closed her red Bible. "Now open it to anywhere you want." Bonita did. It fell on Ruth in the Old Testament. "Now run your finger down the page and let it move till you ready for it to stop."

Bonita extended her finger, and stopped as requested.

"'C,'" said Corina, looking at a boldfaced letter at the beginning of a paragraph. She wrote the letter on a small white pad. Then she closed her eyes for a moment. Her expression seemed slightly troubled. When she opened her eyes, she gently took Bonita's hand and removed the money. She put the money on the table next to the Bible. "The money lay there for success," she explained.

Then Corina recited a Biblical passage which Bonita did not recognize. She thought she heard her say something like "Trough of God" but she wasn't sure.

For the next half hour, Corina, no longer "the Reverend" in Bonita's mind, not in this room, dropped in and out of focus. Sometimes she appeared to be talking to Bonita, and sometimes to voices she called by strange African names. In her own voice, or sometimes in a low growling voice, she told Bonita Rae Doucet all about herself. Most of it she got right. When she was done, she asked if Bonita wanted to know anything.

Bonita hesitated.

Corina smiled. "Spirit say try again."

"I just wondered . . . if I'm able to."

Corina closed her eyes for two minutes or more. Bonita felt uncomfortable. Eyes still closed, she said, "Spirit say something keeping you in your period. Spirit say you don't want your period but you have it. Spirit say you not ready. Spirit say—" she stopped, head dropped back on her shoulders. "Spirit say you need to know if that man love you before you have his baby."

"He loves me."

"Spirit say he don't know that."

"Does the Spirit say it's not true?"

"Spirit say it might be true, or not, but he don't know. Spirit say that why you keep your period. Because it not the time."

Corina's eyes closed again. Her hands tightened on the edges of the Bible. "Then 'C' is for child, Lord? Not for that other? Why you try to trick me like this, Jesus, when I still don't know what you mean the first time?"

Her eyelids opened. Bonita had never seen such a powerful and beautiful brown. But they were not focused on anything or anyone in the room. In a moment, Corina's hands loosened and she let them rest flat on the table. She was speaking to Bonita again, as though she had been all along.

"You know, that Houston man have some Spirit after him, I think. I see him strong around you and I been having him strong around me, too. But I know this, child, you not gonna have no baby with that man right away. Spirits looking after you—Huh!" Her head lurched again. "Spirit say you have good soul in you and nobody put a baby in you until they cleared."

She opened her eyes and shook her head. "I never have seen that before, like that, child. That clear." She moved one hand across the Bible and took Bonita's slender fingers. "You be well blessed today."

As soon as Bonita walked out the door, the cold, damp wind reminded her she had been perspiring. She tugged her pea coat tight against the shivers, but on the way to work she kept her window rolled down. It was as if she couldn't take the air in fast enough.

PICKING THE GIRLS was the easiest part. Miss Angelique's had included voice training and chorale as a part of its curriculum for years. It was a popular choice, perhaps because so many of the girls were musically inclined and perhaps because being in choir was a solid way of getting out of sixth period study hall and a good way to take trips to Atlanta, Chicago, and Dallas, the cities in which Miss Angelique's choir had annual competitive appearances. Nor were they a rowdy bunch, judging by the standards set by their peers within the Academy. If anything, the choir members were considered more or less among the school normals, and, since the music often veered into the seasonally religious, often as not they were reasonably pious, too.

The hard part was convincing them they should get on stage in the Gospel Tent at Jazzfest. Not just get on stage, but crowd around the rear of the tent and generally mingle with the ensembles from black churches throughout the city and even the South.

"We'll be the only white girls there," Cissy Otterton said.

"Mr. Houston, I don't mean that racially, I just mean we'll stand out and look like a bunch of freaks."

"Some of those black girls are mean," said Betsy Druford. "Look, I grew up five blocks from here and you just don't go and do something like this and pretend it's not a problem."

"They don't like us because we're white and also they think we're a bunch of snobs. Mr. Houston, they hate us." That was Cissy again.

All fifteen were talking, but Cissy and Betsy more than the others. Maybe because they were the seniors. Gus was letting them talk. He figured the main thing was to let people who were being forced to do something against their better judgment get all the hard feelings out of their system first. He had observed in the Army, and also in the World, that people were willing to do all sorts of things if they felt like they had put in their two cents. It was saying what they wanted that seemed to matter more than the doing. Gus knew people just naturally liked to bitch. But he wasn't sure if that was going to cut it this time.

"I just don't think you can make us do this, and I haven't even talked to my mother yet," said Cindy Duchamps, of the Garden District Duchamps.

"Oh, come on," said a new voice—Charlotte Percy, a brunette junior who also played on the school basketball team. "Y'all act like you've never been to Jazzfest or for that matter never been outside this school. I've been to basketball games over in the east that were *scary*. This isn't anything. It's just going and singing. And anyway, it's like church or something. Plus Jazzfest is fun and after we can go around to everything else for free. So what's the fucking deal?"

Silence.

"You don't have to curse."

"I wasn't cursing."

"You said 'fucking'."

"'Fucking' isn't cursing."

"Yeah, right."

"'Fucking' is what you do with Jimmy."

Cindy Duchamps didn't move, or throw her books, or anything, which is what Gus had expected. She simply glared at Charlotte Percy. It was a glare Gus had learned to recognize in New Orleans social circles. It meant that the person being glared at was henceforth a nonperson. Response to the causative insult was no longer necessary because the person making the insult was no longer in existence. New Yorkers only knew of the "drop dead" look. Gus had received that one a couple of times during his brief adventures in the advertising trade. In the South the sequence jumped far past mere cessation of life. The death had occurred, the funeral been attended, the earth folded over the coffin, and the headstone moldy with years—all this was implied in the look Cindy flicked toward Charlotte. And even though they were only sixteen and seventeen, it would be generations before anyone in their respective families would have much to do with one another except in required business and financial affairs.

So Gus figured Cindy was off his list. He only needed eight girls anyway, according to Jean-Pierre. He could see natural attrition taking care of the roster all by itself.

The discussion went on for an hour. To his surprise, Cissy wanted to stay, which was good, because she had a beautiful alto that could hold a hymn right in its place. Charlotte agreed, also, and Betsy and Tina Smythe and Marie Graham. In the end, ten of the fifteen agreed to work up a medley in time for Jazzfest. Gus told them only eight could be on the final squad, but that two could be alternates.

He had no idea which ones were the best; to his half-trained ear they all sounded good, and they had won many competitions. Jean-Pierre had heard them himself in the course of his own singing or playing organ in church choirs around the city. In fact, if he hadn't heard Miss Angelique's performing "Ave Maria" at a special Christmas service at First St. John the Baptist he might not have agreed to Gus's idea. But he had told Gus they were "good as almost anybody I've played with," which Jean-Pierre seemed to have meant as a high compliment.

"Give me a couple of weeks and just a few songs, which is all we get anyway, and I'll put them alongside the Angels of Desire," Jean-Pierre had said. The Angels were supposed to be the best Gospel quintet in town, and had made many records and won awards. Jean-Pierre had played a selection from one of their albums for Gus and humbled him.

It wasn't that Gus thought Miss Angelique's could win the competition, but on hearing the Angels, he wondered if the school choir could even share the same stage with the pros and semipros. But in his moment of doubt, Jean-Pierre had lifted him—restored his sense of purpose. In fact, the sound from the Angels that sent Gus into the land of second thoughts simultaneously inspired Jean-Pierre, who, it was fair to say, took up the banner from then on. It was as if Jean-Pierre had accepted some fearsome challenge—teaching white girls how to sing some old Gospel favorites. Gus recognized the feeling. It seemed a little preposterous, but there was no doubting what Jean-Pierre was feeling. He was feeling like a missionary.

16

O N THE IDES OF MARCH, the first day the bulldozer
showed up on Ladeau Street to knock down the
washateria, Corina knew it was all going to get far
worse. Houston had told her it might take forever to get a
construction permit for the SuperBotanica now that the media
had got City Hall stirred up. She had said, "Gus Houston, you
don't know nothing about this city to say something like that."
To which he had laughed, like she was some kind of squirrelly
little old granny who didn't know day from night, and told her it
was just politics and that was one thing he knew about. Which he
didn't know nothing about. Politics in New Orleans was knowing who to give money to, and Elroy must have known, because
it sure wasn't taking forever to get a construction permit. It was
taking no time at all.

She'd heard the diesel engine going as soon as she got to the
shop, and had driven over to check out the racket without even
opening up. Sure enough, it was coming from the old washateria,
or what was left of it. By noon, when Corina went back for
another look, the building was gone and they had jackhammers
out breaking up the concrete slab and rough-looking men in

hard hats jerking metal and pipe out of the wreckage, and trucks full of other men, some white, some black, piling rubble into trucks; dumb, stupid ants carrying off everything in sight.

By nightfall, nothing was left and the lights were on over a big hole in the ground and they were still ant-working, so she didn't go home. She sat in her car and watched. She saw Elroy's Nissan, and thought she saw Julio, too. Then she saw a big flatbed come up with a crane on the back and watched it lift a giant metal cylinder out of the hole in the ground, and then another just like it, which she realized were gas storage tanks.

With all her might, she hoped for the tanks to bust open in midair and spill twenty-year-old Tiger ethyl all over the place and then some dumb fool light a cigarette and blow them all to kingdom come, but her mind was not right for prayer, she knew that, and so nothing happened—except for a moment in her mind where it did, a huge explosion like the end of the world. And then the tanks were loaded on a huge truck and disappeared. And then the crane was hauled away. But the work went on until midnight without stopping, and she left because she couldn't stand to watch anymore, the end of the world.

Elroy was going to do it. He was going to do it so fast she didn't know how to stop him. At seven a.m. a washateria had been on the corner, and by noon the washateria was gone and for a few hours in its place you could detect the bones of the old gasoline station and then that was gone, too, and now there was just a hole. Corina had no doubt that in the morning the hole would be gone, too.

But if Elroy was going to do it, she was going to do something back. She knew what he thought. He thought she would give up. She would bet anything he thought that. He had paid somebody off and he was racing to get his SuperBotanica up and thought that would be that, but it wouldn't be that.

For one thing, there were a lot of black men on that job crew, probably because Elroy was smart enough not to use a bunch of Cubans in the neighborhood. For another thing, Corina had a lot of friends, and clients. For another thing, she had power. By the time she lay down to sleep that night, or really early in the morning, she had called so many people, who had called so many other people, that she was able to sleep the sleep of a general before a battle he knew he would win, that he must win.

Except for the dream. It had been many months since the words had come in that way. She had not forgotten them but she had not had them in her dreams. This time they flashed in lightning across dark thunderclouds that filled the heavens. She knew the words had meaning but she had lost it. The words came with Houston. Houston was because of them. She was bound to him in ways that made no sense without the words, without the power behind the words. "Come Ye to the Trough of God." If she thought she knew the meaning she was a fool. And nothing could tell her. Except Him. Exhaustion overcame her and she almost slept through the alarm.

By nine a.m. every member of the African Spiritual Church of Mercy and a hundred other people too were at the construction site, including Houston, who thought he knew so much about the media and politics but in her mind knew about as much about that as he did about his own life, which was precious little as far as she was concerned. But he did show up. She gave him that. And, like the ones from her church, he wasn't just watching from the street. They were all right there on the site. Sitting down, singing "Power to the People" and "We Shall Not Be Moved" and sometimes walking up to the workers with their jackhammers and tool belts and the foreman, a big Irish-Indian, with his blueprints and telling them they should be ashamed.

When Elroy got there he didn't even speak to Corina, he just talked to some of his workers and they all left, except for a couple to watch the generators and trucks. By eleven, when the TV stations arrived, all the reporters saw were a hundred or more black people walking around a vacant lot next to a stack of lumber and an equipment shed and two Port-o-Lets, male and female, as required by OSHA.

So they interviewed Corina, who vowed to keep "these foreigners and racists" out of the neighborhood and "defend our faith as God has ordered me to do," but not all the stations ran it. Houston said it was because they didn't have good "visuals" or "B-roll" and TV always had to have visuals and B-roll. So at the end of day two, General Youngblood had to take stock again, for her adversary had, on that day, proven as wise as she had been bold. It was a draw, and it left her feeling strangely mean.

Elroy kept looking at the calendar, then at the construction schedule, back and forth, until he thought he had hypnotized himself. It could work, it couldn't. It could work, it couldn't. There was time, there wasn't. Like that, all evening. Thirty days until Jazzfest was enough; but only if they got to work. Day and night crews could do it, tripling the cost, but he didn't mind about that if he could be open. Julio said what difference did it really make, suppose he got a heart attack, would the schedule still be so important? But Elroy had set his pride on Jazzfest and he would have it. She would not stop him.

Work resumed the day after the TV crews left, and although a few reporters came back, Geronimo Casey, the crew foreman, was smart enough to keep things quiet. He gave the men lots of breaks, and had them at work by four a.m., then off around ten, when the protestors showed up, and any time a TV crew came by, which was only twice. It went on that way for over a week. Although at first the crowds were full of fight, by the second week only about half of them were coming back. And it was humid like the Caribbean and they didn't stay that long.

Yet even in small numbers, they were a problem. Besides all the singing and praying, they taunted the workers about being "Toms" and "un-American." Worst of all was Corina. The protestors could be handled, but Elroy didn't think it would stop with the protestors, and since there wasn't anything else Corina could do legally, he waited and wondered. He knew what she might try; he could see it in her face even across the hundred yards that usually separated them. He had been feeding Changó every day since the construction started and knew the battle would take place among the *orisha,* but he wasn't sure how far she'd go. He thought it would be very far, and seeing Paulus every day among the protestors only reminded him.

But he was pleased the second week when the rhythm of the *santos* moved into the work of the crews. The slab set well and even with Geronimo's deliberately weird schedule there was little doubt the prefab would be up maybe even earlier than May 1. Julio was already working long hours at the warehouse making sure the stock was in, especially the new things from Nigeria that they'd ordered earlier in the year—bones, special herbs, candles from the holy city of Ile-Ife, where the *santos* had come from.

Elroy was very proud of his brother. Not only for the inventory checking, but everything—he'd even hired a small ad agency to make sure the ads to announce the opening were in the paper and they were going to shoot a special commercial just before Jazzfest to run on the independent TV station, which had cheaper rates and which more of the blacks watched anyway.

In the commercial, Elroy was going to welcome crowds of specially selected black people into his store and welcome New Orleans to the world of the spirits. He was thinking of even pouring a special mixture of Florida water and flower petals on the sidewalk in front of his store to offer a blessing. It wasn't the kind of thing for Changó, exactly, but he and Julio had decided that viewers wouldn't be ready for real sacrifices yet.

Elroy was very excited thinking about that part of it. It was his dream—gateway to the *santos* for all the people—and he was finally realizing it. It made him especially mad for Corina Youngblood to try to split the browns from the blacks on this. He swore against her to Changó on it. He had misgivings about harming the woman he still had the hots for, but what choice did he have? She was trying to destroy him. She was also, therefore, trying to destroy the *santos*.

She would not. She had not. The war was over. She had lost.

In less than three weeks he would be open for business and become the talk of the city. Perhaps, as a gesture, he would renew his invitation to her to take out a SuperBotanica franchise at a location over on the east side. Or to relocate to Mississippi or somewhere and set herself up. She would never do that, of course. It would be a good idea and Elroy had no doubt she would prosper, but thinking like that was foolish, as Julio constantly reminded him. This was war. Corina Youngblood was the enemy. He must be careful how he apportioned his mercy.

BY THE LIGHT of the half moon by the shallow lake she lay the four slain animals in a circle. Paulus waited to one side with the white-handled *cuchillo*. Each goat pointed in the direction of the cycles of life of the world of Damballah-Wedo, the serpent god she had learned of not through Elroy but through Benjamin, a Haitian she had met at a party at Jean-Pierre's. He had a different idea about the *santos* than she did and they had quarreled but she had remembered much of what he had said and some of it, like the snake-mother circling the earth, she had believed. And Benjamin showed her pictures of the circles the Haitians drew in the earth. She knew those were real just by seeing them, and because Elroy had mentioned such things during her own initiation long ago.

She created the circle and fed the spirits at each corner with the blood of the animals. She prayed for an hour in the center of all that power. Paulus joined her and together they drank blood from the sacred bowl. It made her feel far different than the power of Jesus, but it was a power she knew Jesus let happen and so she felt it was acceptable for her to call upon it.

Jesus let everything happen. Therefore He let the *santos* happen. The *santos,* she thought, were what Jesus sent to the people because He didn't have time for everyone Himself and because He thought people would be more able to talk to the *santos* because the *santos* were not pure of all frailty the way Jesus was. Her own *santo,* Ogun, could have terrible tempers or rage and destroy entire cities and inflict terrible cruelty on his enemies. It was not something Jesus would do but it was something Jesus might allow to be done. Corina believed Jesus had to operate that way. The *santos* had to do things He could not and the people were unable to do. And sometimes the *santos* had to inspire and fill the people so that they could do the unbelievable or unspeakable things necessary to protect themselves. She saw herself thus on that night by Pontchartrain.

Had any white people come across her they would have recoiled in horror. Two centuries ago they would have burned her alive as an evil African witch. Now they would be scared. She was glad. That was her purpose. She wanted to scare people. It was the way of the Warriors—the Cubans called them *Los Guerreros*—to frighten those whom they had to vanquish. She felt the spirit of Ogun slip inside her skin and take her and she felt her face harden and her teeth sharpen and her muscles bulge. It was thus in the night.

Rising from the circle, she told Paulus to leave, for what she had to do was for her. Or perhaps it was not "her" speaking to Paulus but Ogun, and Ogun was unflinching in his might. The Corina part of her did not want Paulus to be too close to Ogun's business, for it could destroy him in a flash and she might not even know what she had done.

When Paulus walked away from the circle, Corina took each of the goats and twisted the carcass backward, with the heads facing out instead of in. She drew upon the opposite side of the *santos*—the propensity for evil that is in all of them and in all of us. She needed that side in the battle for her church, especially against the man who had been her *padrino* but whose spirit role in her life she now foreswore forever and spit on the ground where that which he had been was ground into the mud and blood beneath her feet.

When the goats were rearranged, she walked counterclockwise and stopped at the tail of each one. She carried four small broken coconut shells in her skirt pocket and at each carcass threw the shells. Each gave her the negative sign—two white sides, two husk sides up. If she had been seeking help, that would have been bad, but in looking for the strength of destruction she knew she was reinforced.

On finishing, she dropped to her knees, then fell forward and stretched, arms extended, amid the inverse circle. She called upon all the Spirits whose Cuban or African names she could summon—Elegba, Ochosi, Ogun, Oshun, Oya, Changó, Yemonja, BabaluAyé, Osanyin, Shalako, Oyekun, Elekun, the Ibeji—many, many more and told them of the need to protect their children in this New World and come to her aid and that if they did she would sing their praises and reward them forever.

Just before dawn she awoke with a start. She had been with Ogun, slaying thousands of invaders at the shores of the River

Niger. Paulus was curled along a shoreline, too. Only this one was here, now. She woke him and they drove back to town, directly to the construction site, where two dozen men were already busy in the steaming early morning sun.

She walked up to the generator huffing near what would be the front door to Elroy Delgado's store. While the big Indian pretended not to look, she opened the thermos in her hand. In it was not coffee but thick, warm blood. She poured it over the generator and onto the ground and even if the Indian boss turned away, there were others at work who did not. Corina tried to see as many of their eyes as possible. Each pair she was able to catch, was a pair she fixed. When her eyes were full, she left.

Afterwards, Geronimo Casey ordered two men to hose off the generator and the concrete. It was his policy, and that of Elroy's attorneys, to ignore everything the protestors did. But when he went to his car phone and called his boss, he realized it was easier for him to close his eyes to the hoodoo woman than it was for the others.

17

JEAN-PIERRE had gone down to the construction site several times after work, although he more or less accepted the fact that the Delgados had greased enough palms to get their SuperBotanica. He told his mother that, causing her to become furious, and had decided not to bring it up again. In any case, he had other business with the Delgados. He preferred not to ruin revenge for his brother with a losing struggle against "economic development," which was what the Delgados were calling their stores. In New Orleans, anything which developed the economy, including gambling, was going to prevail. Jean-Pierre considered himself a realist, not a street-shouter. And he had other business with the Delgados. He would not take them on in public, at an area they controlled. He understood his mother's concerns but he was not interested in being a martyr.

He had told her she should just find a new location—what was so great about the Uptown ghetto anyway? She didn't want to hear that either. Jean-Pierre had learned as a child he could not win arguments with his mother. Paulus had absorbed the lesson by becoming like her. Jean-Pierre could never be like her.

Neither could he oppose her. Her will was strong, her temper fast.

Also he loved her. She had taken care of the family and was at heart a woman of substance. She was not educated, as was he, but she had a power he could only read about. For all those reasons he rarely pushed an argument with her. He had set out on his own life's path. And he had other business with the Delgados. He did not want her to know about that or to be a part of that. It was his business with them.

The choir, maybe, was a way of keeping his mother's business separate from his own. Readying Gus Houston's girls to go up against the old-line Gospel groups and the new, strong ones, Jean-Pierre had little time after school for anything except singing lessons and choreography. He had settled on a three-song medley: "Old Rugged Cross," as a kind of white hymn refashioned black, rolled into "Jesus On the Mainline," and finally "All I Got I Got from Jesus," a contemporary Gospel favorite getting good airplay on the religious stations. They also were practicing a possible last-minute substitute, "Oh Happy Day!/Walking with Jesus," a fusion of the call-and-response hit by the Edwin Hawkins Singers with a hand-clapping overlay Jean-Pierre had adapted from something he'd improvised for his mother's church.

He figured the set for a short but high-intensity show stopper. Reasoning that the all-white choir was in context a novelty act, he had seen the key to success as a brief, but decisive, appearance. And he was pretty sure that's what Reverend Lincoln wanted, too. It had taken most of Jean-Pierre's powers of persuasion and years of volunteer efforts at the parish churches to convince Albert Lincoln the white girls should get a place on the program.

But an appearance was all Jean-Pierre wanted, even if it was at six in the evening on Thursday, when the big crowds wouldn't yet have formed and the day people were going home to dinner. Houston felt the same. He didn't seem to care at all when the Academy was scheduled to appear or for how long, just that it would happen.

Jean-Pierre remembered the afternoon he called Houston with the news that the choir had been put in the show. "Son of a bitch," he'd said. "I'll be goddamned." And then he had poured out masses of thank-yous. When they met the next day to work out an audition and practice schedule, Houston's face had the blue aura again, but also something else—a faraway look Jean-Pierre couldn't place. And then he remembered where he had seen such a look. He remembered his mother slumped in her chair behind the altar near the end of a service.

"... *On a hill, far away* ..."

The piercing note caused Jean-Pierre to wince, but it snapped him back into today's work, the last round of the tryouts, and he kept on playing. Unfortunately, the acoustics in the Academy's Performing Arts Theater, which most recently had witnessed the senior drama class presentation of *The Glass Menagerie,* were quite good. Merciless, for the slender soprano on stage before him. Her voice could hit the scales but it cracked too much and wasn't big enough to carry. It was also very white. They all were, except for that big basketball player and maybe one other, the little blond named Cissy. But some were too white.

He glanced sideways at Houston, who seemed to understand, too, and marked an X by the girl's name. Jean-Pierre played out the rest of the stanza, then raised one hand to signal the girl to stop. She smiled and walked off the stage. As she left, she looked back, trying to hide her curiosity. She must have seen the exchange between Jean-Pierre and Gus, because her face suddenly clouded and they could hear a door banging behind the curtains.

"How many we got left?"

"We've got ten you said were okay."

Jean-Pierre looked down at the keyboard and at his slender fingers. He thought a moment. "That's enough."

"That only gives us two extra if we use eight in the choir."

"You expect some kind of sickness at this school?"

"No more than usual."

"Then we got enough. Need to, we can go with seven or even six for the show. As long as we got that big girl and that other one, the alto. After that it doesn't really matter much."

"You don't like them."

Jean-Pierre looked up. "Why you say that? I didn't say that." He ran a quick scale to renew his ears. "They all sing pretty good. Question is whether they can get where they need to for Gospel. They need a lot more . . . 'timbre' I guess is the musical word."

"Fine, but do you think they can compete?"

Jean-Pierre laughed. "I didn't say nothing about competing, if you mean winning. Zero none chance of that, Chaplain." He hung on the word a little longer than necessary. "You never said they had to win. Just get in the show."

"I know. But I mean, will they be embarrassed? More to the point, will I? I got a lot riding on this."

"Like I don't?"

"Okay, we both do. So can you feel happy putting this group you been looking at today up there on May Day?"

Jean-Pierre stood up. "Why you call me if you going to sit there and question my judgment? Would I say these girls can go if I didn't think they could? You think I don't know how to choose a choir?"

Gus put up one hand. "Okay, okay. That's not what I meant."

Jean-Pierre sat back down. He hadn't really intended to leave, but in dealing with white people he often felt it necessary to put up a line of demarcation of power early on. He felt slightly foolish doing it with Houston, since the man had come to him clearly begging him to take charge, but perhaps it was a scene worthwhile.

"Let's look over the list of who's left one more time then."

Houston slid it across. The point of turning back had been breached long ago. They were in. Jean-Pierre looked over the list carefully, putting faces to the names. "She sounds black, this one," he said, pointing to Cissy's name. "This one, too." He indicated Charlotte. "Rest are good enough for backup." Jean-Pierre slid back across the piano bench and began a slow warm-up to "Power," his mother's favorite soul-shaker. "They gonna love us or hang us from a lamp post."

"Make sure they love us, then."

Jean-Pierre continued playing the song. Houston looked at his watch, got up. "I'll be right back," he said.

Jean-Pierre looked at him questioningly.

"Time to inform the lucky winners."

As Houston walked out, Jean-Pierre picked up the tempo, the volume. He banged the keys hard. After a moment her realized he was humming to himself, which he usually only did when he was angry. Or afraid. He played on for another half hour. Outside, though classes were over for the day, a half-dozen girls stood near the auditorium's rear doors, peeking in to see the grim-faced, thickset black man playing and singing with such force, and wondering what the weeks ahead under his tutelage would be like.

BONITA MADE GUS go with her to the doctor, because she wanted him to be a part of whatever was said. And because if it wasn't her who had trouble getting pregnant, but him, she wanted him to be there when the doctor said so. Only it wasn't either one of them. It just wasn't her time.

"I just didn't know it was that big a deal for you," Gus said, driving home.

"It wasn't, but it is."

"It better be. Now I have to whack off in a tube."

"I'm sure it won't be the first time."

He skimmed a yellow light at Napoleon Street. Neither spoke. In Gus's mind was a familiar loop of an old tape. He felt his body bound to the earth at the very moment it longed to soar into the heavens. He did not want to Occupy Space. In Bonita's mind was the knowledge of what Gus was thinking, that he was in the wormhole; also, a determination that it was now, in her life, that she would have her baby. It was with this man. He was smart, he was reasonably good looking, he had no major health problems. He would do. Moreover, she loved him. She wasn't debating it anymore.

Corina had given it context. Bonita had not even been aware of wanting to become pregnant. But that time her period was late woke her up. In wondering if she would have a baby, she realized she did. Now that she realized it, she could not dismiss the desire.

If Gus didn't want a baby, that was his problem. She could feel the tension across the car, but he'd just have to deal with it. He was plenty old enough. Older than her. What would he do, leave just because he didn't want to be a daddy? As she watched him through the heavy traffic heading toward home, she knew that he had already made a decision he might not even have been aware of.

Or he may have. The knowing may have brought back the vision of Elizabeth Hapsenfield's breasts—

"Gus—"

"Shit." He jammed the brakes, veered hard to the left, and just missed a flatbed truck backing out of an auto parts store driveway.

"You better keep your mind on the road."

"Yeah." His hands were tingling slightly and he felt a tremble in his legs. He had scared himself.

When they got home, neither spoke. Gus took an iced tea out onto the porch and watched the park. He wasn't thinking about Elizabeth anymore. He was thinking about which of the girls should go in the front row of the choir and which in the back, and he was thinking about what would happen with his referrals to Corina in the summer, when the girls went home, and he was looking at a squirrel in a tree about fifty yards away. He was thinking about the thing that gnawed at souls, and that were unknown. Or had no names. The shrinks had no vocabulary for this, nor the philosophers. Funny if it worked out that the preachers did.

He had no idea where he was, for the day had been difficult. Yet why? He had merely done what thousands—millions, zillions—of men had done, had always done and always would do. He had gone with his woman to the medicine man to ask if she would bring forth a child. And the doctor had said yes. Of course, the sperm count test was a modern variation, but the basic orchestration was eternal.

All he had to do was beat off in a bottle, although he knew it wasn't really necessary because he'd been tested once and had sperm to spare, but the doctor wanted to "cover all the bases." And Bonita had to take her temperature—God, it was horrible beyond belief. In the prime of his life, in the moment of his access to fame and maybe money, he was having sex with a test tube and his woman was sticking a thermometer between her legs. All in pursuit of progeny! He drank tea and thought he would explode.

Bonita walked around in front of him. She had changed into shorts and a loose T-shirt. Without a word, she straddled his lap and took his head in her hands. She made him look at her. They looked at each other for what seemed a very long time. Her brown eyes were brimmed with something, and Gus realized his were, too. It was true, he loved her. It was a terrible emotion, considering.

"I was lost, now I am found . . ."

But the verse was wrong. You stayed lost.

She leaned forward to kiss him. "I love you."

"I do, too."

She raised her shirt and pressed her right breast against his mouth. He cradled it with his hands and sucked on it. Then the other.

"Come with me."

He followed her into the living room. That was as far as they got. She dropped her shorts. Gus's eyes went immediately to her slender hips and the dark hair around her thighs. A fury of clothes and hands, he stripped off his own shirt and jeans. His cock was so hard it scraped against his zipper. She dropped to the floor and took him into her mouth. She could feel his knees shaking. He said, "I want to fuck you."

She pulled away and turned on all fours, her ass to him. He stuck his cock in and pounded against her buttocks. She came almost at once and then, to her surprise, again. Then he did.

She collapsed forward, her breasts squeezed against the throw rug.

"Roll over," he said. "Put your legs up."

She turned her head slight to see him. He was on his knees, helping her turn onto her back, and drawing her thighs and calves up into an inverted V.

"It's like mashed potatoes. You got to keep the gravy from spilling out."

"What?"

A trained forensic psychologist of the future, scraping away the remains of the brain in Gus's skull, might have detected in the electro-residue of the remark (all thoughts, all speech, leave footprints in the brain, had we but the means to detect them) the subconscious association with school cafeteria lunch food. But Gus was not making such associations and would have banned them had they appeared because this Space was what he Occupied and he was not somewhere else. Nor did he want to be, despite the skull scrapings that twenty-fourth century archaeologists might someday find that would say, as they always had said, that the great flaw in the development of the human mind was that it was never able to regulate itself with any real significance.

She said, "Fuck me some more," and her saying it made him hard, and he did. If it was not on that day that they made the baby, who could doubt the hour would not come round at last?

18

ELIZABETH WAS AS Gus had never seen her. She was happy. "My God, have you seen this?" she said, breezing into his office with a copy of the *Times-Picayune* stretched out ahead. She was reading from an editorial:

> It is rare and reassuring amid this city's ongoing racial unrest for an institution such as Miss Angelique's Academy to take upon itself the bold and openhearted effort to reach out into the rest of the community. Through a novel, if long overdue, decision to participate in this year's Jazzfest, this most traditional of New Orleans institutions has served notice that it is a part of the community at-large. And not just Jazzfest—the Academy has been invited to perform in the Gospel Tent.
>
> Not least because of the—let us be honest—élite nature of this traditional, expensive, and almost totally white school is its offering, however symbolic, to be commended. Many of our city's other institutions, from Mardi Gras krewes to corporate offices, could learn the wise lesson from these young women of the Garden District.
>
> We are delighted to offer this month's "Thumbs Up" to

Agon and Elizabeth Hapsenfield, the delightful and imaginative forces behind the school, for their bringing of new ideas and social initiative to the city.

Elizabeth flopped into the leather couch, beaming. "And then it says to turn to Section F for the story on us that girl came out and wrote." She clutched the paper to her breast and seemed to blush. "I just want to thank you from the bottom of my heart. You are truly a sweet and wonderful man."

Gus squirmed a little in his chair and pretended to look at his blank computer screen. It helped, of course, that the *Picayune*'s publisher's daughter, now a journalism major at LSU, was an alumnus of Miss Angelique's and that the sports editor's fifteen-year-old was currently enrolled. But once you have their attention, you still have to show them something, right? So Gus accepted the praise.

"I really mean it," she said. "At first I wondered if the Jazzfest idea was, to be honest, any kind of thing for the Academy to be involved in. But I have to tell you it's just the best, the very, very best! And then the story!" Elizabeth flipped the paper open to the "Life and Times" section, where the front page was filled with a very flattering picture of her surrounded by the eight girls selected for the choir, which she had named "The Voices of Angelique" for the occasion. At the back stood Gus and Jean-Pierre.

Gus moved around to the front of his desk and read along with the headmistress. He could smell her perfume, feel her heat, but this was not the moment for that. They scanned the article slowly, though each knew the other had already seen it: Gus over coffee at home, and Elizabeth at five a.m. when she went out to collect the newly thrown paper, as she had been doing all the last week. But he pretended for her, as she, perhaps, pretended for him, because it had been made clear from the inception that honesty was not to be the foundation of their relationship.

She read aloud from the second column in Section F.

"'Mrs. Hapsenfield had always seen the Academy as a way of molding not just the student, but the character of the student, and when her chaplain's assistant, Mr. Houston, sketched the idea to her, she seized it at once'—" Elizabeth looked at Gus. "I guess they embellished it a little."

"Not that much. You're good at seizing."

She smiled, a little, and read more. Gus remembered the reporter, Caryn Ames, a young woman just out of Auburn who'd been put on the education beat. She was smart but a little gullible, and Elizabeth had played her like a fiddle.

But the maestro had been nervous as a cat waiting for the orchestration to unfold. In truth, Gus had put it out of mind. He was far too busy with choir practice to think about set-ups in newspapers, the kind of thing he'd done in some previous gigs. Not to mention Bonita wanting to procreate all the time (lab results: sperm to spare), but Elizabeth's anxiety had been more than enough to go around. And now all was well. Gus had played it right. Chaplain schmaplain. Next year he'd be able to pick any job at the school, at double his salary.

As they were reading, Angie Ballew peeped in.

"Oh, I see you saw it. I guess they didn't get Mr. Hapsenfield in it much, did they?"

Elizabeth barely looked up. "I think they got the main characters pretty well."

"*Ciao,*" said Angie. She'd been into foreign phrases spring semester. "Got to run." She looked at Gus and she looked at Elizabeth. Then she was gone.

Elizabeth folded up the paper and said something Gus couldn't hear. Then, "Well, I have to get back out front. I expect the phone'll be ringing off the wall from the parents. Might be a good time to remind them of our fund drive." She looked at the door to see if anyone was there, then leaned over and kissed Gus on the mouth. She licked his lips with her tongue.

"Nice doing business with you."

"Nice to be done."

She studied him a moment, and was gone. Gus walked to his window, peered out, went back to his desk. He sat down. Some time passed; he wasn't sure how much. He was smiling.

"Hey, Mr. H. What's so funny?"

Gus focused on the young woman at the door—Brittany Anderson, he thought was her name. It didn't really matter.

JEAN-PIERRE KNEW where Ocho lived from Maria. In the time they were together, they had driven to his apartment complex out Chef Menteur Highway one night because Maria was scared that Ocho might be following them or stalking her. But his car was home and the lights were on and Maria had decided she was just a little paranoid. At least on that night, Ocho was innocent. Now he was not. Now he had the blood of Paulus all over him and he was not going to get away with it.

Jean-Pierre had never actually been in a pawn shop. They looked like trouble and they always seemed dirty from the outside. This one pretty much fit the bill. He'd crossed the river to Algiers, on the theory that he wouldn't run into anyone who knew him, and he bought the 9mm Baretta automatic for three hundred and twenty-five dollars using a fake name. He had thought of taking Aunt Eddie's revolver from the Ogun pot in his mother's botanica but when he went looking for it, it was gone. Rather than ask his mother if she had it, which was pretty obvious, he decided to just get something for himself. The less she knew about any of this the better.

When he got back to his apartment he cleaned the weapon and loaded the clip and put it in a soft leather briefcase he'd been given for winning a parish-wide Teacher of the Year contest. He'd saved the answering machine tape from the day he had heard the voice and now he got it back out. He stuck the tape in the machine and played it, fast-forwarding through the other messages, from Houston and the others. And there was the voice.

It didn't have much to say—some thick breathing into the receiver and a "Fuck you, motherfucker"—but Jean-Pierre knew the intonation, and he knew the accent, and he knew the epithet. It often had filled Maria's machine in the time they were together and in the end it had terrified her so much that it had ruined what they had. *"Ocho will kill you,"* she had said each time they listened to the curse, sometimes all slurred from the drinking. They had broken up because of that voice.

Jean-Pierre didn't think that Maria had gone back to Ocho or any other of her exes. Probably she had just left New Orleans altogether. Jean-Pierre missed her but there was no finding her. Maybe she had decided just to start over somewhere else. Ocho had marked her and by the time she met Jean-Pierre she was like a puppy hit with a stick too many times. But Jean-Pierre had been good and happy with Maria, and it might have worked for the long haul except that Ocho heard she was with someone and started phoning, following her. Jean-Pierre wanted to face Ocho down as soon as he learned what was happening, but she begged him not to.

He didn't understand that about women—some kind of willingness to suffer, or was it to avoid the fight? He didn't know; he didn't understand. But she said that was the way it was. And so Ocho and what to do about Ocho had become larger than what to do about them and it had poisoned them and it had ended them. "*Ocho will kill you, baby. He's crazy. Look at me. Don't you believe me?*"

And now Ocho had beaten up Paulus. And now he was calling Jean-Pierre directly like he did indirectly before with Maria.

Ocho was a shit, a gangster. Castro had sent such people to freedom in America. And people like the Delgados hired them. Who knew why? Jean-Pierre thought it was a blood thing, a race thing. Same as he saw all the *santería* and the way the Cubans hijacked a black people's faith. At first, Jean-Pierre's mother had defended Elroy, saying he was just giving jobs to his people, but later, when she fell out with Elroy, she saw it like Jean-Pierre did.

Jean-Pierre thought Elroy Delgado had gone even further of late in his relationship with scum like Ocho. Wherever the Delgados set up a business, their competitors gradually disappeared. But until Mardi Gras, Jean-Pierre never thought Elroy actually had his Cubans hurt people—more like intimidated them.

Jean-Pierre's idea was to shoot Ocho in the knees and cripple him. He might kill him in the event, but he wanted mostly to hurt him. He had never forgotten seeing Paulus on that gurney. His face was raw and puffy like cheap hamburger meat and he could barely breathe. Jean-Pierre had never seen his mother really scared until then.

Probably that was when it set in his mind and it would not go away. His mother was denying it, or maybe she was planning something of her own, but it had gotten to where they couldn't talk about it—as if they could talk about anything with all that hanging over them. And so he was going to hurt Ocho. It would be for Paulus and Maria and his mother and himself. But it would be his business and not his mother's to take care of.

If he could do it. He thought he could. He dreamed of doing

it. He had to admit he wasn't sure, though. Just buying the gun was hard. Loading the clip, putting it into the handle, pointing it and imagining putting a slug into somebody's leg, even Ocho's, had begun to seem very real. So he didn't know. But he would do something.

He picked up his phone and dialed the number he knew—could never forget—from when he and Maria were together. It rang four times.

"Hello."

"Hey motherfucker yourself," he said, and hung up.

Jean-Pierre slumped back on his couch. He was glad he made the call. There would be no turning back now. It would be a matter of who got the other one first.

Not a good lesson for his students. He had become a bad example. But he did not feel bad. He did, feel, however, that maiming was not his style and he would simply shoot the son of a bitch in the head.

AGON HAPSENFIELD pretended not to notice the cocked eyebrows when he mentioned the New Primitivism, or the smirks when he patiently tried to explain how it had become the guiding principle in his life, or when they called it "New Age Primitivism," as *Newsweek* termed it. But he did. Still, because of the very beliefs which drew the put-downs of others, he was able to circumvent their disdain. As Elihu said, "Sophistication is the great clouder of minds."

Agon believed that to be true. Take his own case. Sophisticated, cosmopolitan—a Man of the World. He had accumulated much, had traveled widely, was surprised at little. And he was a fool. He remembered the morning after he had spent a night with the youngish mother of one of his first-year students. The woman was bored and filled with hate for her husband and had shared herself with Agon out of little more than spite. Since it was her money, not the husband's, that carried their daughter's tuition, Agon had been only too happy to allow his cock, so to speak, to become the spear with which Suzanna impaled her husband's ego.

But more to the point was how they had sex. It wasn't even making love. It was Suzanna in black leather asking to be chained to the bed in the motel in Lafayette, where they had arranged to meet because of mutual travel plans. It was Agon coming on her face and rubbing it into her hair and it was her shitting all over the bed and it was fucking her in the ass and it was watching on a video and then pouring acid on the video and it was leaving her chained up all night while he took another room because she wanted to see how that felt. It was waking up the next morning and going in and seeing her and smelling the room and her asking him to fuck her again and him doing it. But mostly it was the drive back to New Orleans later in the day, in his own car, thinking about what he had done. It was a sense that—well, he had told Elihu later—that there wasn't anything else to do. It was a sense that he was dead.

Had he not met Elihu at the headmasters' conference in San Diego not long after the night with Suzanna, Agon wasn't sure what he would have done. Most of January had been a blur. During the school holiday, Elizabeth went to Santa Fe, or somewhere, and he stayed in the city but he could remember little of what happened. He had watched considerable TV, something he almost never did, and had read a succession of paperback books bought from supermarket checkout racks.

Blessed San Diego. Elihu's speech was hardly the centerpiece of the conference, but Agon had gone that Tuesday evening out of curiosity. *The New Primitive Primer* was a best-seller, and even if *Newsweek* sneered at "New Age Primitivism" and mocked the "best new est in the West," it was clear in the several pages devoted to Elihu and his philosophy, and to the enthusiasm of those who had attended his "primitive" retreats, that something was up.

Agonistes Franklin Hapsenfield's quite traditional Presbyterian upbringing served to keep self-help fads at a safe distance, but even then he sensed that Elihu Aliesson might be a cut above the run. At the hotel bookstore, he bought *The New Primitive Primer*, intending to skim it before the speech.

He spent the afternoon locked inside its pages, skipping every session of the conference and ordering dinner from room service. The reasonableness, the intelligence, the scope of Elihu's theory made him want to weep. It could be summed up, in Elihu's phrase, as a "Will to Simplicity." Derived from all the great minds who had ever been entranced by the appeal of the simple, the primitive, the unadorned core of meaning, from D. H. Lawrence to Jesus to Heidegger to the Buddha, the New Primitivism put everything in its most elemental focus.

Elihu called it the "Pre-Future." "Now" was a worn-out concept, he wrote. Nor do we live "Now." We live in our own moment of "Becoming." Elihu said he coined the phrase "Pre-Future" so that we would try to think of our Being in a new and fresh way. He said thinking in new and fresh ways was particularly a problem for people who already thought they did.

That was what hit Agon. That was the hook. That evening at the lecture, the man who had left Suzanna Boyse handcuffed in a motel room felt something shatter inside him and then something fill. Supposedly this was what people felt who underwent a religious experience, but Agon had never had a religious experience. He was born into what he thought. In other words, he was born as his Past. He had no Present. He had never had a Now. He had been a Pre-Futurist all his life without knowing it.

By chance, Agon was able to tag along with a group of headmasters taking Elihu to dinner after the lecture and thus meet the remarkable man on a more informal basis. They seemed nothing alike. Elihu was short, ascetic, somewhat Mediterranean in appearance—Spanish, perhaps, with a red beard. Agon towered over him like a Yankee giant. They hit it off. Before leaving California, Agon reserved two weeks at Elihu's "first-step" colony, the Age Zero Primitive Encounter Center in Oregon. There, living communally with a dozen other men and women, dialoguing day and night among themselves and with Elihu, he was changed forever.

Elizabeth had not taken his conversion well. In fact, she seemed to suspect him of something, which was not unusual, given the state of their marriage. Now he could see the sickness of all the games they played with each other. The hideous infidelities, cruelties, plots. The way she had driven Eva Valthenough away—that, as much as Suzanna, had been the final level of sophistication for Agon. He could see it all so clearly now that he was out of his Past.

They had seen each other even less since Oregon. Elizabeth said theirs was a "marriage of old"—by which she meant a business arrangement. It didn't matter if they loved each other (she laughed) or even liked each other, as long as they prospered. Certainly, the Academy was doing well. All he had to do was stay to himself, live his own life in private and let her do the same. That part didn't matter to him.

But lately he was thinking he owed his students more. That he had been a spectacularly disinterested headmaster, all considered, and that just as a chance encounter had changed his life, so perhaps he should attempt to change the lives of those around him. Elihu called it being a "catalyst."

Elihu warned against "secular evangelism" but also said

"providing an example to others is the most important thing a Pre-Futurist can do." Agon had asked what the difference was but Elihu, characteristically, had replied, "Everything is obvious, including this statement."

To say the least, Elizabeth wasn't interested in adding *The New Primitive Primer* to the curriculum. She believed what the press said. She took refuge in the cynical distance. Agon let her be, stuck in the Present, for he knew the Present was merely the Past playing itself out. The Pre-Future was that which was Becoming.

Agon knew he was Becoming and that helped him put those who were mired in the Past/Present in perspective. He thought of them like Dr. Dick Diver thought of his own versions of the sophisticated in *Tender Is the Night*. Agon constantly dispensed benediction on the unaware and the guilty.

Unfortunately, there was another Becoming to negotiate with Elizabeth. Darker, eternal. Primitive, yes, but in a warped way that led not to the Future. He wasn't sure, but he was getting the idea she was up to something. He'd seen strange men come around the school and he'd been hearing things. A few times he thought he had been followed. That was standard procedure before Oregon on his part, too, but he had stopped all that, had told her he had, and had assumed she had, too. But Elizabeth was too much of her own Past. She was up to something.

In that mood of suspicion—better said, Pre-Awareness— had the man Elroy Delgado appeared to him. When the Cuban first called, Agon had almost declined, but the man, whose family Agon knew ran a number of grocery stores, had said he wanted to talk about a business opportunity. They met in the coffee shop at The Pontchartrain, which had made Elroy seem legitimate enough, but what he said was something else altogether.

It was about Elizabeth. And another man. When the Cuban brought up the subject, Agon shifted in his chair and almost left the table, but the Cuban had put up his palms like a man showing he is unarmed and looked downward, almost embarrassed. That look kept Agon from leaving. That look told him he was with a man who was a Pre-Futurist. A man who was aware of where he had been yet knew not where he was going—and, most importantly, knew he was not aware. That was the mark of the Pre-Futurist—"enlightened confusion."

"Let me start again," Elroy Delgado had said. "What I'm really asking you for is a favor for me. I was only offering you something in return. I apologize for offending you."

Agon had looked at the middle-aged man. He wore a clean white shirt, dark blue tie, dark suit. Very Latin, Agon thought. For himself, he did not wear suits and ties anymore. He was in a light knit shirt and cotton trousers. And sandals.

"What is it that you want, then?"

And Elroy had explained it. He had a friend—a politician—who was eager to change his image with the black voters. He thought the best way to begin was to appear before them and confess his wrongs of the past and tell them he would be different from then on. He had thought of going to a large black church, Elroy explained, but had gotten a better idea. He wanted to speak in the Gospel Tent at Jazzfest. He thought that would avoid being tied to any one denomination and, frankly, would draw lots of media attention.

Elroy made no secret that the politician was seeking votes and publicity, but he said he thought it was worth it considering the weight of the issue. "To me it is like Matthew the taxman converting to Christianity, or something like that. And so I told him I would help him."

"And me?"

"I know, we don't know each other, and now I see I was wrong to try to approach you in this way. But when I saw in the paper how the Miss Angelique's Academy was going to have a choir at the Gospel Tent, it gave me the idea to come to you. The paper said how everyone else in the city should follow your example. And Senator Prince, he read that, too. That's how he decided—"

"Joe Dell Prince?"

Elroy nodded.

Agon Hapsenfield swallowed, pursed his lips, looked out the window toward St. Charles Avenue. He shook his head. "Why, he's from the Klan."

"I can't say he is or isn't. But we do business sometimes and I never had any trouble. When he asked me if I could help him get into the Gospel Tent, I asked him all about himself. That's when he told me how he wanted to change and all."

"I still don't see how you came to me. Or all that about my wife."

Elroy sighed, folded his hands on the tablecloth. "I said, that is my mistake. I was not sure if you would listen to me. About your wife, it's this way. I have some friends in the investigating business. I can't say more about them. But one of them has been following a person I have had some trouble with before and in the course of that he turned up your wife's name. This man and your wife have something going on." He paused, but Agon's expression didn't change. "I'm sorry to tell you, but my investigator said this man is having an affair with your wife."

Agon looked into the distance. "She has had many affairs."

Elroy seemed taken aback. He cleared his throat.

"Well, I just thought you would like to know that. I thought if I told you who it was, you might return a favor and allow Senator Prince to introduce the Academy choir."

Agon laughed.

Elroy said, "Well, he is a state senator. Everyone knows him."

"Don't you think he would . . . tarnish our image?"

"Well, yes. But what I was thinking was how good it would look for you if you were the one who inspired this well-known senator to confess his bad ways in public. Do you see?"

Agon frowned. He signaled the waiter for more coffee. He watched the Cuban. He could see it in him. He was definitely a Pre-Futurist. Moreover, he was handing the Pre-Future to Agon. If Agon could only grasp it.

"I suppose that would be exactly what the editorial in the paper was getting at, wasn't it?"

"I think so, yes."

Agon closed his eyes momentarily. Behind him—blank. All he could see was ahead. And it was in his vision. A crowded stage in a crowded tent. A choir of angels. A rank of preachers. A microphone. Agon at the microphone, introducing what he felt might be the most important moment of the entire festival. A moment in which the lamb was already with the lion and the sinner had risen to the heavens and the lame had thrown away their crutches and the jewel was in the lotus. *And now—no, no, hear me out—now I introduce to you . . .*

Agon smiled. "Whether you know it or not, you are a good man. Are your sure Mr. Prince is truly ready for this?"

"I don't know why else he would have come to me."

"You say you've done business with this man?"

"I'll just say he owes me a favor. I like to not say too much about such things. And no, it's not that I like him very much, but, like you, I think some good may come out of what he has been in this way."

"Exactly. You are exactly correct."

"Then you agree to let him introduce your choir?"

"Yes."

Elroy extended his hand. Agon didn't take it.

"But about that other business. Leave it. That's not something in which I have interest anymore."

Elroy let his forearm hover over the saucers and plates. "As you wish. In Cuba you learn to always have some extra thing to offer when you ask for assistance."

"We all must learn to change. Agreed?"

"Agreed."

Agon extended his hand.

Later, when the many questions were asked, it wasn't that important whether Joe Dell had heard of the idea first and wanted to use Jazzfest politically or if Elroy heard of Corina's involvement, through Jean-Pierre, and wanted to make her look bad, and had conned a semi-dotty aristocrat into setting it all up. Unless one can turn state's evidence on the other, co-conspirators don't need to be concerned with who knew what when. They all knew it close enough to the same time anyway. Or so it would play out in court.

As a matter of history, it was Elroy who went to Joe Dell. He said he had an idea that could be of use to the senator's career, especially considering his record with black voters, and would be the sort of event he could become involved in without really alienating white ones either, since it all took place in a "church context." It was Elroy who asked Joe Dell if he wanted to make a speech at the Gospel Tent. It was Joe Dell who agreed. It was Agon who never quite figured it out. Or maybe it was Agon who did.

19

G US COULD SEE that Jean-Pierre was impressed with the rehearsal so he allowed himself to be impressed, too. And they did sound good—if the Academy's Performing Arts Theater had ever filled with this kind of sound before, Gus hadn't heard about it. He slumped low in his plush front-row indigo seat, smiling like a baby to a mother's lullaby. Charlotte's voice had a low roughness in it that, as Jean-Pierre remarked, wouldn't have been out of place in the best black Baptist church. Cissy's alto slid around Charlotte's lead like a vine on a flagpole and the other girls wrapped the whole thing up as the sea surrounds the fish, as Mao might have said had he, like Gus, fallen on strange times and wound up far away from the mechanized infantry teaching hymns to Southern schoolgirls. Anyway, Gus thought they sounded great. And he knew his choirmaster did too, and that was the important thing.

Yet the smile on Gus's face was not simply one of pleasure, nor aesthetic approval. It was a symptom of realization. In the harmony of those voices was the fulfillment of Gus's vision. He had seen it; now he could hear it. It was all coming together. He had really pulled it off. With the newspaper coverage and the sundry attentions that derived from that, Elizabeth was Gus

Houston's No. 1 fan of the moment. He had even heard that Agon had "taken an interest in the project," as Elizabeth put it.

Strangest of all was the buzz within the school—the girls were actually excited about the idea. Gus wasn't sure why and he entertained notions that if the girls of Miss Angelique's liked the plan there might be something deeply flawed about it, but he was in no mood for cynicism with Jazzfest only a week away. So when he saw the promotional posters for the Voices of Angelique that Elizabeth had ordered to be plastered all over the school, and in places like the Uptown McDonald's, where the girls often went for lunch, he did what a hustler should never do.

He believed in his own scam.

Why not? The girls were belting out "Jesus on the Mainline" as dynamically as he'd ever heard it, with the weird twist that half of them were blonds. Gus felt the kind of privilege of discovery that all great cultural explorers have known. Even P. T. Barnum must at one time have been awed at the concept of an elephant balancing on top of a man's head. Would astronauts leaping across the surface of the moon have been any more swept away with their moment of achievement—rare, proud accomplishment—than Gus Houston at the magnitude of the cultural transformation he had germinated? He could see great days ahead.

The hymn was over. Gus drew himself up in his seat to come up on stage to sit in on the post-rehearsal critique.

"Hold on a second," Jean-Pierre called out from his piano bench. He was smiling, glancing at the girls. "We worked something else up."

Betsy and Tina giggled slightly. Charlotte looked mischievous. Gus settled back in.

"We figure on an encore," Jean-Pierre said. "You always got to figure that. This one is ours."

Jean-Pierre initiated an unmistakable R&B line from the bass keys. The girls regrouped in a tight half-circle. From the center came Charlotte's low, moanful husk.

"*Love and happiness . . .*"

She waited until the words had faded and slipped back in at the next opening of Jean-Pierre's progression.

"*Love and happiness . . .*"

The other girls began humming softly behind the beat. Jean-Pierre's rhythm line gurgled deeply into the blues side. Then Cissy picked up the chorus, repeating after Charlotte as the other girls clapped to set up the time, singing:

"*Make you do wrong . . .*"

Singing:

"*Make you do right . . .*"

Gus didn't know a lot about music and less about Gospel. But he knew when somebody was singing Al Green.

Jean-Pierre winked at him and the girls proceeded through a decidedly vampy version of the classic of Green's younger days. But Gus did not associate the music with religion. He associated it with having sex. He watched the girls sway with the rhythm. It had been that way for Gus, too. But now he barely moved. He had two thoughts: these girls were good; and they would never get away with this in the Gospel Tent.

When it was over he clapped spontaneously. Enthusiastically. The girls joined in. Jean-Pierre turned on his bench and did the same. Then Gus stopped clapping.

"That's supposed to be Gospel?"

"Ain't no 'supposed to be.' That's from the Reverend Al Green. Whatever he do, everybody love."

Gus got up and leaned on the apron of the stage. Jean-Pierre thanked the girls and told them they could go for the day.

"Bet you didn't expect that one, did you, Mr. Houston?" It

was Charlotte. Her face and white T-shirt were damp with sweat.

"I'll give you that." When she was almost gone, Gus called out, "But it sounded great. I'm proud of y'all." He heard the stage door close and wasn't sure if she'd caught the last part.

Jean-Pierre sorted his music sheets. He glared at Gus.

"That's what I call damning with faint praise."

Gus hopped up on the stage and sat with his knees drawn under his chin. "It just seemed so, I don't know—profane. In context."

Jean-Pierre noodled a few lines from the song. "You don't know a lot about Gospel, do you?"

"That's not the point."

"Ain't nothing else the point."

"The point is to make this a big success."

"What you mean?"

"I'm just saying, isn't Al Green a funny way to top off a church act? Which is a damn good act, by the way." He paused. "That's all I mean."

"Yeah, it's a damn good act. And this is a damn good way to tell everybody in that tent these girls are serious. Look here, Houston, I been doing this sort of thing for years. You don't think I know what a show-stopper is? They give us an encore, they gonna want something to remember. Now I figure, we could go back with 'Amazing Grace' or some cracker song like that but by now we got everybody moving and we got their attention and they all saying, 'Hey, for white girls, they ain't bad.' So now we just crank it one more notch. We say, they can sing the Gospel and they can sing the low-down, too."

Jean-Pierre shook his head and laughed as he spoke. "Don't you know nothing about Al Green? Ain't nothing that man writes don't come from Jesus." He laughed again. "I'm sounding like my mother. But it's true. Maybe that's where I got the idea.

I just woke up a few days ago and there it was. The Reverend Al Green. White people heard of him, too, so it wouldn't look like too much of a stretch. But this is a black song, right to the core. And we worked on it all week when you weren't here. These girls as proud of that song as any of them."

He trilled a few notes from "Love and Happiness" and then segued into a few bars from the "Oh Happy Day!" arrangement. "Don't you see how these fit in like a glove?"

Gus felt his face flush. "I just was concerned. . ."

"'Concerned?'" Jean-Pierre's tone was unmistakable. Then Gus heard himself repeat the word in his own mind.

"Jesus."

"You got that shit right."

"Okay, okay." Gus lay down on the stage floor. He looked up at the lights. He could feel something in his stomach. He realized he had the jitters. "Maybe we should put it in with the other songs, and not just the encore."

"That's why I'm the director here. You leave the timing to me."

There was a silence as they both thought about it. Then Gus said, "Never mind the white guy on the floor."

"What I say."

"Man," said Gus, after a few moments, "did you see that Charlotte move?"

"That girl got some blood in her somewhere."

"Could be."

Gus lay still, looking up into the rows of spotlights and catwalks above the stage. Jean-Pierre drifted off into some Gospel tune that sounded like "Motherless Child." After a while, he said, "You ever hear of a priest named Gerard Manley Hopkins?"

Gus brought his thoughts back from the Shadow place in which now so unmistakably they had found residence.

"Who?"

"Hopkins. Gerard Manley Hopkins."

It was a long trip. Re-entry took some time.

"Yeah, sure. Hopkins. Yeah. We study him in one of my classes. I always think of him more as a poet, though. Why?"

Jean-Pierre had begun to hum softly to himself. "Just what I say. You always think of Reverend Green as a singer."

Jean-Pierre's fingers moved across the keys as though no longer burdened by gravity. There was no blue aura. He played another half-hour. When he was finished, he noticed that Gus was fast asleep.

AS THE TWO BROTHERS toured the construction site, Julio pointed out the small article in the paper. When Elroy read it he felt as if he'd just been piped directly into the special universe of bad news. Goats, now. On the lake. And dead pigeons and bloody Xs all over the fresh-dried cement in front of the SuperBotanica. Right where he had blessed the site for Changó.

He couldn't stand it. The foreman had said work could be finished in ten days—without interruptions—and that would give another seventy-two hours for stocking. It was just enough time. Julio had everything ready for shipping at the warehouse. They could move it all to the store in one night and get it on the shelves in two days. Even if a few things were waiting, they'd be open on May 1. Jazzfest would start Wednesday and it would all be over.

Now this. Geronimo, joining them as they walked, said six of the crew—all good ones, older guys—had called in sick that morning. And that was just from the dead pigeons. Once they read about the goats, who knew? Elroy sure did. Four goats in a circle, that was a lot. He wished he could see a photo of it but the paper didn't run one. He knew she'd done something with the goats. He could feel it here, miles away, which wasn't much. Spirits didn't count miles. You could make *ebo* in La Habana and someone would feel it in Alabama if you wanted. He had heard of spirit work from Nigeria coming all the way across the ocean to the mountains of Cuba.

"We need to hire some more," Geronimo said. "I done argued with two of 'em over the phone. They say they're sick but it's that hoodoo shit." He spat on the dirt near the water cooler.

"It wasn't just the black ones," Julio said.

"Two of your guys, too."

Elroy frowned. "How long you think they stay out?"

"Far as I'm concerned they're out for good."

"Maybe, but the point is we got to get finished. Can we do it without them? Jesse and Harold were the best we got."

"I can get more down here by tomorrow if you say it's okay."

"Good as them?"

"Good enough, Mr. Delgado. Hell, it's just all finishing up now."

Elroy turned to Julio. "You think the rest will stay?"

"If they're not gone by now they'll stay. I checked. It doesn't seem to bother anyone else that much, the hoodoo part." He paused.

"What else?" Elroy asked.

"You know. It's just a weird job for them. All these people come out to protest. Plus all that about the *santos*—

"Who says these are the *santos*?"

Julio looked at Elroy, then at Geronimo. Geronimo didn't believe in any of it.

"You know it is, Elroy."

"Yeah, well maybe it is, maybe it isn't."

Julio rolled his eyes. "Yeah, right. And it isn't Corina Youngblood, either."

"Shut up."

"Fuck you, man. What's the matter with you? It's not like this is some kind of secret."

"I mean, be quiet," Elroy said, looking around. Although the men were working, words had a way of traveling. Elroy didn't want anything traveling. Except Corina. Back to Africa or whatever hell she came out of.

"Where you get the new men?" Elroy asked.

"I know some union guys not working."

"Can we use them?"

"It'll cost a little extra. I got to make it okay with a couple of people, but yeah, I do it all the time on jobs. With nobody working they look the other way if you make it okay for them."

Elroy looked at Julio.

"It won't cost that much," Julio said.

"Then bring them," said Elroy. He looked at the news clip again, then at where there was blood. This time it hadn't washed off as easily. There was a little stain. "And clean this shit up better."

"You got it, boss."

Elroy and Julio walked on alone, scrutinizing the building. The exterior was all but finished. They were waiting on new windows for the front and the automatic sliding doors for the entry still weren't right, but Geronimo said those were minor things, to be expected. Inside, the fresh concrete and the high ceilings kept the space cool.

It looked like a mess to Elroy, who was not an expert at these things, but he could see progress—the plumbing was finished and the electricians were well on the way. Fortunately, none of the electricians had left, but they were mostly anglos from the Local, which didn't have any blacks. As they walked, Julio checked items off his list and talked to Geronimo from time to time.

Elroy wasn't listening. He was seeing. He was trying hard to see it all done. He was trying to see Corina Youngblood on the shores of Lake Pontchartrain draining the blood of animals to Ogun and bringing down his powers against everything Elroy wanted in life. Tonight, he thought, he would take a goat himself for Changó. He would not tell Julio, but he would do it.

BONITA TOOK THE TRAY over to the two tourists and went back to her perch behind the bar. It was a slow evening so far but that was good. She could barely concentrate on the job anyway. A Baby Schedule was in her head. It started: Day One after period. Then, two weeks later, Egg Descends. After that, Ovulation. Baby. Or Not. To the Schedule was a Routine. It went: Sex Every Night starting a week after her period and continuing until it started again or it didn't.

It had started again. So she was initiating the Schedule again. And the Routine. It was the damnedest thing. The world seemed overrun with teenage pregnancies and people were out bombing abortion clinics and all she wanted to do was to have a baby and she couldn't. She remembered when her friend Margie had the problem. It went on for two years and then she took some pills and then she had twins. And then she and Bernie got a divorce and now she was trying to raise two little girls all by herself.

Bonita thought about that a moment. She looked around The Hellhole. Some life it would be on her own with kids. But that wouldn't happen to her. Gus was infected with her love and it wouldn't get out of his core. She didn't like to think of herself having magical woman or Cajun powers but some things she knew and she knew that. He had his defects as a human being. He had his wormhole. But even with the wormhole he was infected with her and she would never find herself in Margie's position. She could tell by the way Gus fucked her. Men didn't quiver the way he did holding her and not be infected with love.

Only, she wanted a baby now. Not to keep him. She'd seen enough of life to know that wasn't how it worked. She wanted a baby. Corina knew it, too. Her doctor did. Gus did.

"Hello—anybody in there? Two more Heinekens?"

It was one of the tourists. The guy in the gray shortsleeve who thought he looked like Jack Nicklaus. He was leaning on the bar next to Old Clyde.

"Sit down and I'll bring it to you."

Sometimes customers would take offense. Sometimes they would heel like dogs. She must have been putting out the fuck-you rays from her eyes because Jack Nicklaus heeled.

"Sorry, but when we tried to get your attention you didn't seem to be looking."

"I was looking. I was just ignoring you."

She slid off her stool and picked up two mugs from the drying rack. She dug out two beers from the ice chest. Jack hovered, not sure what to do. Whether he was being joked with. Then he saw he wasn't. He went back to his table. She took the beers over.

"I thought people here were more friendly," the other man said. He looked like Donald Trump.

"I think they're more friendly over at Pat O'Brien's."

She went back to the counter. The men spoke to each other in low tones. Just when one of them seemed on the verge of smarting off to her to pump up his manly ego, Thurgood walked in. It was a little early for the bikers and he looked thirsty. The men eyed him, and fed their egos otherwise. Thurgood went directly to the jukebox and punched up some music Bonita didn't like, by Bob Seger, but it drowned out everything. Thurgood sat next to the jukebox and Bonita snapped open a Schlitz, his favorite warm-up beverage, and took it to him without asking. Jack and Donald finished their beers. It was loud and quiet in the bar. Bonita went back to her stool. She was thinking how many days it would be before she would make Gus fuck her again.

OCHO ALVARADO rarely thought about his life, at least in any organized, planned manner, and so tended to drift through it. Maria used to tell him that was the road to nothing and he was already halfway there. But what did she know? Fucking a nigger was pretty much the way to nothing itself, wasn't it?

"May I help you?"

Ocho frowned. He had been drifting again. He didn't like that. He was going to have to do something about it. "The Number 4," he said.

"Anything to drink?"

"I thought it comes with a Coke."

"Pepsi."

"Okay, do that then."

"That's a Number 4 and a medium Pepsi? Any dessert?"

"No. That's all."

"That'll be $3.98 at the first window."

Ocho put the Firebird back in gear and eased forward in the lane. Usually he brought something to eat because he hated most Yankee food but he'd forgotten and didn't wake up until almost five-thirty and barely made it to the job site. His food was waiting when he got to the window. He wished he'd ordered a fried pie but he didn't feel like going through the extra trouble.

He paid and drove a block up the street and parked under a tree near an abandoned grocery store. He couldn't believe it. They gave him regular fries instead of the spicy kind supposed to be in the Number 4. But fuck it, he was hungry and there wasn't time. So he ate in the shade and drank his Pepsi and wished it was four o'clock and he could go home and sleep.

Ocho never forgot the day he found her out. It was by

accident. He'd gotten drunk in the afternoon with some of the guys after a job and decided he missed her. They'd been broken up for a month and he already kind of had a girlfriend in Tina but for some reason he started missing Maria. It was a billboard, come to think of it. For cigarettes or something, with a woman who had coal black frizzy hair like Maria and that's what got him to thinking. So he drove over to her apartment. Which was when he saw them.

At first he didn't get it—she was walking to her apartment and there was this nigger coming from the other way and she said hello. He figured it was a neighbor. And then—shit—he hated to think about. The asshole came real close and next thing they were kissing. Not a big sloppy kiss but the kind you do when you've kissed someone a lot. Something real friendly, that you don't care if other people see because that's only the half of it when you're alone.

He kissed her like that and Ocho knew. Then they went inside. Ocho sat in his Firebird. They came out in a half hour. Ocho followed them. They went to a restaurant. Ocho parked a half block away. They went back to her place. Ocho waited outside for the *chingado* bastard to come out but he didn't. Ocho stayed awake. At six-thirty the *pendejo* comes out the door and goes to his car and leaves. Ocho wrote down his license and had a friend find out who it belonged to. And then he knew, and the guys at the warehouse helped him figure out the *maricón* was that hoodoo woman's son Elroy was having trouble with.

But he caught the nigger prick's brother all right. Fucked him up. He'd seen people fucked up worse, back in Cuba on the docks and really bad in the slums, but he felt good about what he'd been able to do to little brother. It was like that. You get the man or you get the blood. Either way to get your satisfaction.

But Ocho wanted to fuck up older brother, too. He hated him

even worse now that Mr. Delgado was so mad about that little *cabrón* he beat up. So Ocho couldn't work the SuperBotanica job and he'd been on some shit detail clearing an old retail mall site out in Chalmette all the last month. Every day when he was picking up nails and pieces of brick and shoveling piles of junk from one place to another he thought of how everything about Jean-Pierre Youngblood was bad to him. He longed to hurt him. To finish it.

It was eating on him bad today. Javier and the others had been telling him all about the shit happening down at the SuperBotanica. He'd driven by a few times but Jean-Pierre was never there. Once he saw the mother, and once the kid he'd beat up, but never big brother. And then he heard about the Gospel Tent thing and he saw Jean-Pierre's picture in the paper with all those white girls. So maybe he was fucking *them* now.

Ocho finished the steakburger and tossed the rest of the fries into a garbage can. His stomach hurt. Then he drove back to Chalmette. He worked especially hard, for he was strong and could put his back into when he wanted to. And he wanted to. By five o'clock he felt better and decided to go meet Javier and the others for some beers after all.

20

I T WAS already open when Corina Youngblood returned from her dreams the last morning of April and, as was her habit, thanked Elegba for another day before even rising from bed. It was already open when she ate her breakfast of cornflakes and milk, having finally decided to give up sausage and eggs both because of her blood pressure and because she had begun to notice her waistline. It was already open when she parked on the street in front of her church and walked over to unlock the doors of her own botanica.

It was not supposed to be open for another day and so it caught her unawares. The signs had said it would be open May 1 and so it was supposed to be *not* open but it was open. She could tell without even looking up the street at the cars. She could tell without hearing Eudora Johnson rush up to her before she'd even had time to drop her big brown purse on the counter and flip on the air conditioner.

"Reverend, Reverend, God almighty they already open."

Corina said nothing and went to her desk. She looked at a small stack of bills Paulus had left for her to mail.

"You hear me, Reverend? That SuperBotanica done opened for business today instead of tomorrow. We ain't got nobody out there with signs. We was all going to show up tomorrow bright and early."

Corina looked at her sharply. "Miz Eudora, no need to talk so loud. I see it open." Then she sat down and stared at a shelf filled with red and black and yellow candles.

Eudora waited perhaps ten minutes. "You don't want to do nothing about it?"

Corina studied an envelope.

"I guess I be going then, Reverend." Eudora walked to the door. At seventy-four, her steps were slow, but she was strong. She'd been picketing the site for a month, off and on. "You did God's work, Reverend. It ain't no shame if it don't always turn out like you want, long as you do what you can do."

Corina looked at her. She lifted her left hand slightly, in a kind of wave of farewell, and searched the desk drawer for stamps.

ELROY AND JULIO almost looked like brothers. For the occasion, both wore their new Italian double-breasted blue suits and white shirts. Elroy's tie was red for Changó; Julio's was yellow for Ochún. Standing in front of the store, next to the automatic sliding glass doors, Elroy was smiling so hard he thought his face would break. And they looked good. The store did, too.

The bright red letters of the SuperBotanica marquee perfectly set off the building's white stucco exterior. Outside and in, it was clean and bright. Very Caribbean. Floors all polished. Stock in place, except for the five-gallon bottles of Florida water, which had gotten held up in transit but should be there before the week was out, at which time Elroy planned a "Sale for the *Santos*," a loss leader draw-in they'd be using every week. The clerks were bright and beaming, too. Three of them were black, which was good, because Elroy had been concerned Corina's "boycott" would scare everyone off.

"This was the right thing. You had a good idea," Elroy told Julio, looking up at the mid-morning sun. It had been raining the past two days, but since all the last-minute work was inside, the weather hadn't slowed them down.

"I just thought as long as we were finished early, why not open the doors?" Julio smiled, watching the cars which had begun to snake up and down Ladeau Street. Didn't matter if the people in the cars were whites or blacks or browns, they all wanted to see the thing. They'd only been open since nine, but Julio could see word-of-mouth was drawing people in. Which is what he had told Elroy.

Elroy's compliment was more than it sounded like, and Julio accepted it at its deeper level. What an argument! Yesterday morning when Geronimo had them drive over and told them it was done—a day early—Elroy was so happy he promised everyone a bonus. Julio had said they should keep the momentum going and just open a day ahead of time.

That's when it started. Elroy wanted to wait until May 1, because that was the schedule. He said that was when the radio and TV people would come and the caterer had already been booked, and so on. It had taken an hour, sitting and shouting on the checkout counters in the front of the store as a clean-up crew swept away the remaining traces of sawdust and picked up the last of the drop cloths, for Julio to bring his brother around. Finally he convinced him that a "pre-opening" was the kind of thing Hollywood did and therefore had a precedent in American marketing.

Julio's real angle was that even if they opened early, they could still have the grand opening on May 1. Nothing lost. But something gained. By May 1 the store would be open and Corina Youngblood and her people wouldn't be able to say they'd blocked it, which was their vow. So that insane woman would look like a fool. "Plus it will be easier for us to have them arrested for trespassing," Julio had said. He wasn't sure if that was legally true but Elroy seemed to think it was and that was what mattered to Julio.

But by then Elroy needed no more persuasion. He really wanted to open right away, too. The objections were just nerves. They would laugh about it later over beers at Elroy's house. They would go on line a day ahead. Later, any amount of picketing and protest would be secondary to the fact that the SuperBotanica was open. They had worked almost all last night to get ready and they had done it. They were in business.

"They need to finish the fence over on the west side of the parking lot," Elroy observed, rocking back and forth like a maitre d'.

"Geronimo says it should be dry enough by tomorrow. It won't take more than a day—"

"Welcome, come on in." Elroy interrupted his brother and stepped aside for an elderly Latino couple, probably Mexican. They nodded and went inside.

"Good to see such a mix of people," Elroy said.

"What mix? They're all brown, and a few of those weird white people from the Quarter."

"Yes, but there were two black women in earlier."

"That's true." Julio could've added they didn't stay long, and looked a lot like two of the protestors from a couple of weeks ago. But he didn't.

For the eighth or ninth time of the morning, Elroy slapped his brother on the back. "It's a great success. Julio, we did it."

Julio glanced at his watch. It was getting hot. "Let's go inside a while," he said, and they did. Elroy immediately began shaking hands and talking to customers and inspecting everything as though he hadn't already done so a million times since six a.m. Julio helped the old Mexican couple find a shopping basket and then strolled over to one side, near the Community Bulletin Board—his idea.

He counted maybe a hundred people. Not so many but this was all new yet. Pre-openings were to plant the seed, not bring in the crop. Still, Julio thought, they will definitely be here in force before long. How could the people resist? It was a great store. It was a SuperBotanica. "No Need of the Spirit Left Untended"— just like the banner and handbills said.

It would be the model for years to come. New and old customers would see so at once. Instead of the dusty little aisles and junky shelves of the mom and pop botanicas, this one was clean, spacious, easy-to-navigate. Never had so many candles or statues or herbs, or even Bibles, been under one roof, and at such prices. Julio's theory was that no matter how much protest Corina raised and how much she tried to pit the blacks against the Cubans, it would in time come down to prices. The prices at the SuperBotanica were fifty to eighty percent better than places like St. Jude.

Volume was an American marketing idea and they were in America. Corina Youngblood could take that to heart if she was smart. In time, even her best friends, even the best members in her church, would be in the aisles of SuperBotanicas from here to Florida. They would see that the true revolution of the *santos* in America would be to break the old, old tradition of rip-offs in the spiritual supply industry, which is what it was—an industry.

More than Elroy, even, Julio had come to see the beauty of the thing they were doing. Elroy still had a kind of missionary idea about making the *santos* more affordable, but Julio saw the precision and wonder of the economics of it all. And although it was Elroy who was preening, greeting everyone like the father of handsome new triplets, Julio, too, was an immensely proud man.

They had won. He felt something exceedingly strange. Then he realized what it was. He felt American.

ACROSS THE CITY that night lay the mists of spring. New Orleans had gone to hell by most measurable urban standards, true, but the sight of the Great Gateway was still enough to burst the moral armor of the most tightly wrapped visitor and usher anyone of any life's blood at all into its fecundity, its exuberance, and its danger.

Off Elysian Fields, Corina Youngblood slept fitfully, knotting her percale sheets in and around her slender brown legs. Paulus, up late, watched old movies on TV, but turned the sound down because his mother did not approve. Toward the lake front, Elroy lay close to Luz. They had made love and now he snored lightly, thinking of the coming day. Julio, alone in his bungalow, was dreaming of an island woman he had not yet met, and his dreams were the province of Ochún, and she would no doubt deliver unto him this marvelous raven-haired beauty, though not that night.

In Metairie, Jean-Pierre woke from having fallen asleep on his couch listening to the Mighty Clouds of Joy and trying to "visualize," as the athletes did, the performance two days hence. He awoke because his answering machine clicked on for someone to breathe heavily into a phone at the other end and laugh and hang up. That kept Jean-Pierre awake almost an hour but he was exhausted from choir practice every night and school all day and he quickly dropped off again, barely moving a muscle until the alarm went off at seven, not even looking inside his nightstand to be sure the Baretta was still there, a mild compulsion that had begun to creep up on him.

At seven, in her apartment, Bonita was lying on the bed in a sweat, her knees bent and the sperm still warm in her vagina. Gus had rolled to her side and was breathing so hard she thought it almost comical. He hadn't even wanted to do it, but she made him, and of course he liked it a lot once he was hard and inside her. He quivered for her again before he came and then collapsed on her breasts. Then she came, too. She was surprised, she didn't think she would and it wasn't even the point. But it felt good. Last month there had been a false alarm but this time it felt good. She told him so, but he had dozed off. She'd have a Christmas baby. Or one for the New Year. She went to sleep, too.

AS HER SPIRIT spiraled into the void of dreams, its trail of energy drifted far above that of a waking soul from the northwestern suburbs. In a long, low, speckled-brick colonial-style home, the state senator who saw himself quite clearly as governor and had all but moved into his mansion in Baton Rouge stood before the mirror in his study. He was not yet fully dressed—blue slacks and white shirt not yet tucked in—but he had shaved and been twice to the Mr. Coffee. Mary Beth was in Slidell for a party breakfast meeting so he had the place to himself. He liked that. He did not particularly like Mary Beth but more to the point he liked having the house to himself, for one day he would.

Senator Prince looked himself over carefully. He set his jaw and steeled his eyes as he had seen preachers do since he was a boy. He would have to work himself into the appearance and the speech and to do that he had to believe it, at least a little. He didn't, of course, but as Mary Beth had pointed out he needed to consider his position on the issues in relation to the direction of his political career. In that context, she had said, you can believe it because in that context it is true. In the context of wanting to be governor you actually have changed your ideas about blacks.

Joe Dell put that logic inside his head and let it settle. He had studied acting once at Northeastern State and knew about getting in character. In a few moments he felt he had made the transition—it would become a faster process by Thursday afternoon. He would be able to do it instantly. That nutball from Miss Angelique's would introduce him and he would make one of the Big Speeches of his career.

The ball was in play. Yesterday, Finnester leaked word to a favored reporter from the *Times-Picayune*. He said letting the city's only paper in on the senator's otherwise unpublicized appearance would be an irresistible tease to all the other reporters to follow up once the story broke. Joe Dell had been plenty mad, and not just because Finnester didn't clear it with him first. An "exclusive" struck him as a stupid idea because TV stations might show up at the Gospel Tent anyway because of all the publicity that girls' choir was getting.

It was one of the few times Finnester had ever really fought back. He said his "strategy of control" accounted for "random media intrusions" but the point was the speech would still come as a surprise to all but the paper. If the TV got in on it by accident at the actual moment of occurrence, all the better. "It'd be windfall airplay," Finnester had said. "Good visuals." Thinking it over, Joe Dell had agreed. But he was getting tired of Finnester's lingo from that night course in media relations.

Joe Dell looked himself over. A woman had once told him he reminded her of Kevin Costner, "but older." He wanted to appear sincere and open and trustworthy. And a little fallen, for he was going to present himself as a kind of redeemed sinner, racially speaking. Finnester had said, "Blacks love that kind of stuff. So do the white Bible thumpers, for that matter." Joe Dell had turned on him angrily, telling him never to talk like that again and hadn't he learned anything in his damn course other than fifty-dollar words for ten-cent ideas? Finnester had looked at him oddly, as if he couldn't believe it. But then he did. In context.

"Thank you, thank you," Joe Dell said into the mirror, practicing raising his palms before him slightly, as if in blessing. "You can't know how I appreciate being allowed to appear here." He paused. "And how hard you must be working right now to believe your eyes." He waited. There would almost certainly be laughter or feedback. Black people liked to do that, especially in church.

"I won't keep you long. My only point is to tell you that like Matthew himself I have been changed in my thinking. And to no less extent. I—" Joe Dell reflected a moment. What would be the best way to put it? He'd be improvising somewhat, but he had to have at least a game plan for the short speech. "Just as a man who has taken from the people for so long sees through Christ that he must change his ways and start giving back, so I come before you tonight. To change my ways and to give back."

He stopped and studied his expression, his body language. That was good. That was a good way to put it. Now the only thing is to ask for their support for next year and promise them to be a governor for all the people, all colors, all persuasions. And then sit down and let it sink in. As Finnester had said, the media would take it from there.

"My decision to seek the nomination for governor came to me as no less a revelation," he resumed. When he was finished he checked the time on the clock over the fireplace. Four minutes. He figured that was about right.

21

T HE FAIRGROUNDS RACE TRACK spread out before Gus
like a Monet. The soft sunlight of the early evening, the
broad, verdant expanse of the infield, the brightly hued
performance tents and the gaiety of the people were enough to
put an impression on any but the most doltish. And the smells—
andouille sausage, boudin, boiling crawfish, fried catfish, gumbo,
jambalaya, etouffée, shrimp po' boys, cauldrons of red beans and
rice, and the not unpleasant aroma of draft beer displaced the
waning humidity left from the brief morning showers.

It wasn't particularly hot for May, only in the upper eighties,
and as Gus escorted the eight girls from Miss Angelique's in the
general direction of the blue and white striped Gospel Tent
rising like a medieval pavilion at the far end of the Monet, he felt
almost giddy with cosmic satisfaction. This was the way the
world could work out, given the right amount of luck and
human scheming. It shouldn't be all that difficult. Tanks? Where-
fore is there the need of large fully tracked vehicles full of high
explosive ordnance? No need for tanks. No need for human
activity that requires tanks. Nor for disease, woe, death, ICBMs,
advertising agencies—none of that sort of thing.

Sufficient unto the day is the pleasure thereof, Gus Houston thought, strolling past exhibits and tents and couples stretched out on blankets. Outside the chain link perimeter separating the Fairgrounds from the city lay other days, lay lack of pleasure. But this was now, here. The girls stopped in front of the Dixie Beer Stage, where a Nashville band named "Wichita" was finishing a set. They watched a few minutes, then Charlotte led off toward the other side of the infield to see the Bank of New Orleans Stage. People were already laying claims for spots to see the Nevilles, who weren't even on until six.

Gus hoped to catch them. Miss Angelique's was booked for seven, and was to be offstage by 7:20. Jean-Pierre said the schedule had gotten backed up. Art, the Creole ("and proud of it") stage manager, was threatening everyone that he'd just pull the plug on performers who went too long, because there were a lot of acts for the night. The big names, like the Heavenly Hummingbirds, would get an entire hour, but all the new groups, or the "novelty" ones, which is how The Voices of Angelique was being rationalized, got only twenty minutes. Just enough time for the three numbers, Gus figured. Jean-Pierre still thought they might be asked back for an encore, but when Gus asked how they'd do that and still keep to the time schedule, Jean-Pierre snapped, "You just never know about these things."

Gus let the testiness pass. Performance anxiety made people short-tempered. And there was the SuperBotanica. Since it opened Monday, Jean-Pierre had yelled four or five times at Betsy, who was the most timid of all the girls, and had had strong words with Charlotte over "singing like a robot" or something like that.

It was Corina. Gus had avoided her all week, but he knew Jean-Pierre hadn't had the luxury. And what a week. The Spanish language radio station, WXTX, ran an hour-long remote from the grand opening of the SuperBotanica. Plenty of other media showed up, too, although Tom Stanford, the anchor on Channel 11, obviously had no idea what a botanica was until he found himself inside one, and scrambled awkwardly to get out of the five o'clock live shot as soon as possible.

After watching Stanford on a Sony in the deserted teacher's lounge, Gus had picked up the phone to call Corina, but then cradled the receiver. He wasn't much of a psychic, but he could feel her wrath flashing across the city like a high-voltage spider's web. The last time he'd actually seen his co-counselor and spiritual advisor, maybe two weeks ago, Gus had gotten zapped himself. "Why don't you come here more often to help me stop these Cubans?" she'd scolded the minute he walked through the door of her botanica. Busy with choir practice wasn't a good answer. "Just don't you forget it was my son got those white girls into the Gospel Tent in the first place, Candy Man." And so on.

Gus told her he'd try to do better, but of course he didn't. It wasn't just being busy, and it wasn't just that Corina had been in such a funk since March that none of the girls wanted to go see her anymore anyway. It was that Gus had more or less decided to let the referral arrangement die out. With his newly rising star at the Academy he didn't need any more of what Bonita called his "deliberate potential fuck ups." But he didn't say that. He said he'd try to do better.

A bad feeling—having Corina Youngblood disappointed in you. Gus had a terrifying appreciation of what Jean-Pierre had gone through much of his life. He could see that if Corina was upset over the opening of the SuperBotanica, the people around her would be upset, too. He could understand why one night he had seen his choirmaster hunched over the piano, staring down at the keyboard, his hands clenching into fists. There was one other thing. Gus knew that Jean-Pierre had his own reasons to be distracted and angry with all the attention being showered on the Delgados. For he had done nothing about Paulus.

"Mr. Houston, can we get a Coke?"

"You bet." They walked up to a concession tent and Gus bought for the whole team. He looked at his watch. Only 5:35.

"You want to wander around until Mr. Youngblood gets here or go on to the tent and get dressed?"

"I want to see that Cajun band."

"I want to buy something for my mother."

"I'm starving. Can't we get something to eat?"

"Is that the bathroom? God, it's gross."

And so on until six, through the hundred and forty acres of grassy infield of the fairgrounds and race track site. By 6:10, they were at the rear entrance of the Gospel Tent. Jean-Pierre, carrying several cardboard boxes full of robes, greeted them.

"Our night," he said. "Y'all all ready, I hope?"

"We forgot the lines," said Charlotte. Marie and Tina giggled.

"I already carried the other robes and things to the changing tent," Jean-Pierre said. He was sweating and his face was flushed. "We'll go in and change in just a minute."

He took Gus aside. "Mama already here. She's got Paulus and eight people from the church. They been here since two o'clock, she told me. I was going to pick them up on the way but she called and said Miz Anderson wanted to hear as much music as she could and so they all decided to get in and get good seats. They're about four aisles from the right, down in the middle. Take this."

Jean-Pierre unloaded the boxes in his arms into Charlotte's and Cissy's. He wiped the sweat from his forehead and turned back to Gus. "Here's the new schedule." They quickly reviewed the lineup for the evening. "You seen Hapsenfield?"

Gus said he hadn't.

"He better be on time. They ain't gonna wait."

"What if he gets held up?"

"Then we just start straight in after Reverend Lincoln introduces us."

"Right. Good. OK."

They nodded and mumbled and Jean-Pierre asked Gus again if the tear in Cissy's gown had gotten mended, and so on, until they had the last-minute details cold. None of the girls paid them any mind, for their eyes and minds were full to brimming with the sights unlayering around them in the golden shadings of early evening.

They beheld figures from fantasy worlds emerging from the main tent and through openings in the thick ropes cordoning off the nearby performers' parking area. These were the real Gospel singers, and these were their ways. Electric blue tuxes and dazzling white formal gowns; purple robes trimmed in satin; tight green sheath dresses and black sequin jump suits. It was as if Jesus had come back as a rainbow, and in each of the many coats of the many colors of that tribal gathering of God all but the girls of Miss Angelique's were as African as had ever been transported twelve million strong from the bosoms of their own country and delivered unto these hymnals of the Almighty Jesus. "I told you we'd be the only ones," whispered Cissy.

"Shut up," said Charlotte. "Check out the butt on that guy over there." They all looked. He was one of the young men in the black jump suits. "Who are they?" asked Tina. Marie looked at the program Jean-Pierre had given them. "I think that must be the Abyssinian Baptist Quartet," she said. "Why do you think that?" said Betsy. "Because there's four of them, stupid."

"Let's go."

Jean-Pierre led them toward a square white tent behind the main one. Gus could see deepening waves of people outside the surrounding Fairgrounds fence converging on the entry gates.

"Look at that. There must be thousands of them."

"Don't matter how many of them come in the gate, Gospel Tent's already packed full," said Jean-Pierre. "Come on in here." He pulled back the entry flap. "Let's get these robes out of the boxes and see how they look."

The girls filed in shyly and were relieved to find they were alone, that they did not have to reveal themselves among hordes of strange women with bodies that seemed to bulge from the tops of their dresses. Charlotte and Cissy put their boxes next to a stack of others atop a folding table. The girls attacked the pile as though it were Christmas, and within seconds each was holding up a full-length, freshly laundered, robin's egg blue robe with pale yellow crossing along the bodice.

Gus and Jean-Pierre hurriedly inspected each garment. On presenting them to the girls after practice last Sunday, Elizabeth had said that although the robes had incorporated the Academy colors, "only spruced up a bit," they were "as beautiful as your own sweet voices."

"Now y'all go ahead and get dressed and then you can come out if you want 'cause it's hot in here, but remember not to go into the big tent until I tell you."

"But we want to see," said Cissy.

"You can see the act right before ours from the side, and that's it. Just enough to get you interested and not enough to get you scared."

The girls laughed. Gus laughed. Then, while the girls dressed, he and Jean-Pierre slipped around the rear of the Gospel Tent for a peek. A men's group from Atlanta—The Majesties—were finishing their set. Big voices, honey harmonies, choreography from Motown, probably, since all the men looked to be in their forties or fifties.

Watching the faces of the crowd, Gus felt the zing of his

original vision all over again. The girls were nervous and chattering and just barely held together by their excitement, but Gus felt as full of certainty and triumph as ever in his life. This was definitely Occupying Space. He and the Shadow Gus were one and the same and they had gone into the valley of the Shadow and they had emerged whole. What was unhinged and random in his life was finding constellation. He had risked much; would gain much. They all would.

This was the truth of the Shadow. In making your mark was no shame. Seeking personal gain was the way of those who triumphed. What did the mercenaries, the captains of industry, say? Who dares, wins. And they said, "Kill 'em all, let God sort 'em out." But Gus was killing no one, except his own aimless being. He was helping everyone, actually. He looked at the rapture on the faces of the audience and knew that he was about to provide them with more, at an entirely new level, and that they would love and reward him for it, for it was the way of people to seek rapture and to encourage those who provided it.

Jean-Pierre was beaming, too, the nerves replaced by the zing, the arrival of the moment. Gus saw what a handsome man Corina's eldest was—Paulus's prettiness hammered into a rougher texture. Then Gus spotted the source. Tucked among her flock, Corina swayed in her chair to the pounding male rhythm of The Majesties' praise of Jesus. She was stunning. Her form-fitting jet black dress set off perfectly by a gold crucifix on a double chain. She saw Gus watching her. She smiled at him, and at Jean-Pierre, but quickly looked away to concentrate on the stage.

BY COINCIDENCE RATHER THAN DESIGN, the dark green Hapsenfield Mercedes and the dark blue Joe Dell Prince Le Baron arrived in performers' parking at the same time. The occupants of neither car realized the fluke until they had parked side by side and got out. And then not even Elizabeth did, for Agon had not told her of the special guest he was going to introduce.

"My God, I had no idea there would be such a crowd," she said.

"I can only say again we are indebted to Mr. Houston," Agon replied, locking the doors. He looked across the freshly waxed top of the car at his wife. "I just want to say before we go in that I'm glad we could come here together after all."

She looked at him. Her normal response would have been one of feigned boredom, but the tone in his voice seemed sincere. It troubled her. For the last several weeks Agon had been acting not only differently, but in a way she couldn't field. Oregon had been more profound than she had initially grasped. She still couldn't wait to get away from him, but as she looked into his blue eyes, the patrician gray around his temples, she thought, well, he's not a bad-looking man, in a bean-pole kind of way.

She could see why she was once attracted to him. Whatever he was now or wherever he was in his head maybe it would make the future tasks somewhat easier. She didn't take New Age Primitivism seriously, but she had to admit it had made her husband light years easier to get along with and on that account she indulged him. Her own tastes had become, in contrast, increasingly vulgar and less spiritual. What an odd transformation. Two years ago, she'd have pegged it entirely the other way. So she smiled at him warmly. "I think we shall have a fine time. It will be good for us."

"You must be Mr. Hapsenfield."

It was the man in the blue suit from the other car. As Elizabeth turned her head she was reminded of a movie actor but she couldn't think just who. She saw Agon extend his hand. "Nice to see you, Senator. I'd like you to meet my wife, Elizabeth."

The man offered his hand. "Joe Dell Prince. I can't tell you how much a contribution to the city you've made by sending your girls here to take part in this great cultural event."

Elizabeth smiled automatically and withdrew her hand a fraction of a second prematurely. She looked at Agon. "Why thank you, Senator," she said slowly. "I must admit this is the last place I'd expect to find you."

She did not try to hide her disdain. The senator seemed to enjoy it. "I expect a lot of people might feel the same way as you. But sometimes we can have people judged wrong." To Agon: "Perhaps we should go inside?"

"After you."

The trio walked on. Elizabeth looked at Agon, asking with her wifely glance what was going on, but they were inside the backstage part of the big, teeming tent before she could get him away from the senator. By then the music was too loud to hear what Agon said, other than that the senator would be making a brief appearance during the evening and that "some great catalytic convergence of the Pre-Future may be about to take place."

Looking at it later, Elizabeth wished she had pried a little more, but as Agon never had been a really harmful person, except for his infidelities, she shrugged it off as some kind of goofiness to go with his change in philosophy. In other words she had no idea what kind of catastrophe was about to take place. Not that it would have mattered; on that night in history she was one of the people who are witness to the foibles of humanity rather than controllers of them.

In the back of the tent, Ocho Alvarado found a place along the right aisle. He sat quietly, watching the stage. It was hot, but he wore a cream-colored sport jacket over his white shirt and dark brown cotton trousers. He looked very tropical.

THE STAGE WAS ELEVATED more than head high, so even those at the farthest end could see. A purple and white banner trimmed in gold tassels hung from the tent frame overhead. It said, "Gospel for Jesus." Beneath the banner was half-controlled bedlam. Art, the stage manager, fretted among singers, managers, musicians, and one man in a Fire Department uniform who wanted to make sure the various electrical cables snaked under and over the stage were safe, although everyone knew the fireman was only there to see the show for free.

At 6:50, Jean-Pierre led the Voices of Angelique from the dressing tent into the backstage waiting area. Bringing up the rear, Gus could sense the girls tensing up. The sides were rolled and tucked most of the way around to let the evening breeze filter in, but even in its relative openness the Gospel Tent was a like a fortress walled off from the encroachments of the outside world. Gus understood why Jean-Pierre had wanted to wait until the last possible moment. The girls had sung in public before, but nothing could have prepared them for this. Gus himself was intimidated.

The acoustics were much more impressive than he had expected, and much more resonant. The Arkadelphia Angels were finishing a contralto harmony that made Gus's spine tingle. And his stomach sink. The Arkadelphia Angels were mere rookies compared to the other acts, like the Angels of Desire, and they were at least twice as good as The Voices of Angelique.

Gus tried to see if Jean-Pierre might be thinking the same thing, but couldn't be sure. The girls wore the long-distance stares of the dazed. That was good, thought Gus. They are so thoroughly out-of-place and humbled they will lose all fear. And then he smiled. Maybe they would surprise him. For some reason Jean-Pierre looked back at him, glowering, as if he had read his thoughts. Gus flushed with embarrassment. No time for clutch-thinking.

Jean-Pierre guided the girls into a place just outside the crisscross of bodies and stage hands and spoke to them quietly. In his heavy choir master's gown of deep indigo lined with black and scarlet piping, he seemed to them as a great protector from Above. Jean-Pierre put his two hands into the midst of the pale blue half-circle and they all placed theirs on top. They bowed their heads. Jean-Pierre prayed.

Gus couldn't hear what they were saying because of the din from the big amplifier next to him. Nor did he drop his head with them. He probably should have, as the chaplain, but he could not stop marveling at the sight of them. He felt sappy and mushy at their simple beauty, and he felt crass and unforgiven at what the Shadow Gus held in the pit of his stomach, which was the deliberate and calculating use of their efforts pretty much for his own behalf. But he snapped out of it. Recrimination was but a shadow, itself, of clutch-thinking.

Also, from the corner of his vision, he noticed Agon and Elizabeth along the right side behind the stage and out of the way of the crush. Thank God. Gus had been watching for him the last fifteen minutes without success. And then Gus saw the man standing next to Agon.

A thin black woman in green taffeta rushed past, grazing Gus's shoulder with an old flattop guitar. She apologized quickly, and when Gus was able to look again Agon and the man standing next to him were circling along the rear edge, as if to reach the opposite side of the stage. Elizabeth lingered behind, almost squishing herself into the canvas, which in the backstage area had been pegged down to limit crowd access. Gus moved toward her. He was glad she had dressed appropriately—a loose fitting white smock, straw hat. Almost churchish. But the expression on her face was, at the least, secular.

"Was that Joe Dell Prince?" Gus called out as he got closer.

"Hello to you, too."

"Was it?"

She nodded, then shook her head. "Hard to believe, ain't it?"

Gus edged in next to her. Through the bodies, he could see the girls clustered near the portable steps at the far side of the stage—where Agon and the senator had seemed headed. Jean-Pierre was talking, or perhaps yelling, at Art.

"What's going on?" Gus asked, turning back to Elizabeth.

She laughed. Her mouth crinkled the way it had after they had made love that time. "I think my husband has finally gone completely insane—"

The tent broke into applause, which was even louder than the singing. It became impossible for Gus to hear Elizabeth, but she wasn't talking anyway. She was standing next to him but she didn't seem to be there anymore. Her mouth was crinkly, but her eyes were glazed.

The Arkadelphia Angels bowed and turned stage right, leaving single file, followed by their pianist. Gus thought about trying to get to Jean-Pierre to tell him but it seemed a bad time to pass on bad news. Not that it was even possible to get around there in all the confusion. So he remained at Elizabeth's side. Despite having snapped at Bonita that morning for "skipping Jazzfest just because of a bad experience two years ago," he was glad now that she had chosen to go to work. He was very glad.

Stage hands jumped atop the platform to adjust equipment. Audience members busied themselves with readjusting their seats, fanning their perspiring faces, and deciding whether to go to the refreshment tents for Cokes or wait for the fifteen-minute intermission at 7:45.

Gus picked out Corina again amid her flock. She looked immensely happy. Gospel was her music of choice and now her eldest was going to be the center of attention. She twisted this way and that in her seat, talking to everyone around her. Then Paulus, at her side, turned around at some kind of activity coming from the far end of the tent and so did many others in the crowd.

Gus followed their line of vision and saw a black man and white woman come inside. The man was holding a big video camera with a "Channel 12" decal. The woman was someone whose face Gus had seen. That made him feel better. The Academy would be on the ten o'clock news.

"After the girls sing, let's go find that reporter. Maybe they could interview you."

Elizabeth gave him another look.

But the attention of the crowd rapidly returned to the show. Gus looked up to see the Reverend Albert Lincoln, the master of ceremonies, proceeding up the stage right staircase, past his friend Jean-Pierre and a gathering of light blue robes. He was followed by Agon Hapsenfield and Senator Joe Dell Prince.

The three men paused at the top of the steps to huddle and to make way for stage hands moving equipment back and forth. The Reverend Lincoln seemed confused and disconcerted. Agon was smiling and almost beatific. Then Agon followed the reverend to the microphone at the center of the stage. Joe Dell waited at the edge, hands folded in front like a schoolboy.

The reverend put his hand over the top of the mike. He seemed even more confused. He said something in a low voice to Agon, and Agon said something back. The reverend pursed his lips, wiped the top of his shiny pate, and flicked the mike with his finger. The sound popped through the tent, hushing what had become a flurry of whispering from the audience. The reverend broke into a stage smile.

"You hearing the Lord's words sung to you today?"

"Yes, brother . . . Amen . . . Yes, Jesus . . ."

"And you with the Lord today?"

"We with him, Reverend."

"Well, that's as it should be. We got some *glorious* voices for Jesus today right here in the city of New Orleans and we callin' to the Lord to be with us today, brothers and sisters."

"Amen." This time more voices, stronger. Amid them, the sound of paper being shuffled as people skimmed their programs to make sure they were correct, to figure out who that tall white man was. The whispering increased.

"Well then, are you ready for some more good Gospel?"

Applause.

"All right, children. Well, now is the time we see the Gospel goes to all peoples and all colors. It ain't no one color for the Lord. All colors. All peoples."

"Say it, Brother Lincoln."

"And that's why I'm proud to bring on right now something we don't see too much in our city and something we ought to see more often."

"You got that right."

"I'm proud—proud—to introduce a fine group of our white sisters who have been practicing and studying the Gospel of Jesus and now want to show you their stuff!"

More applause.

The reverend put his hand to his jaw, rubbed it, as if still working something out. He could hear the whispers, the shuffling. He smiled again.

"And because this is such an important occasion for us, I

want to let the man who made all this possible come up and say just a few words to us all. And make that just a 'few' words, Brother Hapsenfield, because what these folks come here for ain't to hear us talk but to hear our brothers and sisters sing."

Agon moved forward. The Reverend Lincoln raised his arms.

"My brothers and sisters, let us welcome the headmaster and proprietor of Miss Angelique's Academy for Young Ladies, Mr. Agon Hapsenfield."

Agon bowed slightly, shook the reverend's hand and positioned himself in front of the microphone. The applause died fast. It could have been described as "polite."

"Thank you all so much. Now I don't have much to say about my girls because you'll hear what they have to say for themselves soon enough, although I would like to give special thanks to Mr. Gus Houston, our chaplain, and Mr. Jean-Pierre Youngblood, our choir director, for their bold initiative in bringing our beloved Academy to this revered place at this special time."

Gus watched. It had gone very quiet. Corina, bursting with a smile at the mention of Jean-Pierre's name, nonetheless let the smile drop as Agon continued. Gus felt a rush of blood in the back of his neck at that instant. Agon should have been done, but it was clear he was going to say something more. A sidelong glance at Elizabeth told him the flash of dread was not without justification.

"But the reason I am really here, I think, is not the reason I thought." Agon smiled, and leaned over the microphone stand. He did look like Ichabod Crane. He cleared his throat and continued. "But that is what happens in life sometimes. What you think is not what you get. What I thought was that I was going to introduce the Voices of Angelique and sit down." He paused and looked out. He seemed out of his comma-shaped body.

"But life has offered me a greater role. A greater challenge—and, I must say, a greater privilege. For on this day it has come upon me the opportunity to see a man grow before my very eyes. On this day I can share that vision with you. On this day—" he straightened to his full six-feet-six. His hands raised into fists in front of him. His head bowed slightly.

"I can barely relate my joy. On this day I am pleased to yield my brief time on the stage to a man who, on entering this tent, was one thing, but, I suspect, on exiting, will be quite another thing. And it will be a Becoming, a transformation, all of us can take into our consciousness and grow from. A remarkable moment, I feel."

Throughout the rows of the long tent, people were shifting uncomfortably. So was the man, who, as Agon's long right arm swept toward his side of the stage, could feel the entire weight of the audience's collective gaze. "I would like to offer a very special moment to State Senator Joe Dell Prince of Metairie, who came to me from compassion and evolution of his spirit and asked to allow us to share something from him that I feel will change all of us together."

Joe Dell knew he had to move quickly. He was halfway to the microphone before Agon's last words had left his mouth.

It may have been too late. In the audience, the tension and confusion seemed to alter by the microsecond. Whatever that skinny white man had been blabbering on about was now all about the Klan senator walking out on the stage of the Gospel Tent. Still, for a few moments, the reality seemed too unlikely to be possible. And yet there it was. Same face that had plastered the political posters of election campaigns and TV news. Same face that went with the motto, "It's All Right to Stay White." It was him. It was not possible but it was him. But it was not possible.

"What's this?" came the first cry.

"Reverend Lincoln, what going on?" An older, bearded man in a gray suit near the front row stood and faced out into the audience. He called out even louder. "I said, Reverend Lincoln, what is going *on* here?"

But the reverend had left the stage, glowering, slapping his hands to his sides with great force, calling out for Art.

Joe Dell clutched the mike stand. "I know what you may be thinking," he began. The amplifiers screeched. He let go the stand and tried again. "I know what you may be thinking. And I know you have your reasons. But what I'm doing here now is to ask you to just hear me out. See if you won't know that things have changed for me as they once did for Matthew and Paul. That as I once was, I am no longer—"

"Hear the man out," came a female voice.

The senator tried to seek her out and ride with the sentiment. "I have come here to tell you of a great change in my heart—"

"Get off the stage," came another woman's voice. "How dare you come to this place!"

Joe Dell couldn't see where that one came from. Nor the sustained booing that rose up like a drill hole ready to blow. For an unhinged moment, Joe Dell wanted to think the booing might be directed against the woman trying to silence him.

"I am here to tell you that although my past was one way, my future lies in another—"

The booing continued. It grew. It became a wall of sound.

"We don't need no Klan in here—"

"As I said, my past was one thing. I could explain that, but I am here to tell you I have surely changed—"

A red, round seat cushion sailed out of the audience and whipped past Joe Dell's head.

"Now there's no call for this," he said, dodging. "I came here to say I'm your brother—"

Three more cushions were launched. The first hit the mike cord and took the stand down with it. Feedback scratched through the air again. Joe Dell's face squinched up in pain. The second cushion hit an amp, and the hell-noise went off and on, like madness. The third round caught him in the stomach.

Then something harder bounced off his right elbow, and then, in a matter of seconds, the place where the Angels of Angelique should have been standing and interfacing as promised became ground zero for seat cushions, flying ears of corn-on-the-cob, chicken wings, wadded-up paper cups, an occasional rock.

Transfixed, as if it could not be comprehended therefore it must go away—a nightmare, only, nothing real—Joe Dell held stock still. Neither did Agon Hapsenfield move. Pocked with food bits and ice balls, assailed by cushions, he scarcely even ducked, never lost the blank, peaceful expression which gave no indication of his circumstances.

Joe Dell was the first to tune back in. At the next salvo, a deep crimson flush raged across his face and neck. Mouth, eyebrows and even his nose contorted and he did not look like Kevin Costner. Staring at Agon, he said something no one could hear in the din, and hurried off stage, pelted all the way.

Finnester, trying desperately to shuck the *Times-Picayune* reporter he'd escorted in for the "exclusive," took his boss by the elbow as he came down the stage stairs. Joe Dell pushed him away, nearly toppling the reporter, and made directly for an opening at the rear of the tent. Finnester ran after, and they disappeared into the evening. The reporter followed a few paces, paused, looked back inside the tent, and returned to the real action.

Agon was still on stage. Alone. But the barrage had not lessened and he was covered in muck and his face and arms were already welting. It all seemed in slow motion, and he could not believe what had come of the most recent three and one-half minutes in his life. He looked out at the audience. A spare rib caught him on the jaw. He winced, touched his cheek, felt blood. People were beginning to mount the stage. It had cut him.

His cheek throbbed. He suddenly knew why. Covering his head with his arms, he scurried off to the stairs so recently also used by the man whose political penance and rebirth Agon had fervently believed would have triggered the rebirth of the future of the state.

Elizabeth was laughing. Gus moved in front of her, protectively. Among the scrambled and overturned chairs, people of every color, age, and gender had begun to brawl. Even the performers were crowding and shoving each other to try to get out of the tent. Jean-Pierre was among them, trying to lead the girls through the maelstrom.

Gus put his face next to Elizabeth's ear. "Go. Get out. Now. I'm going to help Jean-Pierre." She stepped back and stared at him. Whatever she was going to say, Gus didn't hear. From out of the pit that had been an audience of Christians a whirling folding chair struck him in the lower back. Sagging, unable to catch his breath, he dropped to his knees. Elizabeth backed out under the tent flap.

Gus tried to get up, but was knocked down again by several men in deacon-like black suits yelling, "Get him, get him." Gus thought at first they meant him and covered his head to ward off the blows but the men were heading for someone else. He lowered his arms just in time for a shoe to catch him full on the left ear. He saw a flash of light amid a pitch-black universe deep inside his brain and before he lost consciousness he felt a coolness on his cheek. The compressed ball of grape Snoball slush that had arced in from an unknown hurler left only a small abrasion and fell onto the ground inches from Gus's forehead to melt without a trace of culpability.

JEAN-PIERRE KNEW HOW BAD it was going to get before the first cushion was thrown, which, he reminded himself, could not have come from his mother because her bad back wouldn't give her that kind of range. When it started, the girls were in single file behind him at the base of the stairs, waiting for their cue.

That was when he had first seen Joe Dell Prince. Jean-Pierre had stopped cold, and held his arm back to halt the girls, too. He knew right away. He should have reacted without hesitating. He should have turned back and found Art and found out what the hell was going down. Whatever that man was doing up there on stage, it couldn't have been good.

He should have paying closer attention. But everything was bedlam and Betsy and Tina had gone pale even by white standards with stage fright. So he'd been calming them and only half-listening to the introductions, mentally readying himself to lead the girls up to the stage and make his way to the piano, and hoping Art had it set up in the right place.

Maybe that was why he froze. He was preparing to give praise to the Lord and he saw that man instead. Even when the man moved across the stage and started speaking, even when the first volleys of cushions and food found their marks, Jean-Pierre had held back. In that moment, a moment he would rethink until it made him want to scream, he had been paralyzed by a force he never even knew existed. He did not understand the stopping power of a random chaotic visitation from an uncharted future.

He might have taken comfort had he known he was but one of many others that evening around whom chaos lay like an infection, that he was but one of many disparate souls selected to learn how easily things can happen that are not supposed to. He would have learned why pilots must trust their instruments; that vertigo, the disbelief of gravity, is the siren of universal chaos itself. But he did not and there was nothing else to do. Spinning Charlotte around by her shoulders, Jean-Pierre had pushed her forward. "That's it," he said. "Get outside."

The girls, who below stage level had been unable to see what was happening, bunched up and shoved back. "What is this?" Marie asked. "Shut up and run," said Charlotte.

Jean-Pierre hopped to the ground and headed them up like wild cattle. "Don't run. Just get out quickly." But by then it had gotten crazy.

A human wall had already formed along the tent's outer perimeter as more and more onlookers rushed over from the other shows. Backstage was the only remaining respite from the crush, except for a small opening at the far front end of the tent. But in no time the wall of people gained mass, pushing farther inside, until the stage itself was overrun like some enemy position and there were no safe spots at all.

Cissy had started screaming and Betsy was crying. Charlotte took Betsy's hand. Jean-Pierre kept them moving in as tight a shell as possible, although it was slow and, as whites, the girls stuck out too much. When he saw a hole to the left he powered two young men in muscle shirts out of his way and was rewarded with open skies and cool evening breeze.

They were clear.

"Oh, Mr. Youngblood—" It was Marie, fallen to her knees.

"Go, go. Keep going. Get them as far away as possible," he said to Charlotte, then bent over Marie. He picked her up and almost gasped when he saw a gash across her forehead, blood trailing down into her eyes. "Something hit me."

"It's okay." Jean-Pierre held Marie close to his chest, their robes a complement to each other, though bloodied now. He moved through a whirl of bodies trying to get somewhere, who knew where or why. The din of voices and curses had become immense, and now in the background he could hear police sirens from the streets.

Charlotte had made it to the fence line. She had shepherded the others to a clearing between two parked delivery trucks. Jean-Pierre carried Marie over. "Hold this to your forehead," he told her, giving her a handkerchief. The cut was bleeding, but minor.

"I'll be right back," he told Charlotte. "Don't go anywhere till I get back or Mr. Houston does. You should be okay here. Get the first policeman you see."

Then he raced back to the tent to find his mother and brother.

AT FIRST, CORINA AND PAULUS had ducked in their seats, and then, as it got worse, they knelt between the rows of chairs with Arletta Wynnewood and Estella Bourgeois and the others from the church. But after a minute or two even that was not safe. Everyone seemed either to be trying to get up the stage to find that Prince man or trying to get out to stay away from the trouble. Corina wanted to get away. Miz Johnson was too old to be around this kind of riot, and Paulus was too young, and she herself didn't care to get beat up, come to that.

So as soon as she could see a clear spot behind her, she kicked some chairs out of the way and led her flock out. A small stream of like-minded folk parted the debris like the Red Sea ahead of her and she followed them to the farthest end of the tent. Miz Johnson and the others were scared and wanted to leave. Corina told Articia Sloan, the strongest among them, to lead everyone out to the front gate and wait there.

"You not coming with us, Reverend?" Miz Johnson asked.

"I got to see my son is okay. He up there somewhere with all those white girls." She gestured toward Articia. "Go, get on. I be with you directly."

They left. Corina went back in the tent. Paulus had picked up a chair and wedged it next to a tent pole near what had been the ticket booth. Corina stood on the chair, holding Paulus's shoulder for balance. She looked, but she could not see him.

OCHO HAD LONG SINCE THROWN his seat cushion, and a rock he'd found on the ground, and was well forward in the first assault wave on the stage, but the two white men were gone and now people were fighting with each other, mostly over shoving and crowding. Ocho liked it, and it was making his life easier. In truth, he'd had no idea how he was going to get to Jean-Pierre or get away, other than to follow him around until the moment came, but now—this was the moment. He pressed on, but there were too many people, and it was hard to see anything.

He felt an elbow sharp against his ribs and turned to see a black man making a face at him, so Ocho hit the man across the face with a wooden stake he'd found lying near the stage. The man toppled. Another came toward Ocho and Ocho hit him, too, and then the swell of the crowd pushed him far around the right side of the stage to the rear.

Which is when he saw Maria's lover.

All the black singers in their robes and the other ones who'd just come in to see what was happening had the place cluttered up but over on the side Ocho could see Jean-Pierre coming from outside back into the tent. He was wearing a robe, too. It made him easy to track.

Ocho moved forward, careful to keep a few people between him and his target. But his target kept getting better. As he got nearer, Ocho could see that Jean-Pierre was trying to get on top of an overturned amplifier.

Ocho felt something take over, as he had often felt it in his life and he was sliding around the back side of three young rednecky looking white women in cutoffs drinking beer and yelling at someone to get out of the way. At the same time, his hand went inside his jacket and down into his belt. His hand found the little Walther he had brought from Miami. Then his hand was up and the gun was in it and he was yelling, "Hey, you fucking asshole motherfucker," and Jean-Pierre was turning slightly to see him.

Jean-Pierre's body twisted sharply to the right as though a taut wire had been jerked suddenly from the center of his shoulder blade. Ocho fired again. Jean-Pierre slammed into the amplifier, crumpled forward onto one knee, then fell on his side onto the ground.

Ocho was moving quickly back into the crowd and to the other side of the tent. Now the yelling had turned to screams and a few people had dropped to the ground and others were looking around and then the sound of the shots and the fear of the people was swallowed whole in the confusion and Ocho was outside the tent and walking quickly along the fence line.

He was going so fast he nearly didn't see the group of white girls in pale blue gowns, one of the gowns spattered with blood, huddled against the chain link. And he could have missed them, too, except they were singing. It was a weird song, Ocho thought, making for the big concession tent near the Louisiana Pepper Stage. Not like a hymn, exactly, something else.

He did see the police running toward the Gospel Tent and had he been able to he would have seen Agon Hapsenfield resting on a small set of bleachers surrounded by two state troopers and a fireman, nursing various cuts and lumps. He would not have seen Elizabeth, for as soon as the first cushion struck Joe Dell

Prince she had ditched Gus and walked away without looking back to hear the zydeco band in the Bud Lite tent. It was said that sometime later an attractive middle-aged woman had taken off her dress and was seen dancing in nothing but her panties and a straw hat in front of the Johnny Winter band but it was never really established that it was Elizabeth, because the night was too filled with alarm and nakedness was far down on the priorities of the available police.

AT THE SOUND OF THE GUN SHOT, Corina saw what had happened. "Oh God, they done shot him," she said, barely audibly, to Paulus. And then they were running up to Jean-Pierre's side. But the first wave of police beat her to her son and only by crying that she was his mother was she allowed to behold him, soaked in blood, as the officers pushed back the onlookers and called on a walkie-talkie for paramedics.

Paulus tried to get in close, too, but seeing his brother like that and his mother like that dropped something cold into his soul and he did not press. One of the policemen asked him if he had seen who did it and he said he hadn't been able to see anything and he just sat down on the trampled grass and debris and stared through the legs of the surrounding cops at his brother sprawled on his back, bleeding into the ground and his mother crying as if she would die.

Off to the left, outside the tent, a crowd of people had assembled around the white girls in the powder blue robes. They were rocking softly, side to side. The big girl carried the lead. "Love and happiness," she sang, while the others filled in, sweet to her eerie low moan: "Love and happiness . . ."

At first the voices only made Paulus angry, but amid the police radio chatter and his mother's crying he found himself drifting away on the rhythm.

"Moan for love . . ."

A stocky black policeman with a black mustache came and squatted next to him. He had a notebook in his hand and was writing something. His name tag said B. F. Saunders. It was one of the cops who had first found Jean-Pierre. "The EMS just came through the gates," the cop said.

Paulus turned in the direction of a siren—there were many sirens but that one was a little different—and saw an ambulance trying to thread through the crowd. It was unclear whether people were trying to leave or get in free through the gates amid the confusion. Paulus watched as the vehicle got closer. The siren went off but the lights were still flashing.

"Make you do right . . ." she sang.

"Make you do wrong . . ."

"We stopped the bleeding," the cop said. "I think he'll be okay." Paulus nodded and tried to get closer. In a moment Jean-Pierre was on a stretcher. Something was over his face. Paulus vaguely remembered the sensation of an oxygen mask. Then Jean-Pierre was in the ambulance. His mother climbed in with him. "Get Miz Anderson to bring you over," she called out to Paulus as the doors were shut by the fireman who had hung around for the free show. His uniform was splotched like a modern art painting, and there was a gash along the bridge of his nose.

"It's okay," he said to Paulus. "They'll take care of him."

The ambulance pulled away. The sirens went back on. Paulus followed a tall blond lady cop and B. F. Saunders to a squad car just inside the gate. On the way to the hospital, as the lady cop drove, Officer Saunders asked Paulus why anyone would want to shoot his brother. He wanted to know if he was involved in drugs.

ALONG THE FENCE LINE BEHIND the tent, a halo of music spread itself over those who had gathered within earshot of the white girls. Born of desperation, it was a haven; within it, recalled many who found respite there, was perhaps the best show of the week.

"*Love and happiness . . .*"

The big brunette was red in the face and sweating profusely, and there was a distance deep in her gaze. The seven others bunched up tight next to her had become all of a body, moving in sync, to and fro, dipping and stepping, clapping in time, Motown with melancholy, utterly hypnotizing. The onlookers took up the clapping in time, too, as though nothing was playing itself out not fifty yards away.

Just then the smaller blond with the high and honeyed voice lifted her arms upward, closed her eyes, and flew off to some other place. She took the rhythm and the lyrics with her.

"*Oh happy day . . .*"

From Cissy's lips, the simple words of the Edwin Hawkins Singers classic washed fulfillment on Al Green's lament like waves on a tropical shore. Low at first, and then louder:

"*Oh happy day . . .*"

"*Oh happy day . . .*"

"*When Jesus washed . . .*"

—the other voices joining now—

"*My sins away . . .*"

Then the big brunette looked at the blond and added her strength to the change.

"*Oh happy day . . .*"

All the little sisters were in harmony now, their voices joyous from a place they seemed to have just discovered:

"*Oh happy day . . .*"

Charlotte and Cissy called out; the choir responded. So

perfect was the pitch, so vibrant the emotion, that just the first notes brought tears to even the cops and busybodies standing nearby, the way music can disarm you in that way, a way even Paulus would have accepted, that Jean-Pierre might have felt worth his wounds.

"Oh happy day . . ."
"Oh happy day . . ."
"When Jesus washed . . ."
"When Jesus washed . . ."
"When Jesus washed . . ."
"Oh when he washed . . ."
"When he washed . . ."
"When he washed . . ."
"My sins away."
"Oh happy day . . ."
"Oh happy day . . ."

Charlotte ran with it, her voice reaching and rambling like a blues singer from Memphis. The girls were locked arm in arm now, swaying. They were blood now, all of them, even Marie, whose own blood was drying on her cheek.

"When Jesus washed . . . my sins away . . . oh happy day . . ."

And then, as they had practiced seemingly so long ago, Tina, quickly joined by Betsy, moved the medley into the words from Jean-Pierre's mother's church. The beat shifted just slightly but still was anchored in that fundamental Gospel time.

—*"Walking with Je-sus . . . walking with Je-sus . . ."*

Lost from their troubles now, the girls unlocked arms and clapped, rocking in their robes like candle-flames: Those specially-designed robes, conceived in a form of deceit but now transformed, those robes now auras of blue over white skins which, like those in their immediate audience, actually had no color at all but the One, the one that in that moment in history could be neither distinguished from another nor extinguished from the common light.

—*"When I'm walking with Jesus/I'm walking with the strength of the Lord . . ."*

"Oh happy day . . ."

—*"Walking with Je-sus . . ."*

The songs now fully entwined. Charlotte and Tina picked up the new lines, Cissy and Marie leading the response.

"Oh happy day . . ."

"When Jesus washed . . ."

—*"Walking with Je-sus"*

"When he washed . . ."

—*"Walking with Je-sus"*

"When Jesus washed . . ."

"My sins away."

"Oh happy day . . . Oh happy day . . ."

—*"Walking with Je-sus"*

"When he washed . . ."

—*"Walking with Je-sus"*

"When he washed . . ."

—*"Walking with Je-sus"*

"When he washed . . ."

—*"Walking with Je-sus"*

"My sins away."

"Oh happy day . . . Oh happy day . . ."

More than a hundred souls, maybe twice that number, joined on every line, learning as they went. All you could hear, in that corner of the Fairgrounds—until the sounds of sirens covered everything and police were everywhere and the soiled salvation of the evening was all but forsaken—was what a happy day it had turned out to be.

22

G US DIDN'T EVEN KNOW there had been a shooting until he got to the Tulane Medical Center, and even then he was too groggy to take much of it in. The news came from two extremely unpleasant detectives, one black, one white, like in the movies, who "interviewed" him for two hours as soon as the docs in the ER had stitched the cut on his cheek and X-rayed his head and ribs and found only a minor concussion and bruises.

It would be the first of many such interviews, indeed, the first of many slow pirogues down the bayou to hell, but on that night, time and careers and guilt and the wrath of Corina Youngblood were not really distinguishable entities to Gus. He was okay and Jean-Pierre would probably live. The police said his condition was "serious but stable," with a puncture of the right lung and a big hole but not bone break through the left thigh.

Since he was not a member of the immediate family, they would not let Gus see Jean-Pierre, so he sent a message to the recovery room to Corina, asking for her to come out. She didn't, but Paulus did. He said, "Mama say she don't want to see you now." After that, all in the world Gus wanted was to get out of the hospital. All he wanted was to see Bonita and have two or three hundred shots of Jack Daniels. And so he went down to the Quarter.

He could see right away he would pay for much in which he had erred, and that the first installments were due. It was in her look, which began as soon as he sat down. She didn't even walk over—more like a quick inspection from afar to see that he was in one piece. Had she heard? Oh, yes. Many people had heard. It had been quite a story, on the news from just after seven p.m. until now, nearly midnight. In fact, not much else had been the topic of conversation.

"You could of fucking called, you know?"

"I said I was sorry."

Every head of every male along the bar swiveled toward him, on his corner stool, and back to her, at the register. Monotonous, stupid, tennis-watching drunks. Each one capable of inflicting harm had the fury of the brunette attending their besotted needs so indicated by the least flick of the brown iris rapier that was now her sidelong gaze.

"I'd like a beer."

"In a minute."

As it often happens in public houses, she was quite busy just then. Glasses had to be washed, tickets rung up, liquor stock assessed. The Slim Jim rack was almost empty. Old Clyde needed a fresh one, too. Yet she did love him, for even amid the heavy demands of that hour, Bonita eventually found time to carry a Dixie to her brave and wounded knight. She leaned across the countertop to touch his face. He wasn't sure exactly how she meant it and he flinched a little.

"Yeah, they got you all right." She withdrew her hand. It was an odd moment for Gus. He realized he had many conflicting expectations. One was that he wanted to be comforted. Another was that he wanted to be understood. Another was that he wanted to be long gone because there was at that moment between him and Bonita a delicate cosmic seam.

On one side of the seam was a possible future and on the other was a past in which Gus had undertaken what very possibly may have been an ill-conceived venture. Not even an isolated misstep, fluke, momentary lapse of good sense—more like a sustained, conscious series of fuck-ups, from the chaplain's job to the Gospel Tent. In undertaking said venture, Gus had loosed upon himself yet again the destructive weasels hiding in his shadowed soul.

That was a dire reading but it was a possible one and it was probably a true one. Only the delicate seam lay between the playing out of the consequences of that hubristic Rube Goldbergian past—putting the best possible spin on it—and the possibility of a future which Bonita represented. Gus knew, without her saying anything, that was what her touch meant. She was touching his skin to see if she felt anything beneath it. He wondered what would have happened had she slapped him. Would the skin have collapsed over a void? He was not sure.

"Jean-Pierre is going to be okay. He lost a lot of blood, though. I gave some and so did Paulus."

"You got the same type?"

"No, but they said they could trade and it would keep the cost down."

"Corina?"

"She's still at the hospital. I think she's spending the night in his room. She wouldn't leave."

"She get hurt?"

"No."

"She blame you?"

Gus rotated the beer bottle between his hands. He looked out over the room. He didn't say anything.

"I just want to know one thing."

"What's that?"

"Whatever was Joe Dell Prince doing there anyway?"

Gus tried to laugh but it hurt. The resident in the ER had wrapped his ribs as a precaution and although they weren't broken, spasms of pain raced up his side with untoward frequency.

"Is that funny?"

"No."

"And what about the girls? Did they get out okay? We couldn't tell on the news."

"They're okay." As he spoke, Gus realized most of the deeply concerned patrons in the bar, except for Old Clyde, busy doodling on a napkin, were still trying to eavesdrop. The jukebox had stopped and no one was putting in any more quarters.

"Everything's fine, folks," Gus smiled, as he often had to tourists at the Garden of Dixie. He raised his bottle in a toast. "Just a little fracas among the Baptists. It's all over." He realized they were still looking, and he could not help himself. "So y'all can just get back to minding your own fucking business."

The silence was grim, sustained, fraught. A dozen heads looked at Bonita for instruction. She turned her back to Gus and walked to the cash register. Gus drained his beer and slammed the bottle on the bar. "I'd like another, please."

"She'll get it when she gets it," said a concerned patron in a red T-shirt.

"Somebody oughta kick your ass, boy," said the stocky bald man in bermudas and auto parts gimme cap. His name was Henry. He worked at the post office.

"Yeah, well, somebody already did." Gus stared at as many of them as he could.

"Leave him alone, he's an idiot. Here, Henry, go play something loud." Bonita gave Henry two dollars in quarters and took a new Dixie from the ice chest and carried it back to Gus.

"You are, you know," she said.

He stared at the circular stains in the dark varnish on the bar. The faded rings were like little planetary orbits; entire galaxies. A universe of alien presences memorialized here and forever through the high intensity electron signatures cleverly captured by this special detection device cleverly disguised as an ordinary elbow rest for an entire continent of drunks. At last, for the Air Force, interstellar footprints—proof of UFOs and other life forms. Which he possibly himself represented. He could not look at her.

"Did you hear me?"

"Yeah, I heard you."

Henry played "Gimme Shelter" by the Rolling Stones. Gus smiled. Henry had a pretty good sense of humor for a mail carrier.

"I wish we could go home," Gus said.

Bonita touched his hand, rubbing little ringlets into his skin. *"If I don't get some shelter . . . Lord, I'm gonna fade away . . ."*

BY SUNDAY THE WORST of the calls from the parents had tapered off, and with the exception of Cissy Otterton's prick of a father everyone had been managed. Cissy would finish the year, it being so close to the end of term, but the "appalling bad judgment of you and especially your husband" would preclude his daughter from coming back in the fall, Dr. Otterton said. And firing Mr. Houston didn't make it okay.

All considered, Elizabeth considered the damage sustainable. In a way, she might yet see an upside to it all. For one thing, no one was blaming the Academy per se for the riot. She stretched her legs out fully on the lounge chair on the patio and reached over to the piñon end table for something to browse while she waited. Monday's *Times-Picayune* was exactly where she'd left it. Not much housecleaning going on in the Hapsenfield abode lately. Not of that kind.

She dug out the editorial page and read from it again. She read it aloud. "We should not let the unfortunate events at the Gospel Tent cloud the memory of our consciences regarding the essential good faith of Miss Angelique's Academy in attempting to cross the racial lines which have yet again proven so uncrossable in our city. And, we must add, that applies to the less defensible, but not less idealistic, actions of headmaster Agon Hapsenfield."

She stopped reading and listened. Nothing but the sound of him shuffling through boxes in the bedroom. Just as well. She had been deliberately provocative. He had let it go. That was probably better. He was hoping to leave for Portland by late afternoon. He was taking the Mercedes; she was keeping the Chagall. The rest they would sort out later.

She decided she hated the sound of her voice.

She scanned the rest of the old paper. She'd bought several copies, intending to clip them. She tried to remember where she'd left the others. Maybe in the den. She turned to the city section. A small follow-up article on the "Gospel Riot," as they were calling it, said Jean-Pierre Youngblood was recovering and would be out of the hospital before June. Elizabeth and Agon knew all about that—they were picking up the bill just to be on the safe side, legally. The rest was no longer her business. The police were looking for a Cuban construction worker. Senator Prince had issued a statement saying he blamed "rabble-rousers and drunks," and that he was "rethinking my political agenda."

She put the paper down and went into the kitchen to refill her coffee mug. She heard a thud, then a "goddammit," and some more moving of boxes. She thought about going to help him but instead leaned against the counter and looked out the window. She wasn't sure if she'd miss Gus or not, especially with Agon gone. That was a good time that afternoon. Nor did she really blame him for anything. It was clearly Agon's fuck-up with the senator. But Gus was a teacher and Agon was the headmaster and for the sake of the Academy fingering the appropriate scapegoat was necessary.

When she called to tell him he was fired he hadn't even protested. He only asked if she could box up his things and send them over with Ralph the deliveryman.

"Need any help?"

"No, I'm fine. Just a little clumsy."

"Let me know."

"I will."

It had been an easy decision, Agon, under the circumstances. It was like with Gus, only more so. Yesterday afternoon, on the patio, the very same one where she now lingered, they agreed to tear asunder what God had put together. He had been sitting on the sea-green chaise longue. In his white shirt and eggshell trousers he seemed almost like a pearl. Herself, she was without makeup and wearing the same cotton shift she'd had on since the previous evening.

Far from feeling remorse for the riot and the shooting, Elizabeth's soon-to-be-ex-husband was convinced it may have "freed minds." He told her, "The hallmark of the primitive consciousness is the expression of our basic instincts. What could have been more basic than that upheaval of violence and hatred? I'm not saying it wasn't frightening but even the fear was part of the instinct."

He had laughed lightly. "I remember trying to explain it to the lieutenant and honestly Elz, I think he thought I was crazy. But to be seen as crazy is not an insult to me. It may the proof of how sane I have become." His eyes were bright and glowing. Her eyes held them for some time. But hers were not glowing. She had looked away and he had sighed. "I know you don't see it."

"No. It seemed a disaster to me. And people were hurt."

"Pain is the first plateau."

She had slumped on a rattan armchair. "What's the next one?"

"You can't know that until you are there."

"Oh, Agon, for god's sake."

He sat up suddenly and held his right hand at a rigid right angle in front of his face. He seemed to stare past it as though it were a rifle sight. He said, "I see *our* plateau."

She said nothing.

He shifted his gaze slightly toward her. "It's yours."

She cocked her head.

"What do you mean?"

"This. The school. It's yours, Elz."

"Why do you say that?"

"Because it's the time." He held her in his sights. "Everything that's been happening has been leading to this. All of it, don't you see? The women. The girls." He winked. "The men. Mr. Houston. The detectives. Everything. And the glorious brawl and the revelation of it all—it was all headed here. And now it's time. I will continue on my journey. You will stay here. This is your journey."

He dropped his hand. He was smiling in a way that both infuriated and disconcerted her. "I know you have your doubts about me, but you must see the rightness of this."

She had looked at him. In all her thoughts, she had never figured on it ending like that. She had anticipated lawyers. Fights. Property battles. A terrible mess. But now he had just waved it all away. It left her feeling a little unfulfilled. It made her want sex. But she did not want it with him and she could not have it with Gus.

And so it was over. Agon had risen from the chaise longue and walked to her and leaned down and kissed her on the forehead, and then she raised her face and kissed him on his lips and then he pulled away and they looked at each other in a far less hateful way than she ever might have envisioned. He went out for a walk and she went to take a shower and change clothes and go shopping. And it was over.

And now the Academy was hers. Agon wouldn't discuss any details, saying that's what lawyers were for. He wanted his last days there to be free of strife so he could continue to feel the "joy of the purge of rage." So he had been mostly packing or gone somewhere in town, she didn't know and didn't ask.

Today was the end of it. The movers would come for the big things tomorrow. What he needed at the retreat for the next several weeks he was putting in the car.

She went into the bedroom. He was beatific again, except for the occasional swearing at banging his knees on a chair or dropping a suitcase on his foot. He had never been graceful.

"Actually," he said as she walked in, "I think I'd prefer to finish this on my own. If you don't mind."

She stopped. "No, of course not. Do you want me to be here when you actually go?"

He looked up from a well-stuffed bag. "Maybe it would be better to let the stream flow as it's going."

She shrugged with some effort. Speaking had become a terrible burden. "Then good-bye."

"I want to be part of something."

That was the last she ever saw of him, too.

23

CONSIDERING HE HADN'T even gone to Jazzfest and been around any of the trouble personally, Elroy was suffering mightily from the fallout during the past two weeks. The Saturday after the Gospel Riot had seen decent business, maybe because of spillover from the grand opening, but by Tuesday the SuperBotanica was so empty you could hear the clack of a person's heels on the linoleum floor six aisles away.

Worse, "Boycott Delgado" posters were back, stapled up on utility poles all over the neighborhood. No matter how fast Elroy had them taken down, they reappeared. He hadn't seen a black customer for more than eight days. And with the people picketing again on Ladeau Street it wasn't likely he would. Calling the cops did no good. They said the picketers had a right to be on public thoroughfares. They didn't even hassle them. And the TV stations had been around twice doing stories. It was almost as bad as during the construction.

Only now it wasn't the usual "Buy American" thing that Corina had tried before. Now it was about how Elroy had lined up "the Klan Prince" to ruin the Gospel Tent. Elroy could never explain how he got into it on camera and now everyone in town thought he was some kind of racist nut. Someone had spray-painted "Gusanos Go Home" and "Ku Klux Kuban" all over the storefront stucco. Julio had a couple of employees wash it off but

Elroy could still see the day-glo green residue in his mind.

It was just a big mess. Prince had gone "on vacation" and didn't have anything to say, and Hapsenfield was out in Oregon or somewhere, which was bad, because even when Elroy tried to blame everything on his stupid ideas it didn't seem to stick. So Elroy was furious. Corina was turning all the blacks against him because he was brown, and now the media were turning everyone else against him because he was a Cuban.

The only thing he had been spared was a lot of questions about Ocho Alvarado. The cops had got his name from Jean-Pierre Youngblood and they were looking for him and they knew he'd worked for Elroy, although thank god nowhere around the SuperBotanica since Mardi Gras. The truth was Elroy had no idea about anything about Ocho, except what Julio had found out, which was about the girl Maria. But Elroy didn't tell the detectives any of that, because he'd only found out after the shooting anyway and anyway, fuck Ocho. Elroy was sorry he hadn't just fired him a long time ago, like Julio wanted. But Ocho was a Cuban, and Elroy felt he had some responsibility. Which was stupid.

No matter how hard he tried, he couldn't understand why it had gone so wrong. He took a chance to cut his enemies off at the knees and it didn't work out. But it might have. What he told the reporters and most people except Julio was that all he'd done was introduce that skinny *gabacho* Hapsenfield to a state senator in the course of business—networking, he called it, at Julio's suggestion. The rest was none of his doing. But Elroy didn't lie to Changó, and he didn't lie to himself. It wasn't that bad a plan and it might have worked. But it didn't.

He pitched his empty Bud can up the fresh-polished tile between the aisles. It skittered. It was midnight and that was number six. Julio was wrong. It might have worked. Julio said,

"That's your trouble, Elroy. Even now you still can't even see what a stupid idea it was to have that Klan man up there in front of all those black people. You can't see how stupid you were to have anything to do with it. You say you're so glad we're in America but you don't get anything about this country at all. It was a stupid thing and you ended up fucking us up and you ought to admit it."

To which Elroy had exploded, "Fuck you, Julio. If you knew half as much shit as you say you did you wouldn't be following me around like a dog all the time—"

To which Julio had swung at him, missed, and cracked his knuckle against the wall in the back office. And then Julio had looked at Elroy as though at a pile of garbage and turned and walked out, with his knuckles raw and bleeding. So they hadn't spoken in two days. Elroy figured Julio would get over it, in time. Or maybe he could tell Julio he was sorry. Or—oh, fuck it.

He wandered amid the empty, well-stocked shelves. Sometimes he bumped into them. They were the kind on roller tracks so you could change the aisle widths whenever you wanted. It was easy to forget after six beers which aisles were this wide and which were *this* wide. He sat near a display of painted statues of the Catholic saints. Julio had installed viewing seats—"like in the art museums—"so the customers would have time to think over a purchase. It was a brilliant idea. The whole store was.

Elroy looked over the enormous space. They'd strung a rainbow of banners across the ceiling—a color for each of the *orisha.* A big red one in the center for Changó. The PA system alternated Gospel hymns and Caribbean music. Every other hour they ran a raffle to give away something. They'd had to stop that promotion, though, because there were so few customers that one Venezuelan couple won three times in as many days. Elroy didn't want to give them the prize the last time because he thought they were somehow cheating, but Julio said they didn't need any more trouble and handed over the case of Florida water. But what an idea this SuperBotanica! And yet there were no people to see it. Even the employees had begun to turn sour. All three of the black ones had quit, and one of the Mexican women who ran the snack counter.

Elroy drained number seven and slumped in his chair. He looked at the statue of the Virgin of Guadalupe. She was very beautiful, he thought, with all those sun rays around her. Julio said if the customer flow didn't pick up they'd have to consider selling the grocery store on Melpomene to "increase liquidity." Fuck that, too. Elroy's liquidity was in the can in his hand.

He knew Julio was right. But he still had hope and Julio didn't. Which was typical. Which was why they had the fight, really. Which was why Elroy didn't know if he and Julio could ever be right again. Hope was the whole thing. What did they say here, "the whole enchilada"? Hope was the whole enchilada. Elroy thought that if they could just weather it out a few months, the trouble would die away. Elroy could make some donations to some of the black churches and community groups and that would square the racism crap.

Before long, the people would get tired of paying three or four times as much for things at the other botanicas. They would begin trickling back. America and its nutball people notwithstanding, he had great confidence in the free market. Cuba had taught him that. You can believe what you want, but you put your money where it does the most good. Fidel probably knew that, too, which was why he turned into such a bastard. He knew it but tried to keep it from happening.

So Elroy would wait them out. He was a force in the market.

He crossed himself for the Virgin, got up, steadied himself, and threaded the unpredictable aisles to the front where he had left the Igloo. He reached into the ice for another beer and popped it. He was the fucking invisible hand. He had his store and it wasn't his fault all that shit had happened and people would forgive and forget. At least they would forget. And then they would forgive with their pocketbooks.

Fuck the market and fuck America, and fuck Julio, he thought. And most of all, fuck Corina Youngblood. He realized he was pretty drunk and therefore decided to drive home. Luz didn't even turn over when he got in bed. Maybe she didn't see him, for he was the invisible hand. And fuck enchiladas, they weren't even Cuban.

CORINA UNWRAPPED the brown paper around the package carefully. She had stayed after the shop closed so that she could do this by herself. She didn't even want Paulus to be there because the *ju-ju* was strong and she wasn't that sure of her own ability with it. She took the bone out of the paper and carried it over to the iron pot in the corner. Eddie's .38 was back inside, among the wooden sticks and the dirt and the old handcuffs, railroad spikes, nails, razor blades, the cat's bones and goat's head and a thick settlement of High John and other herbs she had gathered over the years. She rarely took anything from the pot—and was glad she had put the pistol back in there. But now she was adding something different.

The *palo* witches said the human bone is the strongest but sometimes if you don't know where it is from it can carry the spirit of something bad. Like if the bone belonged to a murderer or a rapist, then you might have the spirit of that murderer or rapist in the pot. But on the other hand you might have a spirit with great strength to bring evil upon your enemies.

Palo wasn't like the *santos* or the *orisha*. A *palo* pot was a cauldron from hell if it wanted to be. But Corina wanted the strongest thing she could find and she was willing to take a chance. And so although she had drawn on the bones of animals for *palo* and fed animals to Elegba and Ogun and the others, she had never courted the mystery of the human.

Doctor Joseph said he found the bones when a graveyard near Vicksburg was dug up for a highway. Doctor Joseph said they were for sure human but he wasn't sure exactly who. He said he had kept the bones for five years and nothing bad had happened so he thought they must be from a saved soul. When she had touched the one she wanted, a yellowed rib, she felt that, too, and she paid the two hundred dollars without trying to bargain. Corina's mama had known Doctor Joseph back when Corina was growing up. Corina never took much stock in root men, especially since she got the *santo*, but when she knew what she wanted she knew who to find in Mississippi to get it.

She put the bone in the pot, pushing it down into the dark, pungent soil and covering it over. She put the Ochosi, an iron bow with an arrow running through it, on top, and she dragged an iron spike over next to it for Ogun. Then she picked up one of the razor blades and drew a line across her forefinger until it sprouted red and she dripped the blood over the spot where the bone lay. She stood back and looked at the pot and then around at her botanica. The lights were on. She turned them off. A glint of moonlight spilled in from the side window. In Corina's soul was the soul of Ogun and of her *santos* and of her Jesus but the one that guided her now was from a place she was scared to enter but into which she had to go and it filled her head to toe. She could feel the power surge throughout her body as she stood before the pot, what the lady from Dominica called an *nganga*.

The power rose up through her strong legs and then to her cat and she could feel the blood in her cat bulge out and she knew she was wet. She could feel the power in her stomach and her kidneys and up in her lungs and leaping through her breasts and around her dark nipples and then up her long neck. She felt it fill her head, glint off her teeth like diamonds, and then she was on her knees before the pot, chanting a tongue she did not really understand, sounds from her throat she did not know—guttural, low, moaning.

She unzipped her dress and stood up long enough to let it drop to the floor and then she took off the rest of her clothing and she was naked before the pot and filled with the power. Again, she knelt, then stretched forward, full on the floor, arms toward the magic, the *ju-ju*, the thing she needed to prevail in holy battle. This she felt, still in the tongue she did not know.

She did so for an hour but it seemed like thirty seconds and then the words in the other tongue stopped and she was silent. And then her own words came into her head. They were not words, exactly, but a thought. A kind of command, as though she wanted something to happen and it had no words but it had a shape to it and that is what was in her head. The thought-shape was a wish. It was a solid, hard focus of all her mind. It had no words. She saw the focus coalesce on the image of Elroy Delgado.

She awoke before dawn, on the floor, face down. A line of saliva had run out of her mouth and had wetted her face and matted her hair. She rose up and let her hands roam across her body. Then she crossed her arms over her chest and prayed to every Spirit she could remember.

Then she put on her clothes. She was hungry so she drove to McDonald's for pancakes and sausage and coffee. She was not tired. She was filled with the Spirit and the Spirit was full of power. It had been hard and she had been wounded and her loved ones had been wounded, too, but the Spirit was strong in her now and it was time to turn her attention to other matters. The Delgados were finished. This was her way.

CROSSING INTO MEXICO was never a problem. The problem was always getting out, but Ocho didn't plan a return trip. As he walked across the International Bridge into Nuevo Laredo he didn't care in the least he'd never see the gringo land again. Maybe the money would be harder to come by but he was still fairly young and strong and things would go his way. Mexico wasn't Cuba, by a long shot, but he knew the language and all the other would be behind him.

On the Mexican side he walked straight ahead as the cop in the brown hat and green uniform barely looked at him. He went to the bus station and bought a ticket for Monterrey. He had heard you could find work there, especially if you had experience. And so he would make his life. Not once, slumped in the Greyhound seat watching Louisiana and Texas zip into his past, had Ocho squandered a single thought on remorse for killing that *puta-fucking cabrón,* any more than he had for beating up the kid brother.

The only thing that made him mad was how the Delgados had treated him. Like shit. No money, nothing. Fired from his job, even, after smacking the kid around. And when he got his friend Elusário to see if Elroy could sneak him some money to leave town after the other, he not only got nothing but got the strange feeling Elroy might even try to send the police after him.

So he was never going back to New Orleans, especially, or America, ever at all. Gringo shit place. Mexico was more for him. He walked up past a little tree-lined square where bootblacks played cards in the shade and boys pushed along carts selling cold drinks. He felt almost like he was home. He called one of the carts over and bought an orange drink. He sat down and waited until bus time. He thought about things.

24

J ESUS, HE'S GONNA BE our next governor." The freckled, sandy-haired young man in cutoffs and Tulane crewneck slid a newspaper across the table to his pale, brunette companion.

"Act like you're surprised, Billy."

"Yeah, well, it's still a piece of shit."

Gus interrupted with a half-full pot of Costa Rican coffee. It was the house special every Tuesday.

"Notoriety has a mind all its own," he said, offering another refill. They seemed badly hung over.

The woman's wristful of silver bracelets jangled as she reached for her cup. She had violet eyes and a small rose tattoo next to her right earlobe. They were regulars. He thought her name was Jane but he wasn't sure. She studied him a moment, then seemed bored and continued reading the article. Gus had seen it. A poll showed Joe Dell Prince was picking up new white voters in his gubernatorial campaign. The poll said whatever the Gospel Riot had cost him in black votes had been regained among whites. It said if the trend continued he could win in November.

"Fucking Louisiana. It's like living in a sitcom," said Billy.

"Who cares anyway," said Jane. It wasn't a question.

"You want any more croissants?" asked Gus.

"Yeah."

"No."

"Coming up."

Gus went back to the glass pastry case he'd bought second hand at a going-out-of-business sale. His bakery was delivered each day from La Coupole. "Look on the bright side," he said. "Election's still four months away. Things can change."

"Yeah."

Gus shrugged and walked out of the coffee nook into the main part of the bookstore. Mid-morning was always slow and he hoped he could finish the restocking before afternoon, when it picked up again. For a moment, he'd felt like telling Billy and Jane how it went down in the real world and how the comment about notoriety and change wasn't just conversational kibitz. But he wasn't up to it.

He picked up an invoice which had toppled from the front counter. The mail had come early and he'd piled it all next to the register. He re-stacked the letters so they wouldn't fall again and dug into the bulkier fare, mostly in the two gray postal-delivery bins. Most of that took the form of filament-taped cardboard packages from his suppliers.

Right on top were three fresh copies of the latest from Portland. The one string Agon had attached to the grant last June was a request that Gus devote a section of at least four shelves to Elihu Aliesson and writings on New Primitivism. So Gus did. Weirdly, the stuff sold.

Agon was way out there now, but Gus tried to think well of him. Fifty thousand produced nice thoughts. The note that came along with the surprise check from the New Primitivism Foundation had thanked Gus for "being the catalyst of the Pre-Future." It said Aliesson's upcoming book, *The Savage Redeemer,* would make everything clear. So Gus read it. It said that anger should be given more esteem as a human emotion, because it serves as a "catalyst" to the true peace of the human future. It said people who serve as catalysts do as much good as the peacemakers—"indeed, pave the way of peace itself."

Gus sorted through the rest of the bins. A new John Grisham, a new Garfield, a new Anne Rice. At the bottom were two more copies of *The Savage Redeemer.* He stacked them on the counter to put away later. Bonita's position was that Agon wasn't so crazy and that the money was just a way to buy Gus's goodwill, avoid lawsuits, and piss off Elizabeth. And a tax write-off. But she had agreed to take the check.

And she liked the bookstore/coffee shop idea. She said it would keep Gus put. She even came up with the name: No Quarter Books. Gus liked her choice so much he began to think of Bonita in an entirely different and perhaps more enlightened way; part of that enlightenment was realizing he had not appreciated her insights nearly enough in the past and that the price of not doing so had been high.

After two months, No Quarter Books was going okay. He might not make a killing and he didn't get all the tourists from the Vieux Carré, but being near Tulane and Loyola meant pretty good customer traffic, too, and with the food service angle he was breaking even. Bonita's paycheck filled in the rest and they got to use her insurance. At first the store attracted a minor notoriety because Channel 12 came down and did a story— controversial canned chaplain's new career kind of thing. But that died down pretty fast—it was New Orleans. Scandal was a constant enterprise and not a mark against you.

Maybe that's why Joe Dell was rising from what should have been his own karmic muck, Gus thought. If Gus had gotten out of it pretty much in one piece, and Agon, too, and even Corina, if you wanted to look at it that way, why not the senator who wanted to be governor? Even Elizabeth wasn't suffering. Only Jean-Pierre, but he was getting better.

Girls from Miss Angelique's came in fairly often in the late afternoon, and, as Charlotte said, "Nobody really gives that much of a shit about the riot. They think it was sort of cool." In fact, all the Voices of Angelique except Tina had been by to ask how he was doing and tell him they didn't blame him. He had accepted their good wishes. It would have been cruel not to have. It was not their fault.

"Okay if I get more of the decaf?"

"Go ahead." From a convex mirror on the opposite shelf Gus could easily monitor the coffee room. The two Tulane kids were digging in. He was glad. It was good to have someone in the place, and good not to have too many. If the notoriety had brought business and attention, Gus was glad it had died out. He had given up on his idea of taking the city by storm. He had given up on deliberate potential fuck-ups and the other sorts of things Bonita said came from his wormhole.

He had banished the Shadow Gus. If it returned, ever, it would render upon him a judgment from which he had been saved by the blood of sacrifice. He would not go back there. He was in a different place. He was not where he had been, when lost. He was Occupying Space.

He began shelving the books. On impulse he opened a copy of *The Savage Redeemer* and scrawled Aliesson's name on the fly-leaf, stuck a yellow Post-It on the cover saying "Autographed Copy" and set it in the front window. Then he walked outside onto the sidewalk. It was September and it was hot and muggy like it always was that time of year down where the Big River began spending itself into the Gulf. The shadows of morning were drawing up into the rising sun. Soon even the buildings and trees would be unable to offer protection and his side of the street would be awash in unfettered light.

Traffic down Prytania was light and Gus found himself listening to a scattering of sounds: a tree filled with grackles, a distant car horn, the whoosh of a passing bus, indistinct voices from an elderly couple leaving an office supply store on the other side of the street. The sunny one. It had been many months since he himself had lingered over coffee, strolled around Jackson Square, read the paper, wondered what the day would bring. He went back inside and busied himself with his chores.

FIRST IT WAS JUST what the lawyers call a TRO, which only lasted two weeks, but then they called it a "permanent injunction" and the same day a herd of little chickenshits had come over from the city and taped up signs on the front of the SuperBotanica and now it had been three months and Elroy and Julio now had to decide if they would keep fighting it or if it would be cheaper to just pick up and open somewhere else.

Nobody had to tell him it was Joe Dell Prince doing it. The only thing that surprised him was the reaction when he threatened to tell about Hindfoot Davis.

Joe Dell said, "Elroy, the experience of the last couple of months has told me two things. I got to play to my strengths, and I don't need to fuck with you anymore. You want to say I hired you to scare the shit out of some nigger ten years ago, go ahead. You know what I think? I think I'll take out an ad and claim it for myself! And you know what else I think? I think if I had a business trying to sell this mumbo jumbo shit to a lot of niggers and spics like you are and if I was in as much trouble with them as you are I'd be *damned* careful about anything else that could backfire on me. So fuck you, Delgado."

Elroy drank his Bud Lite—he was getting fat from the booze—and slapped a mosquito. The house was quiet with Luz gone. The night was cool but the bugs were bad. He almost got out of his lawn chair to light a citronella candle but instead he squirted himself with Cutter's. He hated the stuff because it smelled but there was no one to smell it on him now. He looked up. For the first night in a while he could see the stars. No clouds or rain. No ceiling inside the SuperBotanica to block the view. He thought himself back to a beach in Cuba where the sand was white and the water was blue and warm. But he could not hold such memories.

Joe Dell wouldn't even take fifty thousand dollars to call back the city people who were saying the "environmental variance" was overturned by the EPA. Joe Dell said there wasn't enough money in the world to do business with Elroy again. "You damn near got me killed and I damn near didn't work my way out of that hole you dug for me. What I mean is I take it personally. I mean I'm finished with you and I don't know you anymore." That was when Elroy brought up Hindfoot and wound up telling the senator to fuck himself, too, and that was about it.

Elroy slapped his left ear. Shit, he thought, I'm not putting that stuff on my face. But he wasn't feeling the bites anyway.

Period, end of sentence—the SuperBotanica was closed up. The fight with the city was a nightmare. The lawyers said if nobody could be "reached" it might be a year—or *more*—before they could reopen the place and then only after a lot of new "environmental studies" and then there would be delays and— the SuperBotanica was basically history. Period, *finito*, end of sentence.

Julio figured they would lose a million and a half before it was over but that they might lose double that if they went to court. So Elroy was all but decided. Luz said she needed a rest. She actually said, "I'm sick of this shit, Elroy, and it's all your fault. You just better think about what you want to do and you better think about what you think I'm gonna do." She was in Miami with her cousin Cici.

Now Elroy's life was talking to lawyers all day and fighting with Julio and getting shitty letters at the store from people calling him names. "The Ku Klux Kuban" and so on. On top of everything else, Elroy had heard from his lawyer that the immigration had been snooping around about illegal aliens on his construction crews. The lawyer said Joe Dell Prince was behind that, too. And those detectives had left a message with Corvette that they wanted to come buy and talk to him some more about what he knew about Ocho.

It looked like another two six-pack night just to get to sleep. Too many of those; worse, he always had a hangover until he started drinking again. Against all his pain, his *santos* were silent. Not even the blood of a goat and a dozen guinea fowl brought words to Changó or Elegba nor any of them, nor power to Elroy. And he couldn't even think of it all as a dream, not even a bad dream, because it wasn't. It was just an empty building. Or would be by tomorrow when the last of the loading trucks took everything back to the warehouse for storage.

"MAMA SAY SPIRITS DO THAT." Paulus drove slowly down Ladeau Street and looked at the plywood boards nailed over the windows. The SuperBotanica marquee was still up but a black paint bomb balloon had hit it and left a jellyfish-shaped blotch in the upper right corner. The security guard mostly stayed inside. Graffiti covered the front of the building like a mural. It was like nobody cared, and people said at night the trucks were taking stuff out of the store and supposedly it was nearly empty, but Paulus didn't know for sure.

"You believe her?" Jean-Pierre asked.

"Yeah, I do."

Now that Paulus had his license he liked to figure out a way to drive by the devastation at least once a day. Each time he did it was like some new wound inside him healed shut another centimeter. But the sight was new for Jean-Pierre. His wounds were fresher. Marks were still fresh where the metal staples used as stitches had zagged diagonally across his abdomen, where the first bullet, through his lung, came out. Where it went in was sewn shut and almost ready to scar. His leg was pretty much okay, except they said it would be months before he wouldn't need his cane.

The exit wound was the one. Slow to mend; ugly. This was the first day he'd been allowed to ride in a car, other than the ambulance that took him back to his house for bed rest. And this was the first night he'd been able to come to one of their mother's services. He moved slightly to adjust a crease in his new black robe. It was a gift from Gus Houston. The old one wasn't any good anymore.

"They reaping what they sowed."

"I think Ogun sowed them pretty good," Paulus replied.

Jean-Pierre smiled. He knew his mother's ways. He couldn't altogether rule out what Paulus said, though he didn't want to admit it.

"How you doin' with all this now? You not planning anything crazy like mama used to talk about, are you?"

Paulus shrugged. Jean-Pierre could see how his younger brother was filling out in the shoulders. He would be stocky, too, and maybe a little taller. Jean-Pierre was stricken with a flash that something could happen to interfere with that process.

"I want you to leave all this up to me," he said.

Paulus looked at him, then turned the corner to find a parking place near the church. "Leave what up to you?"

"Don't play games with me." As Paulus eased in behind an Oldsmobile on the other side of the botanica entrance on Eldora Street, the front tire banged against the curb. Jean-Pierre winced and held his right side.

"Watch out, dammit."

"Sorry. I'm really sorry. Are you okay?"

Jean-Pierre exhaled slowly. It was gone now.

"I'm okay. But did you hear me? I know you been thinking about this to yourself and we got to talk about it soon but what I want to say is this is going to be our business, you understand. It's not mama's business anymore. This isn't about that dumb store or any of that spirit stuff between her and Elroy. It's about me and you now. And Ocho and the Delgados. But mama's out of it. You understand what I'm telling you?"

Paulus stared ahead and pulled the keys from the ignition. He reached for the door handle.

"Wait," said Jean-Pierre, reaching over to touch his brother's forearm. "You taking this in?"

Paulus drew back from the door. His face darkened. His hands formed fists around the steering wheel of his mother's El Dorado. "You don't have to tell me nothing about 'Something going to be done' or 'We gonna do something.'" He turned sharply. "I'm going to find that fucker sometime. You can count on that."

Jean-Pierre tightened his grip on his brother's arm. Paulus was a quiet, studious type. But now he was getting big. He could drive. He could find a gun, just as Jean-Pierre had done. Only Jean-Pierre had left his piece at home that day and Ocho had not.

"I understand," Jean-Pierre said. "What I'm saying is I'm

your brother and it's up to me to look after you. I'm also saying I'm in this with you. Damn, Paulus, what you think I'm wearing under this hot old robe right now? I'm all wrapped up in bandages and limping like a cripple from what those people did and I can tell you we are going to have our day. What I'm saying is I see something in you mama might not because I'm your brother and I'm your blood and I know how you carry things inside. I'm saying don't do nothing before we talk it out."

Jean-Pierre looked across the street at Arletta and another young woman from the neighborhood turning the corner toward the church. Each wore a lace coverlet in her hair. "We'll find a way with our business just like mama surely did with hers."

Paulus looked at him. His eyes were round and wide, and a little moist. "That night," he said, "I wasn't doing nothing. I was just walking."

"I know."

"I never done no harm to that man."

"No, you didn't."

"Then why, Jean-Pierre? Why he do that to me?"

Jean-Pierre let go Paulus's arm and looked out the windshield. It felt hot in the car, now. It was time to go in for services. In a way, he could maybe see why Ocho had shot him. It was stupid and Ocho would have to pay but to the question Paulus was posing, Jean-Pierre could say of his own encounter, "He was a jealous fool." But that wasn't the question. It was why Paulus, who had done nothing?

"God doesn't give us all the answers, you know."

"I see it every night in my head, and then I wake up and I think I was dreaming it but I wasn't dreaming it. I go over it all the time in my head but it don't make any sense. I pray but it don't make any sense. I ask the *santos* and it don't make any sense to me why my face got all busted up and when it rains my jaw hurts still." He shook his head. "You know what I'm saying, Jean-Pierre? Do you?"

Jean-Pierre opened his door. The air felt good.

"I know. But I don't know why." He looked over. "But I know we going to have our day. You down for that with me?"

Paulus opened his door, too. When they were both out and the younger had gone around to take the arm of the older and help him across the street, for he struggled with the pain of his wounds, he said, "OK."

Jean-Pierre leaned on his brother and on his cane, and they made their way through the front door of the African Spiritual Church of Mercy. "Welcome home, Brother," Miz Anderson called out, and "Amen" came from everywhere and then they clapped for him. He nodded quietly and took his place at the organ and for the first time in months the sanctuary filled with the delicate strength of his fingers on the keyboard.

Paulus checked the altar to make sure the Bible was in place and his mother's chair was straight against the wall under the crucifix. He noticed her *palo* staff, wrapped in twine of purple and white. He almost put it behind the lectern she had begun to use for her sermons but thought it better not to disturb anything. Then he lit two plates of incense and took his usual post near the door. As Jean-Pierre played, he looked over the congregation, as was his duty, to count heads and take attendance.

It was then that Paulus noticed the Candy Man and his girlfriend in the second pew on the right. They had been coming quite a bit now she was having that baby. Bonita, she was Cajun, also visited his mama for readings, but she never said much, just went into the back room and left out of the side door.

Jean-Pierre saw Candy Man, too, and Paulus could almost feel the electricity zap across the thick and holy air. But then it seemed still, calm. Paulus gazed out the half-open door onto

Beauchamp Avenue. Steam lingered along parts of the pavement from a late afternoon shower. She came in.

THE SONGS HAD GONE ON for nearly an hour, and only Jean-Pierre's sudden fatigue had brought them to a halt and no one had even realized how long they had been praising the Lord and swaying together in the pews. The first possession had come after only the second hymn, as Clothilde Samuels fell out into the middle aisle, eyes rolled back inside her skull, arms limp as rags until they shot up over her head and "Yes, Jesus! Yes, Lord!" raged from her lips and she spun like a top until she fell into the arms of Brother Jones the plumber, who, like some of the others, had joined the church after the Gospel Riot. From then the Spirit was so vast throughout the room it had nowhere to go but into the souls and bodies of the worshipers and the hour was gone before anyone knew. Even Jean-Pierre had not known until his body could no longer sustain the forces inside it and he slumped atop the keyboard, his face ashen.

They stretched him out on the pew and took off his new black robe, soaked in salty sweat, and inspected his bandages. He seemed to breathe easier in just his slacks and shirt and said he was okay. Paulus got him a glass of water and turned the air conditioner down to the coldest setting, and then the Spirit said they would return to the services and they all did, Gus and Bonita among them, together, hands clasped together, being with and only with each other, and with the one that Bonita now carried inside.

Corina favored John and Corinthians and the Twenty-third Psalm above all others, and read from them, but she never really took her eyes off Jean-Pierre. Presently it became apparent she was no longer reading from the Bible at all, or even reciting, for she had long since memorized most of it, but was moving off into her own terrain, something about the routing of her enemies and the vengeance of the Almighty and the power of the African soul.

Abruptly, she fell silent. Rock rigid behind the lectern, she seemed to not be there even as she was. Her eyes seemed fixed on the Black Madonna on the opposite wall, although they might have as easily been looking into another universe. No breath in the room went unheard. Time itself unhinged. Out of that she turned quickly to her right, grasped the *palo* staff and raised it over her head. She whirled and talked in a tongue no one could understand until she came to a stop before the center pew. The words fell out in the voice that sometimes came to her when her own was not enough:

"And it came to me in my dreams that I was wandering through the desert."

"Amen, Sister Youngblood."

"I was hot and beaten down and I was going to perish in the wastes when suddenly I saw it."

"Tell us, Reverend."

"And I will tell you I did not know what it was, and I came closer, and—" She held the staff above her and thrust her head backwards.

"God save us," said Estella Bourgeois.

"And in my need and desperation the Trough of God lay before me."

"Say it, Sister."

"I say this: I say I was thirsty and I heard the Archangel Michael at my ear. I say this is what he say to me." She lowered the staff, then dropped it to the floor. It rattled and rolled to a stop and when it stopped so did all sound from the room except the voice of Corina Youngblood.

"The Angel of the Lord, he say to me: 'Come Ye to the Trough of God. Though it be deep, it be not abiding. They who drink thereof will surely drown in their own thirst, for it not God's bounty but his Spirit which is for us to imbibe, and all else is illusion.'"

Her robe also was black, also heavy with sweat. Her eyes came back from that other place and sought out those of Gus Houston, and found them.

Jean-Pierre lay quite still. His skin had gone very cool. He was breathing erratically. He began to perceive the answer.

∾